A SOFT ECLIPSE

Film maker, literary editor and corporate communicator, **Jayabrato Chatterjee**'s first novel, *Last Train To Innocence*, published in 1995, opened to excellent reviews and won the Hawthornden Fellowship that facilitated his spending a month at the International Writers' Retreat at Hawthornden Castle in Scotland in 1997. He was Writer-in-Residence at the University of Stirling, again in Scotland, in the spring of 1999 on a Charles Wallace India Trust Fellowship where he began work on his second novel, *Beyond All Heavens*, published in 2003 to much critical acclaim.

An English Honours graduate from St Stephen's College, Jayabrato Chatterjee has directed over thirty-five documentaries focusing on issues relating to the girl child, education for the marginalised and altering public perceptions of disability in India. He sits on the Governing Body of ADAPT (Abled Disabled All People Together) Mumbai, the NGO that pioneered the cerebral palsy movement in India. His latest feature film in English, *Lovesongs: Yesterday, Today & Tomorrow*, starring Jaya Bachchan, Om Puri and Shahana Chatterjee was given a red-carpet premiere at the BAFTA-Tongues On Fire Film Festival in London in 2010 and went on to receive critical approval at international and Indian film festivals. As artistic director of the audio-visual, *Jaya Hey*, commemorating Rabindranath Tagore's 150th birth anniversary in 2011, he transcreated all five verses of *Jana Gana Mana* (the first verse being India's National Anthem) in English and directed 39 of the country's most celebrated musicians and singers in a unique album sponsored by Ambuja Realty.

An incorrigible traveller, Chatterjee's creative energies find divergent expression both on celluloid and in the written word. He lives in Kolkata, his favourite city.

A SOFT ECLIPSE

Jayabrato Chatterjee

This edition first published 2014
AMARYLLIS
An imprint of Manjul Publishing House Pvt. Ltd.
7/32, Ground Floor,
Ansari Road, Daryaganj, New Delhi 110 002
Tel: +91 112325 8319/2325 5558 Fax: 91 112325 5557
Email: amaryllis@amaryllis.co.in
Website: www.amaryllis.co.in

Registered Office:
10, Nishat Colony, Bhopal 462 003, M.P., India

ISBN: 978-93-81506-42-4

Printed and Bound in India by
Replika Press Pvt. Ltd.

For Subhra

Aaro durey cholo jaayee
Ghoorey aashi –
Mon neeye kaachhaa-kaachhi,
Tumi aachho aami aachhi,
Paasha-paashi!

~

Let's travel on
Far and wide
Heart touching heart –
Just you and I
Side by side!

—BENGALI FILM SONG

CONTENTS

I'm wife; I've finished that,
That other state;
I'm Czar, I'm woman now:
It's safer so.
How odd the girl's life looks
Behind this soft eclipse!
I think that earth feels so
To those in heaven now.
This being comfort, then
That other kind was pain;
But why compare?
I'm wife! Stop there!

—EMILY DICKINSON

Book One

YESTERDAY

One for sorrow,
Two for joy,
Three for a girl,
Four for a boy,
Five for silver,
Six for gold,
Seven for a secret
Never to be told!

–THE MAGPIE NURSERY RHYME

When I was seven, my mother told me about her vivid dreams before my two elder sisters were born.

'For Shubha, it was a resplendently caparisoned elephant,' she said one afternoon, combing out the knots in her hair and remembering. 'Nobody believed me then. Not even Dolly. But I knew that my poor baby would be in for a tough time.'

'What rot! Shubha's quite happy not going to school,' I countered, looking up from the book I was reading.

'*Happy?*' Ma reprimanded, amazed at what she thought was my utter insensitivity. 'How can she be happy when your father hasn't managed to find her a good husband even after all these years?'

'Perhaps she'll marry an elephant,' I joked.

'Getting cheeky, are you?'

'But you said you'd dreamt up an elephant, hadn't you?'

'I had indeed,' Ma recalled, turning to face the beveled mirror. 'Before going into labour, I saw the animal ambling down our street. It was a quiet afternoon. You could hear the shaleeks flap their wings madly and quarrel. And then, suddenly, it went berserk.'

'Berserk?'

'Yes, yes! Completely mad! It began a wild dance and trumpeted in loud snorts. Before I could reach for my prayer beads, it bounded into our compound and uprooted the old jaam tree. Then, in a state of frenzy, it charged towards the house.'

'Really? What did you do?'

'Nothing! I was flat out on my back, you silly girl, telling the midwife I was about to die! But old Beejee – bless the faithful maid – did everything she could to appease the beast, sprinkling marigold petals and ringing the prayer bell with all her might. Then, Bishshonath, the priest's son, appeared miraculously on a puff of cloud, his skin aglow and cleared of all those wretched pock-marks. Matador-fashion, he waved his tattered naamaaboli as he sailed down from the sky. Perhaps Ram Thakur and Krishno Thakur's name printed on the scarf took the animal by surprise. In sudden panic, it went down on its haunches and shat near the jasmine creeper. Can you imagine? Before I could recover from the shock, the animal had melted into thin air after creating such a stinking mess! Beejee knew what this was all about. She immediately collected the dung on a silver salver, drizzled it with holy Gonga water and smeared the muck all over the baby. Shubha was spared any physical damage but the poor girl grew up an absolute nervous wreck!'

I often protested at Ma's implausible tales but poor Shubha had neither the stamina nor the will to fight. An onslaught of men had been constantly inflicted on her just after her eighteenth birthday so that she could settle into an arranged marriage. But much as Ma and Dolly-kaakima tried, Shubha failed to attract a suitable groom.

My father, Barrister Bidhushekhor Dotto, had named his first born with much fanfare as a tribute to Mother India.

'Shubhaashinim... Sumadhura-bhaashinim...
Sukhadaam baradaam Maataram...'

But Mother India would have fallen off her pedestal in a dizzy fit had she seen Shubha trapped in her plight.

Huge spectacles started dangling from her nose when she was barely eight. Over the years, the frame and the lenses grew thicker. They made her large and lambent eyes seem like 'Chinaman' slits. Every time Shubha pushed her spectacles back and scowled, her fingers trembled and her tongue got hopelessly tied. She was thin and dreadfully flat-chested. Her anorexic appearance became a big joke. At last, with a deep sigh, Beejeepishi proclaimed that Shubha was a sad reminder of the year she was born. The Great Bengal Famine of 1942 had depleted the shops of all food and grain immediately after Shubha's arrival. Bishshonath's father, who was actually our family's official head priest but made his son do all the dirty work and daily pujos, had apparently pointed out that this was, indeed, a portentous omen. The news was heart-rending. But he had been forced to break it to Ma to keep his professional reputation spotless. The girl would never wed. And if she did, her husband would surely die within three months of their marriage. The only way to rid the all-pervading power of such evil would be, of course, to make a fat donation. He was building a temple, you see, in his distant village in Purulia. It venerated the powers of Mother Kaali. She'd surely protect the child and save her from the clutches of the ill-fated Saturn if she were sufficiently bribed.

'On hearing such a cock-and-bull fib,' Beejeepishi told me years later, 'your father went mad and instantly kicked Bishshonath's father out.'

But, ominously, Shubha became sick and used her ill health as an excuse to draw attention to her plight.

Lanky and awkward, even a spray of ordinary acne got her all worked up and edgy. I remember my mother and Dolly-kaakima doing all they could to rid her of the terror. But Ma's mud packs and Dolly-kaakima's homemade unguents only managed to aggravate matters. The more they plastered her face with herbal concoctions, the wilder became the crop. Shubha was happiest when the family left her alone to daydream for hours in her tiny bedroom at the farthest end of the corridor. She watched the mango tree outside the window standing tall and talking to her, its foliage full of flickering tongues in the evening breeze. These conversations soon became Shubha's nemesis.

At school she hardly had any friends. The nuns found her reticence annoying. Not once would she open her mouth in class. She never talked about her special interests, her favourite books or even about the subjects she disliked. Much as the teachers tried, she paid little attention at group discussions and was soon forgotten, relegated to the back of the class. Only once, during break-time, Mother Bernadette had caught her in the chapel, down on her knees and weeping earnestly at the feet of the Virgin Mary. She found this odd and confronted her. But Shubha stood before the nun's imposing desk, hung down her head and remained infuriatingly silent. Exasperated, Mother Bernadette dismissed her from her office and told her to go back to class.

Shubha's only solace lay in prayers. She spent hours in the prayer room, casting sidelong glances at our mother's self-imposed suffering. Ma's perpetual torment pervaded even her long and tapering fingers that always remained surprisingly elegant and bare. Not a ring glittered past the knuckles; no fancy baubles decorated their beauty. Her nose, dotted with a diamond clove, and her thin upper lip, marked by a mole on the outer edge, imbued her face with a touch of anguish. Shubha found such tragedy extremely beautiful. She woke up every morning at the crack of dawn to worship with Ma. They bathed and readied themselves before the rest of the house could stir and crept up the stairs to face the gods. Safe in the arms of Krishno Thakur and Shib Thakur, they went down on their knees and prayed. They thanked the gods for letting them breathe. They thanked them for the blood running warm in their veins. They sang many keertons for them, clashing little cymbals and burning incense. And they thanked them for not letting them down, despite their grief.

To usher in Mrinalini, my middle sister, Ma had dreamt up a storm.

'With every contraction, I only saw streaks of lightning flash through the corridors,' she revealed one afternoon, picking up the stitches she had dropped from her knitting needle. 'I tried to call out to the maids to help me, but who do you think hovered at the door and prevented them from entering?'

'Who? Baba?'

'No, my dear, it was your wonderful Dolly-kaakima! Slyly, she blocked their path, fiddling with her Muff chain and flaunting her brand new gold bangles, as she proceeded to tell me that Joga, the driver, had come back from the market with a pair of eelish maachh. She wanted to know whether she should marinate the fish in coconut and mustard, or just steam the fillets with green chillies and a dash of cumin seeds. I kept yelling and warning her about being struck but do you think she listened? "Don't worry, Didi!" she had mocked. "No tempest can defeat me! Can't you see that my Bachchoo will take care of me? I have a son, but you'll only have another burden tumbling out of your womb!" Some cheek, cursing me in the midst of that terrible storm!'

However, our cousin, Dibaakor-da, alias Bachchoo, didn't bear out Dolly-kaakima's prophecy. But that's another story.

Dibaakor-da, Mini's hero, actually depended on me for tea and sympathy. Mini, the dolt, would go all weak-kneed whenever she was left alone in his company. But I'd have none of his swagger. Over the years, he learnt to respect my independence. We'd spin tops together and discuss the books we enjoyed reading, especially the escapades of the Cossack warrior, Taras Bulba, or the adventures of Tarzan raised by a bunch of African apes. He was our only male cousin on whose forehead I would place a tilok on the morning of the annual bhai phonta ceremony meant to venerate brothers, fervently pleading for a ring of thorns to sprout around Jom's threshold and keep him safe.

'Bhaier kopaaley dilem phonta, Jomer duaarey porlo kaanta!'

If only the King of Death had listened to my prayers!

Unlike Shubha, Mini was a chirpy little sparrow happily flapping her wings. Baba had christened her Mrinalini after Robindronath Thakur's obedient wife. Mini was anything but docile. I had seen her in the bath once, her slender, boyish figure naked and rebellious. The pubic bush had just about begun sprouting at that time as she lathered it with great delight. Mini's sloe-black eyes narrowed at every scrap of kitchen gossip. She'd thrust out her firm little breasts whenever Dibaakor-da descended for his meals and gave her appreciative looks.

'Ayee, Mini-winnie,' he'd mock, pulling at her pigtail, 'are you always dreaming about boys? Or are you also concentrating on geometry?'

Mini would shriek and tilt her head to one side.

'Why Dibaakor-da, why do you want to know?'

'Because Jethaamoni said your marks were abysmal.'

'Did Baba really say that to you?'

'He did. Do you need help?'

'Yes. But why should you want to help me?'

'Because I'm in love with you, you silly girl!'

'Dhat!' Mini would giggle, blushing, and run into the boitak-khaana.

Neither Shubha's gentle persuasion nor Ma's threats could make Mini get out of bed in time for the morning prayers. She just didn't give a toss for any seductive god at Amherst Street or even the meek and mild Jesus at Loreto Convent. Pulling the cover a little tighter, she'd dream, instead, of the handsome Hollywood stars her friends at school had introduced her to. I had gone with her once to pore over their pictures in the suffocating locker room. Mini would slobber over William Holden, Gregory Peck and Cary Grant. Her delusions took wings on monsoon nights as the rain outside came suddenly, shouting in sheets. She'd hug her bolster tighter, rubbing herself against the pillow. The heat of the night made her bloom like a flower, cunningly waiting for the petals to wither.

Mini began to menstruate early, just after her tenth birthday. Instantly, she was banned from the kitchen. Isolated from the rest of the family, her resentment manifested itself in awful tantrums. Ma became alarmed. Her little girl was still a baby, she cried to Krishno Thakur and Shib Thakur – how could they betray her? But the idols only smiled, embarrassed, and let a lizard slip across their altar.

Over the years Ma decided that all our family troubles had been predicted in her dreams but, foolishly, she hadn't taken heed. She hadn't consulted the family astrologer or gone to visit the clairvoyant at Tarapeeth to find out what the premonitions augured. Now it was too late, she lamented, turning away her sad, impassive eyes from me.

Unfortunately, there were no visions when I finally arrived. I wasn't the son Ma had begged the gods to deliver. She was so disappointed when the midwife told her it was yet another daughter that she refused to even look at me. Years later Dolly-kaakima explained that a virulent attack of jaundice, followed by a mysterious viral infection had laid Ma up in bed for almost six months before I was born. The reality of death had loomed large. But, foolishly, she had hoped that Shib Thakur would compensate with the gift of a male child. She bore her pain stoically but my arrival had reduced her to tears. At the end of the ordeal she wondered how I had dared to scream my way into this world with such audacious nonchalance, disguised in the wrong sex.

Poor Ma! In small but bitter doses she came to learn that even her omnipotent gods had little control over mortal vagaries.

Ma always blamed my recalcitrance to our English education. She had kicked up a huge fuss when Baba initially decided to send Shubha, Mini and me to study under the Irish nuns at Loreto Convent. But he was adamant. Education for his daughters was something he wouldn't allow his uneducated wife to tamper with. So what if beef-eating and poor charity girls from Anglo-Indian homes shared the same class with vestigial Hindu virgins? English education was, after all, *English education*! And it would stand us in good stead once we were married and sent away from the strict environs of 189/A Amherst Street.

For Ma, it was a losing battle. According to her, the convent had undone us and put all sorts of imprudent ideas into our heads. Shubha, perhaps, was the only ray of hope. Mini had turned into a rebellious idiot and I had openly put Ma to shame by getting into divided skirts, exposing my knees and playing basketball! Was I a hooligan? A cheapskate chee-chee prostitute? Were the nuns off their heads, making delicate Bengali girls run around in the sun, ending up looking like charred, 'kaak-taaraani' scarecrows?

'Will Mother Bernadette find you husbands?' she had shouted. And to add insult to injury I had had the audacity to bring back a photograph of the entire team, all sweaty and dishevelled, grinning from ear to ear and holding high the trophy! Hai Bhogobaan, even in her wildest dreams she hadn't imagined I'd do this to her!

My mother's views about bringing up girls were severely

conventional, abetted by Dolly-kaakima's jibes and taunts. My father, however, was the quintessential Brown Sahib who, under parental pressure, must have succumbed to a marriage that had produced three daughters but left the nuptial bed hopelessly arid thereafter.

Every wall in my father's library was stacked from top to bottom with legal tomes in glass-encased cupboards, excluding one shelf that displayed an array of unpolished trophies. In his youth, Baba had won them at assorted tennis tournaments in the city when he had been part of Calcutta Club's regular team. Now, of course, he could only nostalgically recall his victories when his older clients came to visit, unmindful of the ugly ormolu clock that broke the stillness of the afternoons with its persistent, irritating ticking. His mahogany table dominated the far end of the room, next to the French window. Beyond the slats swayed the branches of an oleander tree constantly smothered with a profusion of flowers. In another corner a Lazarus sofa invited visitors who had the gumption to brave walking across the tiger skin, replete with the taxidermied head of the beast snarling across the floor.

Baba tried cultivating western manners in his fussy waistcoats, spats and gold-plated watch-chains. But his heart, alas, remained inexorably dwarfed by old-fashioned mores. He hated admitting this and hid the contradictions in ambivalent behaviour, leaving the task of running his home and disciplining his daughters to his wife. Only his broken nose gave away his brooding inconsistency. He had injured it some years ago, trying to lend a helping hand to Dibaakorda who was bringing home the Durga idol we worshipped in our thakurdalaan every autumn. Ma's comment, while the bleeding was being stemmed with cubes of ice, was – as always – wry. She had pointed out that Ma Durga had a way of knocking the noses of those who insisted on eating beef on the sly. Baba had only grunted and been rushed to the local dispensary.

Over the years my father, inevitably, lost his slender build. His neck coarsened and grew two collar sizes thicker, though he insisted that he walked up and down the steep High Court stairs at least fifty times a day. Normally, such vigorous exertion should have helped him escape the inevitable swelling of middle age. Ma knew better. She blamed his tendency to put on weight squarely on the endless pegs of Scotch he drank every evening with his colleagues and clients at the Calcutta Club after work. Baba dismissed her allegation with irritation. But shami kebabs and whisky-soda turned out to be obsessive mistresses that ultimately ruined his health. Flicking through the obituaries before actually looking at the headlines in *The Statesman,* Baba would remain sprawled on his favourite easy chair, sipping umpteen cups of Lopchu's Flowery Orange Pekoe and scanning the column that announced the previous week's 'hatches, matches and dispatches.' He read the newspaper for at least an hour, unduly fussy about his privacy in the mornings, and still fussier about his tea. The servants brewed it to perfection so that their master's bowels, aided by a dose of Isobgul the previous night, moved precisely at seven thirty-seven. Nobody was allowed to disturb this ritual, not even the gods or their daily proshaad that would be brought to him only at breakfast. Lifting his eyes from the silver salver dotted with scurrying little ants under the sugary bataashas, Baba never forgot to ask whether the flies had also got at the offerings. Once Beejeepishi had confirmed that they hadn't, perfunctorily he'd accept what had been proffered, briefly nodding his balding pate as a concession to his self-conscious supplication.

Sundays, however, were less rigid. Baba would come down at midday to have lunch with the rest of the family in the kitchen, wearing a dhuti and a Sandow vest in an attempt to imitate the pioneering Prussian bodybuilder whom he admired with all the candour of a starry-eyed school boy. Sitting cross-legged on a floor mat, he'd eat off the gleaming bell-metal plates as Bijoy-kaka would riddle him with a variety of questions that fanned legal gossip. Baba would grunt out perfunctory explanations and Dolly-kaakima would proceed to frown and instruct Bijoy-kaka not to try her brother-in-law's patience. But Bijoy-kaka loved his role as the family wastrel.

In his youth Bijoy-kaka had escaped to Benares and learnt to sing tappas and thumris at the feet of an assortment of gurus and baijees tucked away in the city's ancient lanes. He was a difficult customer to please. Not for him the temporary solace of gaanja or the lure of Maghai paans laced with stronger narcotics. Little could Lord Bishshonath's ubiquity do to curtail Bijoy-kaka's initial enthusiasm frittered away, as the days went by, on the endless bounty of musical thirsts quenched between teachers of repute and dancing girls of equal notoriety. But, alas, the boredom of routine soon made him impatient. And the minute he began feeling like the aimless bulls ambling down the gullies near Dasashwamedh Ghat, he upped and quit. Neither Ustaad Daulat Khan's melodic raspings nor Motibibi's carnal capers could hold him back. When he decided to return home at last, to the relief of his mother, he was married off within a fortnight. My Thaku'ma had found him a bride with a mulish mouth set indomitably in a face that had soured before she stepped out of her teens. Bijoy-kaka never recovered from the shock of lifting her sequin-speckled veil on the wedding night – all lovey-dovey and romantic – to confront a pair of cross-eyes staring at him in unmitigated fury.

Dolly-kaakima's married life revolved around three insurmountable impediments – a sullen mother-in-law with a vicious 'black tongue' that spelt doom; a big, black wok in the kitchen; and a bigger and blacker phallus in the family prayer room, incandescent with mystic heat. The husband didn't count. The genesis of her foul temper lay, perhaps, in the combined dark deeds of the formidable troika. No one was quite sure. But once the wok had been conquered, the phallus appeased and the dreadful mother-in-law conveniently packed off on her final journey to Boikunthho, Dibaakor-da arrived to fill her days with udiminished sunshine. But according to Ma, most ironically, when no one was looking, the mother-in-law suddenly turned her back to the Gates of Heaven, removed her dentures, spat fire, stuck out her bum and farted loud and long. Then, laughing hysterically, she vanished into a cloud of smoke. Dolly-kaakima's menstrual cycle immediately went haywire and her rotund figure swelled to crush any residue of Bijoy-kaka's undomesticated libido. Poor Bijoy-kaka! He was forced to seek relief in other arms as Dolly-kaakima turned fat and diabetic.

Bijoy-kaka started teaching music to a bunch of giggling novices in the stifling humidity of summer afternoons. The intricacies of classical ragas certainly helped cheer their dreary lives as they arrived wrapped in Dhoneykhaali saris and reeking of Lokkhibilaash Hair Oil scenting their locks. His lessons came at ridiculously low rates. Every time a new trainee stood simpering at the door, pulling at her plait and swaying from side to side, her face smeared with Boshonto Maloti or Himalaya Snow, he'd blow around himself a blizzard of musical garbage and welcome the victim with: '*Ami toh tomaarey chaahini jeeboney, tumi amaarey cheyechho...*'

I didn't want you in my life my dear/ It was you who sought me out, I fear!

Rajanikanto's songs were a time-tested ploy. And once the sweet resonance of Raga Megh or Raga Behaag had died, he'd invariably toil over his wards beyond the call of musical duty. Pretending to teach them how to bellow the harmonium, he'd let his fingers stray away from the keys in search of their budding breasts. The girls would be suitably delighted because these extra trappings came at no extra cost.

189/A Amherst Street, under the cover of old-fashioned norms, swam in the undercurrents of sexual predilections. Any overt talk, though, was considered ill-bred, even after my sisters and I were finally paraded in the marriage market. Our home would only ripple with whispers and innuendos. Ma and Dolly-kaakima would constantly remind us that on certain days girls were 'impure'. Any further explanation had to be covert. When 'the monthly curse' arrived, unannounced, it flowed out of my body in a hot and sticky lava, catching me unawares.

How embarrassing!

As the blood seeped through my sari or my skirt, I'd have to wait for the men to clear out before I could get up and hurry to the bathroom. Ma instructed me with her darting eyes, telling me when to sit or when to rush back to my room. My sisters and I were urged to bear the mess without too much fuss. Sanitary napkins were hidden away in the dark recesses of our cupboards and I initially saw a condom in my last year in school, when Sylvia D'Silva brought along a packet. Shepherding us into the locker room, she had giggled and casually blown into one, making it swell like a balloon. It had left me repulsed and fascinated.

Our weekdays flew by, being carted back and forth from Loreto Convent in the curtained family Studebaker, under Joga-kaka's hawk eyes. There was no question of lingering at the school gates to buy a stick of Magnolia's iced lolly or catch up on some eleventh-hour gossip with friends from senior classes. The minute the nuns set us free, we were herded into the car and deposited at home where we had to contend with Ma's ruthless commands and sneers. Our evenings were equally dreary. Old Bishnu Babu, in his threadbare dhutis, ground-glass spectacles and canvas pumps slightly budding at the toes, helped us wade through Physics and Chemistry. Shona Didimoni came every Tuesday and Thursday to teach us '*Khoro baayu boy begey chaari dik chhaaye meghey...*' and other assorted Robindroshongeet that would shoot up our value in the marriage market. And then, of course, there was Shaky Bomi who had juddered her way into our lives to render Math tuitions, replete with a woebegone expression that seemed to convey that she badly wanted to run to the loo.

Shaky Bomi had been accidently discovered by an over-enthusiastic neighbour who had sung paeans to her algebraic acumen. In reality, however, the mistress of mathematics was certainly no nubile nymph of numbers come upon us from some enchanted wood. She had the slyest pair of eyes separated by a startling, bulbous nose. Her hair, oily and spotted with dandruff, was drawn back into a no-nonsense knot; her face, lit by a ghostly allure, remained burdened under the weight of Cuticura talcum powder. And a slightly sickening body odour pervaded our study the minute she entered, all helter-skelter, dripping with perspiration that left permanent spots on her blouse, especially under her armpits. An emaciated bag of bones, Shaky Bomi was thus christened by Mini for often skipping classes and then crying foul the following day.

If Mini ever asked her irritably, 'Kaal ki holo? Why didn't you turn up yesterday? We were waiting for you all evening!', the Math wizard would roll her eyes and describe with a theatrical flourish, 'Shey ki bomi, didibhai! I got sick as a dog and threw up all my lunch! Right from the shukto, the dalna and the daal to the katla macchher patla jhol! Shey ki bomi, ki bolbo! How could you expect me to come here and tackle Pythagoras after I'd been little better than a dying duck in a thunderstorm? Have a heart, didibhai!'

Regrettably, Shaky Bomi and her excuses became an erratic part of our weekdays along with sewing lessons and hours in the smoke-ridden kitchen learning to cook exotic dishes like muri-ghonto or a robust loitta shutkir jhaal, made famous in Chittagong from where some of my mother's family had ultimately immigrated after the Partition. But the weekend afternoons, thank god, were usually spent playing cards. I'd team up with Dolly-kaakima, while Dibaakor-da was left to partner my mother. A vigorous game called '29' always lifted Ma's spirits, though she never stopped fearing Dolly-kaakima's awkward questions.

'Didi, are you going to turn your girls into prissy little mems?' Dolly-kaakima insinuated one afternoon, filling the centre of a fleshy betel leaf with cardamom, fennel seeds and shavings from the shupuri nut. Overhead, the fan whirred noisily and beyond the crackle of the old Murphy Radio, as if it were grating into a pair of particularly uncomfortable dentures, Hemonto Mukhopadhyay burst into song, contemplating a river's treacherous journey from its source to the sea. The heat of the afternoon added poignancy to the lyrics.

'O Nodi re, ekti kotha sudhaai shudhu tomaarey...'

'Didi, you're not listening,' insisted Dolly-kaakima, popping the paan into her mouth and egging Ma to retaliate. 'Tell me, why do girls from perfectly respectable Bengali homes have to study in alien convents with filthy, half-caste sluts?'

'Why do you ask, Dolly?' Ma sighed. 'To sprinkle salt on my wounds?'

Dibaakor-da shuffled the cards and winked at me slyly. Immediately, Dolly-kaakima shouted in her shrill falsetto, 'Bachchooooo, abaar chottami korchish!' Then turning to Ma with a mocking smile, she produced a tiny silver box from her ample bosom and pinched out a bit of scented tobacco that she proceeded to tuck into her mouth.

'My Bachchoo goes to a perfectly respectable Bengali medium

school and is in no way less clever than your girls,' Dolly-kaakima remarked, chewing away at her paan with relish.

'Do I have any say in the matter?' Ma pleaded. 'Whoever listens to my views?'

'But surely you can protest. They are your girls as well.'

'You know their father. How can I argue with the head of the house?'

'That's a pity! Because I know exactly how to treat my husband if he tries any hanky-panky.'

'You're lucky, my precious Dolly. Some people have all the luck in the world!'

Ma dealt out the cards listlessly. Dolly-kaakima collected her lot and spread them out against her face like a Chinese silk fan, chuckling pleasurably after her verbal victory.

Dibaakor-da inspected his hand and shouted, 'Eighteen!'

'Nineteen,' Dolly-kaakima immediately countered, not budging an inch. The edge of her sari momentarily slipped. Dolly-kaakima's blouses were always cut low and she didn't believe in wearing brassieres. Dibaakor-da stared at her cleavage and blushed a beetroot red.

'Pass,' Ma whispered, turning her face away in desolation as she threw down her cards.

'Ayee Meye!' Dolly-kaakima said, smacking my back and flinging back the sari anchol in place with studied indifference. 'What's so grand about your stupid convent? Do you think by chattering away in English you'll find dashing husbands? Arrey baba, Bengali men like eating fish fresh from our local ponds!'

'The convent is a true paradise. You wouldn't know because you've never been to one,' I retorted. 'Can you imagine, Dolly-kaakima, the nuns are actually Christ's brides! And they pine for his company, turning into bats as they fly down the corridors, shrieking out his name at night!'

Instantly, I got a reproving look from Ma. I lowered my eyes, trying not to giggle.

'Twenty,' I challenged, staring at my saviour, the dandy Jack of Spades.

'Are the nuns really from Dublin? From the land of Celtic hounds that bark at the full moon and Bean Nighes who are condemned to wash blood from shrouds?' Dibaakor-da asked, showing-off his half-baked knowledge of Irish mythology picked up from Baba's old copies of *The National Geographic*, a magazine that all of us loved to pore over whenever we got an opportunity. Then, forgetting about alien apologues, he spotted a home-grown Queen of Clubs resting on his fingers, right in front of his nose. Without batting an eyelid he announced, 'Twenty-one!'

'Even if the nuns were from Timbuctoo, I'd say "Double" and catch you out,' I declared. 'Do you agree, Dolly-kaakima?'

'Redouble!' laughed the dragon, pouting her lips and wiping a stream of red spittle that had dribbled down the corner of her mouth.

Dibaakor-da granted me the very special privilege of flying kites with him, though these jaunts on our rooftop proved to be anathema for Mini and my mother. Mini felt threatened and snooped around, hoping she'd be able to intercept me and carry tales to Ma.

Ma, of course, simply hated my tomboy habits.

Once she had risen from her midday nap, washed her face, eaten a round of Marie biscuits dipped in tea and found that I was missing, it was time for Armageddon. But I remained stubborn, unmindful of Ma's scoldings, determined to flee to the roof before the rest of the house stirred from their afternoon siesta.

'I'll fly that kite today, I will! Or my name isn't Mohini Dotto!'

I'd swear, dashing past the prayer room and humming the Ave Maria, in defiance to the Hindu pantheon crowding the shelves.

As a little girl, when I was barely seven, I had once asked Ma if she knew who had filled the moon with so much light. We were standing on the veranda, I remember, looking out into the autumn sky. It was the night of the Kojagori full moon.

'Shib Thakur,' she had barked, annoyed at my interrupting her prayers.

'How do you know?' I had persisted.

'Oh, do be quiet!' she had snapped, rattling her beads harder.

'How do you know it wasn't Ma Du'gga?'

'Because dealing with lights, fuses and wires is a man's job!'

'Why? Why can't a woman do all the things that a man can do?'

'This girl will be my death!' Ma had shot back and smacked my head.

Just then, a sheaf of clouds had blown over and my question, alas, remained forever lost in the sky.

Now, squinting at a rush of sunlight, I spotted Dibaakor-da at the far end of the roof, leaning on the parapet. If only I were a boy like him, free to do as I chose! As free as the kites! If only I could dip and bob in the breeze without a care! If only I could run away from a hundred irritating regulations Ma set up for us! That's when I decided never to succumb to her threats again, never to get provoked by Dolly-kaakima's sarcasm. I certainly didn't want to grow up into a mealy-mouthed ninny, with foolish, regressive ideas floating in my head, without a heart that could feel, a mind that could think and feet that could help me stand tall.

What irony that my father had named me Mohini, the heart's enchantress!

I was born the year after India became independent. But on my way to the roof that afternoon, I suddenly wondered what use was that freedom. At class, when the Anglo-Indian girls giggled over Mother Angelina's dark skin and strong South Indian inflection, I found such hilarity irritating.

'What did Gandhiji give us after *sooooo* many years of struggle?' Mother Angelina would ask during history lessons, and then, turning to face the blackboard, she would answer the question herself, her eyes sparkling as she scratched away with a piece of chalk.

'Yef-ar-ye-ye-dee-yo-yum!'

But what had that 'yef-ar-ye-ye-dee-yo-yum' done for me?

Away from taboos I longed to be my own person, without the shame of my womanhood. How was I to know then – I, all of thirteen and bubbling with life – that the only way to be at peace would be not just freedom from fear, but, alas, also from hope and expectation as the days went by. Already my sisters were being groomed to fit a time-tested pattern as ideal girls from a solid middle-class home. To be signed, sealed and delivered to men who'd never understand their longings or their hurts. Poor Shubha! She had been compelled to leave the convent after failing twice in the Senior Cambridge exams. What option did she have now but to get married? And Mini? What would Mini do? If she had guts, she'd run away from home and start a new life. If she didn't, she'd be condemned to whimper and fade into the crumbling walls of Amherst Street, waiting for a groom and cursing her luck. I was in a defiant mood when I met Dibaakor-da.

'Where on earth were you hiding?' he asked. 'I thought you'd never turn up!'

'I was being watched as usual,' I retorted.

'Rubbish!' Dibaakor-da exclaimed. 'Jethaamoni always supports you. He'll fight your case to the last.'

'One swallow doesn't make a summer,' I said. 'Where's my loot?'

Dibaakor-da rummaged through a packet before whipping out the prettiest kite I had seen in a long, long time. Shaped like a butterfly with gossamer wings, it was spangled with silver dust, a vision out of some fairytale. It smelled of wild flowers and wilder dreams. Certainly, this creature had been born in a mythical garden and flitted over the most fragrant rosebuds before coming to our home. And I was ready to set it free.

'Oh, Dibaakor-da, it's beautiful,' I cried and waited for him to quickly attach the contraption to a spool wrapped with thread he had personally strengthened with powdered glass. I picked up the wooden spindle and ran to the farthest end of the roof. Dibaakor-da lifted the butterfly with both hands. The string turned taut. He clutched the wings lightly and pulled himself into position. Little beads of perspiration started to form over my upper lip. But I disregarded the heat and stood poised. Just then, urgent footsteps broke the silence. They seemed to hurry up the staircase in angry slaps. Dibaakor-da and I simultaneously turned to look and were horrified to see Ma emerging into the sunlight. Her voice, sharp like a surgical knife making brutal incisions, shouted at Dibaakor-da for leading me astray. Then she quickened her pace to come and grab me.

'I don't care what anybody says,' I said to myself defiantly. 'I'll set my kite free. I will! I will! Or my name isn't Mohini Dotto!'

With no prior warning, Dibaakor-da tossed the butterfly into the air. Ma froze. I let out a hoot of joy and pulled at the string. And without much ado, the butterfly soared into the autumn sky, away from the claustrophobic confusion of our home.

The burden of her ordinary looks weighed Shubha down. She could always hear surreptitious whispers in the kitchen as Ma confided to Dolly-kaakima about yet another 'rejection slip'. The accusations hurt her deeply. She had no abiding interests that could help her tide the constant remonstrance. She could neither sit on a cushion to sew a fine seam nor learn to cook exotic dishes under Dolly-kaakima's instructions. Reading, of course, was out. Her span of concentration couldn't beat that of a buzzing bee. Shubha couldn't even flip through the pages of a film magazine without yawning. Ma did give her Bengali classics to browse through but the trials of *Biraaj Bou* and *Bindur Chheley* left her exhausted. Secretly, she just couldn't comprehend why, after so much poking and prodding, she was always tossed back on top of the garbage pile.

Aggravating the situation was Beejeepishi's mumbo-jumbo. When the roots of herbs hidden inside copper charms and tied to Shubha's arm didn't produce the desired knight in shining armour come charging on his white steed to our gates, Dolly-kaakima decided to take custody of such a hopeless situation.

'Don't sit and fret like a stupid mouse,' she admonished. 'Buck up and try to look nice! Why can't you dress smartly? Why can't you line your eyes with kajol? Wear a little jewellery? Make an effort to be cheerful? Go and put on a clean sari, Shubha. Go on!'

'But I know I'm no good,' Shubha wept.

'Nonsense,' scolded Dolly-kaakima. 'You just don't want to try!'

Shubha did try. But only half-heartedly. Her efforts instantly paled when Mini began mocking her and said that a crow could never turn into a swan, hard as it struggled to whitewash its feathers. Shubha burst into tears and locked herself in her room.

One summer afternoon Dolly-kaakima saw her sitting alone in the veranda, hair dishevelled and staring blankly at the krishnochura tree in bloom. The profusion of flowers did nothing to uplift Shubha's heart.

'Why on earth are you looking so shabby?' asked Dolly-kaakima.

'Because I know I'm useless,' said Shubha, not bothering to face her. 'I'm dark and ugly and nobody loves me!'

Infuriated by her obsessive melancholy, Dolly-kaakima rushed to the kitchen and returned almost immediately, hiding something under the folds of her sari. Stealthily positioning herself behind Shubha, she pounced on the poor girl, making her shriek in fright. Dolly-kaakima pinned her down and slowly opened her palm.

'Just to compare,' she whispered, narrowing her eyes. 'Can't imagine anything blacker!'

'Compare what?' asked Shubha, whimpering.

'Your complexion with this,' said Dolly-kaakima.

Only then did Shubha notice a piece of unlit charcoal in Dolly-kaakima's fist.

Shubha had always been inordinately shy and hated crowds. Not once did she demand an extra sari or an extra piece of jewellery from Ma. We tried persuading her to come out with us to picnics and birthday parties. But she preferred staying at home. Even family weddings mortified her. She'd only make a reluctant appearance at Shoroshwoti Pujo that drew the curtains over Calcutta's winter season, hiding behind Ma and biting her nails.

The priest was kind. He always encouraged Shubha to come and stand up ahead, past the gaggle of visitors. He'd give her the first flower that fell from Ma Shoroshwoti's garland and let her be the first to place her hands over the flaming lamps and wipe the blessed heat over her crown. But the fire being circled around the goddess, the pounding of drums and the chanting of prayers always left her flustered, and she was only too happy to escape to the house once the oblations had been offered. Then, one evening, Shubha encountered Mohit Ghoshal, our father's junior assistant, as she was fleeing to her room.

'Shubhashini!'

The low and urgent voice made Shubha start. She stopped, flabbergasted, and looked around. Mohit Ghoshal strode forward from the shadows. Recovering from her shock, Shubha managed to say, 'Oh Mohit-babu, you frightened me!'

'I'm so sorry... But I had to talk to you.'

'What about?'

'About...about us...'

'About us?' Shubha asked, stupefied. For a moment she found the situation unreal. Overwhelmed, she stood rooted to the ground, fiddling with the edge of her sari. In the distance, the dhaaks kept up their steady frenzy. The fairy lights edging the wall twinkled in fits and starts.

'Yes, Shubha. About us,' said Mohit Ghoshal.

Shubha managed to push her spectacles firmly up her nose and snap, 'I don't understand what you mean!'

'You will, if you ask your heart.'

'Mohit-babu, please let me pass!'

'Shubha!'

'This is ridiculous! How dare you take advantage of me?'

'I'm only telling you the truth.'

In the pale light of dusk they stared at each other. Shubha could see a pair of apprehensive eyes. For his twenty-three years, Mohit had an innocent face, accentuated by a sensitive nose and an equally feminine jaw littered with a scanty stubble.

'I don't want to frighten you, my dear,' he blurted out. 'I don't want to push you. But I only want to say that I know you have a kind heart. I know that it is full of love, waiting to be recognised.'

He could not help but impulsively grab Shubha's hand and press it against his chest. Shubha felt his heart thump. She wrenched her wrist free. Never had she imagined, when she used to tiptoe past

Baba's chamber, that Mohit Ghoshal had been watching her through the window. If only she had had the courage to look back, she would have heard him call out to her silently, willing her to turn and discover his longing. She knew she was dark and ordinary. And yet, for the first time, beyond the gloom, she felt stupidly reckless.

'Mohit-babu, you're not in your sane mind,' Shubha said softly, attempting to calm his ardour. 'You must never try and intercept me again.'

'Why?'

'Because...'

'Because?'

'Because you have no right!'

'Shubha, you don't understand! If only you will tell me that you care, if only you will let me know that in your heart there is a tiny little place for me, I'll speak to your father at once.'

'Mohit-babu, please let me pass!'

Listlessly hanging down his head, at last Mohit moved away. Shubha hastened her footsteps and then broke into a run. She fled past Beejeepishi who called out, concerned, wanting to know what had happened. But she didn't stop to answer. Dashing up the stairs, she ran into her room, panting, and banged shut the door. Resting her back against its solid comfort, she stood frozen, watching a shaft of light ripple across her dressing table. In a while, once she had caught her breath, she walked up to confront the mirror. She could just about make out the outline of her face in the light of the faint moonbeams that poured in through the window slats and melted the numerous blemishes. Shubha couldn't help staring at herself. It seemed as though, in that pale yellow light, she were discovering a stranger – an astonishing and beautiful apsara she had never met before. She ran her trembling fingers lightly over her face to reaffirm the vision. And overwhelmed by her emotions, she started to cry.

Through the coming weeks Shubha sat with Ma, confused and distracted, in the prayer room. With every drift of the joss stick smoke, her mind too kept wandering elsewhere – away to some enchanted land only she had the ability to inhabit. Shubha's private island did not carry the burden of remorse. No questions were asked to embarrass her; no wisecracks passed on her looks; no god or demon came there to bother her – not even her beloved Krishno Thakur – and in the end, reconciled to her lot, she followed Dolly-kaakima to Bijoy-kaka's special classes and began learning to sing a fresh bhojon.

Then Ma found out about Mohit Ghoshal and there was utter pandemonium. Her incessant questions, her vindictive insinuations made Shubha cower with guilt. Accusing fingers were pointed at her by Dolly-kaakima. A storm blew through our kitchen and within a month, Shubha started to incoherently mumble in her dreams.

A week after the commotion, there was a soft knock on the door of Baba's chamber. He knew at once, even before turning the next page of a fresh petition, that it was his wife. Ma hardly crossed his threshold unless she was in dire trouble. Certainly, Shubha's illness had alarmed the family, but he wondered why she was seeking him out alone so early in the day.

'Come in!' he called, as if summoning a criminal or a client. Ma drew apart the curtain and entered, unrepentant.

'I need to talk to you urgently,' she said, framed against the door.

'Do sit down,' he commanded, folding away the papers.

'It's about Shubha,' Ma muttered, walking up.

As she eased herself into a chair across his desk, Baba saw her wince at the sudden whiplash meted out by her sciatic nerve. He saw the delicate blue veins meander up her throat. He peeped at the vermilion in the parting of her hair. The mother of his daughters. Yes, she *was* the mother of his daughters. And yet...and yet...who *was* she?

'Shubha says she'll never marry,' said Ma, lowering her head.

'Why?'

'I don't really know. I can only surmise...'

'Go on... Tell me what's the trouble.'

Without looking up, Ma whispered, 'Mohit Ghoshal.'

'Mohit? You mean our Mohit?'

'Yes,'

'I'm completely stumped! He's such a coward!'

'Every night she tells him to go away. "Let me pass, Mohit-babu," she repeats over and over again in a delirium. I never seem to really know what is the matter.'

'What do you want me to do?'

'Talk to the boy. Find out, for god sake!'

Baba brought down his fist violently on his desk. His greatest weapon, a combination of audacity and conceit, suddenly failed him. It was a miserable collapse. Ma shot him a quick, jubilant glance. Then, without another word, she left the chamber.

Despite innumerable threats, Mohit Ghoshal was too weak to admit to his feelings. Perhaps his faint-heartedness had fortified him with sly ingenuity to defend himself and refuse to disclose that Shubha had been a convenient pawn in his machinations to extract a fat dowry by condescending to marry her. He pretended complete innocence and even tried to feign outrage at the accusations. Nothing would make Mohit budge and confess – neither the dire consequences spelled out by Baba that threatened to ruin his career nor the cajoling by my harried mother who wanted to get to the bottom of her daughter's convulsions. In the end, Mohit offered to quit his job.

Then one evening, following Ma's footsteps, Dolly-kaakima also swept into Baba's chamber, unannounced. Her eyes kept sparkling and her right cheek was swollen with a wad of betel leaf. She was like a breathless schoolgirl ready to confess her first affair. Baba's new subordinate, Romesh Haldar, took one look at her and fled from the room. He didn't want to face any embarrassment of witnessing – God help him – Dolly-kaakima unbosoming!

If only he had known what she was about to reveal!

'Dada,' Dolly-kaakima exclaimed, 'Narayon Moharaj has blessed our family at last.'

Baba looked up from a pile of books, irritated. What new trick, he wondered, had his sister-in-law hidden up her puffed sleeves edged in lace. He possessed neither the tact nor the patience to handle her.

'Chhotobou,' he muttered, scrutinising her over the rim of his glasses. 'Why should the venerable Narayon Moharaj come to us and, without reason, shower his droppings – I mean blessings – upon our head? Does he have nothing better to do?'

Unfazed, Dolly-kaakima flung herself into a high-backed chair. Her smirk said it all as she frisked out her little box of scented tobacco and mouthed a generous pinch.

'How long will Shubhashini remain in this house?' she demanded.

'Oh, as long as she wishes,' Baba said, taken aback. A slight displeasure laced his utterance. 'Or have you decided to banish her from our home as well?'

'Seven ponds brimming with katla and catfish,' Dolly-kaakima sighed, fidgeting in her chair.

Baba squeezed his eyebrows. 'What on earth are you talking about?' he asked.

'Miles of paddy fields and a granary overflowing throughout the year,' lisped Dolly-kaakima, shifting the wad of betel leaf from her right to her left cheek.

'Chhotobou,' said Baba impatiently, 'is this some silly joke I'm supposed to laugh at?'

'Of course not,' shot back Dolly-kaakima. 'But, Dada, imagine orchards of mangoes and guavas pregnant with fruit! Imagine the fresh air of a bountiful village! Imagine her personal jewellery casket laden with goodies in pure gold encrusted with rubies and emeralds and diamonds! Imagine her being waited upon hand and foot by a string of personal maids, a filthy rich landlord's undisputed queen! A right royal jomidaar ginni!'

That evening Dolly-kaakima threw herself into a well-rehearsed performance rarely witnessed in north Calcutta's numerous professional theatres. She raved and ranted and fell headlong on the barbs of her own facetiousness. Thank Narayon Moharaj, it did not slice straight up her underbelly and disembowel her, even as her histrionics failed to impress her brother-in-law.

'You've lost your mind,' Baba barked at last and rose from his seat. So did Dolly-kaakima. As he stared at her, ready to battle, she pulled the errant anchol of her sari closer over her forehead.

'I have brought a marriage proposal,' she announced triumphantly. 'And this time it will work!'

The revelation was so sudden, like a stunning slap, that Baba slumped back in his chair. Dolly-kaakima preened, fiddling with her noa-bangle. From its rim she unlocked a safety pin.

'Shubha to be married into a family in a village?' growled Baba at last, thoroughly miffed at Dolly-kaakima's rash speculation. 'Are you crazy? Have I educated my daughters in a convent to marry them off to bumptious country yokels?'

'Dada,' said Dolly-kaakima, thrusting the pin between her molars to dislodge a stubborn fennel seed. 'You know as well as I do that our Shubhashini is no paragon of beauty. As she grows older she'll turn surlier. Don't you think we should find her a home before it is too late? Don't you want to be blessed with grandchildren? The people I am talking about are distantly related to my maternal cousin's wife. They are well-known landlords, one of the oldest jomidaar families from Bankura who have tremendous goodwill in their village. And the groom has just sat for his B.A. exam and hopes to clear it at one go.'

Outside, day died on a funeral pyre of fleeting flames and night was born in utter darkness. Dolly-kaakima chewed harder and secured the safety pin back on her bangle. Baba must have recalled the face of his ugly duckling and found his heart instantly sinking. No amount of dowry or western demeanour could wipe the pimples off Shubha's dark and pitted cheeks. Much as he tried imagining her in bridal finery, he only saw an awkward, lanky child in huge glasses fretting away. She was as doomed as her ebony complexion.

Baba looked at Dolly-kaakima, defeated, and said, 'When do they want to come and see her?'

They came. They saw. But, alas, they remained unconquered.

Their rejection, in the form of a rude postcard, arrived to strike Shubha like a thunderbolt, and she immediately succumbed to the hopeless struggle of living up to everyone's expectations.

The missive described Shubhashini as a weakling. The family of the prospective groom feared she wouldn't be able to bear children; that she had been spoilt by her convent education. What use was a woman if she were no better than a barren piece of land? No thank you, my dear! We refuse to accept a girl who has such poor health. Fat dowry be damned – we know when bad fruit is being passed off as farm fresh. We wish her well but do not want her in our backyard! Yours sincerely...

For the next month Dolly-kaakima breathed fire. Her black wok wobbled dangerously over the flames every time she fiercely scrapped it with her spatula. Her temper and the mutilated stem of a banana tree simultaneously came to a slow boil. Wiping the perspiration from her brow, she cursed Shubha's bad luck. Even Shib Thakur's phallus in the prayer room wasn't spared. For weeks she remained stubborn, refusing to bow before its dense magnificence. Thank heavens, Bijoy-kaka had moved into the spare bedroom, impervious to her yellings. Not once did he shout back or create a scene. As the month went by, the rest of the family got used to hearing him sing passionate Shyama-shongeets dedicated to the scimitar-swinging Goddess Kaali over Dolly-kaakima's hollers. But Baba was not amused. He sent his brother a note, threatening to evict him if the bickering did not end forthwith.

Ma, of course, slipped into a world of make-belief to fight her severe depression. Every afternoon, after lunch, she went and lay down on her four-poster and turned the pages of the latest *Ultorath*. Yet photographs of actors and actresses tinted purple left her mood dark and messy. Even gossip-laced articles insinuating a torrid affair between Suchitra Sen and Uttam Kumar did little to lift the gloom. Her own fantasies were like ghosts leaping off her lids. Soon insomnia and indigestion came to keep her company. Antacids and barbiturates took their toll. The combination was lethal – her mouth became twisted and bitter, her breasts sagged and her hair began thinning at an alarming rate. Ma had always managed to defy middle age but now, without protest, she slipped into that raddled, indefinite realm from where there could be no return to youth. Recurrent bouts of ill-health saw her losing weight so rapidly that Beejeepishi had to force her to eat at least one proper meal, even if it meant boiled rice and plain, boiled vegetables. To liven up the dull fare, Beejeepishi sliced a fragrant gondhoraaj lemon into thin wedges and placed a piece alongside a mound of salt and a hot, green chilli. But no temptations, fiery or sour, whipped up Ma's appetite.

Just as dark clouds over 189/A Amherst Street threatened to burst, a ray of stubborn sunlight pierced the gloom. Dolly-kaakima received an urgent missive, this time from her younger sister. Pulling out a pin from her bun, she slit open the envelope. As she read Molly's letter, her heart leapt into her mouth. Akaash Baba, wrote Molly, would be arriving next month at a devotee's home in Baghbazaar from his ashram in Rishikesh. What a wonderful stroke of luck! With his vigorous occult powers and spiritual energy he would set things right! Of course he would! He'd surge through his band of faithful devotees and find Shubha not only a worthy husband but also another lease of life!

With tears coursing down her cheeks Dolly-kaakima rushed to the prayer room. There she lay prostrate in front of Shib Thakur's phallus, brought down to her knees at last and begging for forgiveness. She had undermined the lingam's divine tumescence. Surely if Shib Thakur wished, Shubhashini would not have to remain a frustrated spinster! How impetuous she had been! How foolish! Only Shib Thakur could work things out and save the family! This was no task meant for run-of-the-mill women in the pantheon – the Lokkhis and Shoroshwotis and Shitolas of heaven! It needed a virile god to end a virgin's plight! Holy Notoraj, forgive me! I'm stupid! Only your mercy and cosmic dance can drive some sense into my thick head!

'Bholey-baba paar karega! Bom-bom Bholeynath!'

Dolly-kaakima couldn't wait to break the news to Ma. She lingered in the kitchen during lunch, hoping that Ma had not decided to fast that afternoon.

Ma's sciatica was playing up again. Nowadays she could hardly lower herself on the floor to pray or eat. She limped in at last and, groaning, sat down with great difficulty. Dolly-kaakima smiled from the shadows. Ma didn't notice. Instead, she listlessly fiddled with the rice and mixed it with some daal poured out on her bell metal plate by Beejeepishi.

Eating a very serious slice of a very serious-looking pabda fish, Dolly-kaakima said, 'Didi, we are blessed by Narayon Moharaj.'

Ma was instantly stung. She had lost faith forever in Narayon Moharaj's celestial supremacy. He had done nothing to save her from the affront of Shubha's numerous rejections. Throwing Dolly-kaakima a withering glance, she hissed with great acerbity, 'Why, Dolly, what has He come to bless us for? Does Narayon Moharaj have bleeding gums? Does he have flatulence and nowhere to fart? I give a damn for His blessings after the embarrassment He has made us suffer!'

'Haribol!' Dolly-kaakima murmured, completely stupefied. Her sister-in-law had more spunk than she had imagined. 'Didi, have you really lost faith?' she asked, looking askance at Ma's face.

Fat teardrops rained all over my mother's mound of rice and lentils. Realising her sacrilege, she chose silence for atonement. On the bell metal plate opposite hers, a coriander leaf draping one glazed eye of the pabda fish fell back into the gravy. Dolly-kaakima immediately popped the head into her mouth. Crushing the bones with relish, she removed the residue and placed it neatly on the floor.

'We women have to live our lives under His thumb, Didi,' she confided. 'We have no right to question Him, such is our lot. I can understand your frustration but believe me, I did my best.'

'I know, I know,' said Ma, wiping her tears. 'Shubha was born unlucky!'

'Oh, don't say that! Worse could have befallen her! She is saved! Molly's just informed me that Akaash Baba will be coming to Baghbazaar soon.'

Ma looked up from her soggy plate, astounded. She couldn't believe her ears. 'Akaash Baba? You mean Akaash Baba from Rishikesh?'

'Yes, of course,' said Dolly-kaakima, feeling like a cat propitiously born under Pisces.

'Oh, Narayon Moharaj, Narayon Moharaj! I have sinned! Pity me!' cried Ma. 'Dolly, we must go visit the holy man as soon as possible.'

'We will, we will, don't worry. I fret for Shubha as much as you do. You know I've never discriminated between your daughters and my Bachchoo.'

'God bless you, my sister! You're the only person in this wretched house who understands my plight.'

'Let's leave things to Akaash Baba now. He has hundreds and hundreds of devotees from all walks of life. He may find Shubha a groom who's more our kind.'

'Why not? Why not?' Ma consoled herself. 'We can't undermine Narayon Moharaj's infinite mercy, can we?'

'Or his bleeding gums and flatulence,' giggled Dolly-kaakima, jingling her gold bangles and lifting her bulky frame off the kitchen floor.

But the distant stars had charted a different path for Shubha. The wounds that had been inflicted cut deep. And in the following week she became violently ill.

Even after a fortnight, when her fever would not subside, Baba decided to consult the city's most eminent physician. He was a trenchant old bachelor, doubling also as the state's chief minister. But he had gone to college with Baba, depended on his legal expertise and found time now, despite his hectic schedule, to come and see his old friend's ailing daughter.

To the conch-shell blasting for the twilight orison, Dr Bidhan Roy was ushered into 189/A Amherst Street and escorted straight to Shubha's bedroom. Ma hurried behind him, adjusting her sari over her head. Baba followed, carrying his briefcase. Dolly-kaakima trooped in, chewing her paan. Beejeepishi lurked near the door, fretting. The air over the little room hung heavy with expectancy. Nervous fidgets slowly gave way to quiet prayers as the doctor began his routine check-up.

At last, having counted her pulse, he gently let the patient's feeble hand drop back on the bed. Dr Roy now glanced through the blood report. Then, very matter-of-factly, he pronounced that Shubha was down with a severe attack of typhoid.

'Typhoid!' repeated Ma from the shadows, pressing her sari's anchol over her trembling lips.

'Typhoid?' questioned Dolly-kaakima, almost starry-eyed.

'Yes, typhoid,' growled Dr Bidhan Roy, scrutinising his audience with impatience. The soft scratching of his Parker pen on the prescription pad sounded ominous. Then he folded his stethoscope and remarked, 'What can you expect after making your children consume all that rotting fruit you serve your wonderful gods and goddesses? Can they purify the filth carried by buzzing flies? And what about the foul water from the Gonga that you drink as part of your silly rituals? I repeat, the girl has a bad bout of typhoid. She must be properly nursed if you want her to recuperate fast!'

Day by day Shubha's speech grew incoherent. Most mornings she woke up with a splitting headache. All kinds of medicines were administered to relieve her pain. From homeopathy to Ayurvedic drugs – between Ma and Beejeepishi, no stones remained unturned. But Shubha refused to pull herself together as the weight of rejection ripped apart the silk of her precious memories. Finally, she asked for a string of prayer beads. Ma happily provided her with the new toy. Shubha took to reciting the rosary through long and exhausting hours. The mindless repetition of Krishno Thakur's name gave her some solace. She often slipped into a daze and had to be shaken awake. Perhaps she had misjudged her god in her petty anger. Perhaps he had really given her a second lease of life. To repent. To weep. To fall at his lotus feet. To tell him, without reserve, that he was her one true lover.

'Dinobondhu! Korunashindhu!'

Oh friend of the poor! Oh ocean of Compassion!

'Forgive! Forgive! Pity me! Have mercy!' cried Shubha's heart at last, as she tossed and turned in her sleep, flinging away the cover sheet and staring into the dark.

Finally, Krishno Thakur spoke to her in her dreams.

'Weep, my girl, and I will gather you in my arms,' he said, smiling and offering her the peacock plume from his crown. 'Weep and let your tears wash away all hurts. I am there, waiting for you. You cannot run away from me! Which man will give you the happiness you truly deserve? I have the power to change your life. I have the key to unlock all that hidden pain in your heart and let it flow away in the dark waters of the Jomuna. Look at your mother – is she happy? Look at your aunt – is she content? Of course not! They are too engrossed with their petty little wants to come to me and seek forgiveness. But if they want peace they will have to surrender at my feet, without looking back. I am Krishno, saviour of the world! I am the mischief hidden in the heart of every child! The passion buried in the bosom of every lover! The wisdom concealed in the pronouncements of every philosopher! I ride the head of deadly serpents! I hold mountains on the tip of my finger! I draw the chariot of my true disciple through every battle! I am Krishno! I will guide you through darkness! My flute will call you again and again and fill your heart with longing! You will be my Radha and dance the raas with me! You will lie in my arms and I will smear you with my all-forgiving colour! I will wipe away your ugliness and make you beautiful and blue like me! I will love you forever, do not fear! I am Modhushudon of a thousand identities – which name will you call me by?'

Not for a moment did Shubha count the sleepless hours Ma and Beejeepishi had spent by her bed to speed up her convalescence – the quiet afternoons when they had sat beside her, draping her forehead with strips of muslin dipped in cold water scented with 4711 eau de Cologne. In her new intoxication, she forgot the umpteen times Ma woke up at night to administer the pills and take her temperature. The tray brimming with medicines had been removed from the dressing table. The thermometer dipped in a glass filled almost halfway with opaque Dettol water had disappeared. The reality of her illness became more an awful dread for those who had witnessed it than for Shubha herself. She was convinced that she had survived because of a miracle.

And she was hell-bent on fighting her way back to heaven.

One evening, once her fever had subsided, I found Shubha strolling in the garden near Baba's library. In a while she went and sat on a wrought-iron bench under the jasmine bower. The old and weather-beaten seat was almost hidden by a shock of trailing tendrils laden with early buds. A flock of shaaleeks quarrelled near the marble birdbath. The silence of the sun caught fire and spoke at last, briefly, through clouds that bruised the sky. Finding her humming, I waved out but she pretended not to see me. So I went and sat beside her, listening to her song. Startled, the shaaleeks flew into the air in a sudden explosion of wings.

'Raag Boshonto?' I inquired, curious.

'No,' Shubha said, smiling vaguely. 'Mollhaar.'

I was taken aback.

'But we're still in the middle of spring,' I said. 'Isn't Mollhaar sung to welcome the monsoon, Bordi?'

'Didn't you hear the papihas warble?' Shubha demanded.

'Papihas?' I asked, puzzled. 'I only saw a flock of stupid shaaleeks fly away.'

'Papihas, my dear, papihas!' Shubha insisted. 'You don't want to see or listen; that's why you don't notice or hear!'

'Bordi, give me a break! How can papihas sing in the middle of March?'

'They do! You're so busy flying your kites that you shoo the poor things away. But I can hear them all the time. I love their songs. They are constantly singing for me!'

'You must be longing for the rains then.'

'Oh, but why should I long for the rains when it's pouring already? Can't you see the raindrops dripping from the bower? Aren't you wet? I'm soaked through, Mohini. I'm cold and shivering!'

Completely flummoxed, I blamed Shubha's gibberish to her tryst with typhoid and quickly changed the subject.

'Bordi, don't you want to go back to school and meet your friends again?'

'School? You mean the sea, don't you?'

'No, I mean school. The convent. I wanted to tell you that your friends still remember you. In fact, just the other day, Mother Bernadette was asking after you.'

'Oh, *Mother Bernadette!*'

'Yes, she sends you her very best wishes.'

'She's an evil old witch!' Shubha spat out, rolling her eyes. 'You mustn't go anywhere near her! She has claws, my dear. And she hammers Mary's little boy black and blue every single day! Slap, slap, slap, slap, slap! Hammer, hammer, hammer, hammer, hammer! Can you believe it? The poor child's been crying his heart out! Didn't you hear him? And haven't you set him free yet, Mohini? Mother Bernadette has had him locked up in the chapel, without telling Mother Superior. Don't you know?'

'Bordi, are you feeling unwell?'

'Oh I'm fine, darling; I'm just fine,' Shubha turned to look at me and gave me a sudden hug. 'You're so impatient, my little one! How can I describe the sunlight or the sound of a wave or a bird to you? How can I explain that those wicked nuns are abusing Mary's boy child day in and day out? And all the wretched things that they make him do! It's shameful! But you're so restless that you don't notice these things!'

My curiosity got the better of me and I couldn't help asking, 'What do the poor nuns do?'

'*Poor!* They're depraved, darling – they're not poor! They lock the chapel door after vespers and strip down to their cami-knickers, can you imagine? *Their lacy cami-knickers!* And they pretend to murmur prayers and dance around that poor, bewildered child. Then... then they fondle his little willie and his little marbles and... and... and call him all sorts of names. And, and...' Shubha's voice trailed away and came to an abrupt halt. 'You're too young to understand! You're still a baby,' she sighed, flushing.

'Would you like me to take you back to your room?' I suggested, stupefied, not knowing what else to ask.

'Let's sit here a bit longer, Mohini. Stay still and you might listen to Krishno Thakur play the flute for me. He was playing Raag Mollhaar just before you came! Can't you hear the music? Darling, hush a bit! Don't go on and on and on! Do be still! Krishno Thakur is playing for both of us. Can't you hear his flute?'

'No, Bordi,' I said dully.

'Listen hard! You're not listening hard enough, you silly girl. But then, I can't really blame you,' Shubha broke into a giggle. 'You're not in love.'

'Are you?' I demanded.

Shubha blushed and nodded, swinging her legs to and fro. She pulled at a leaf and began tearing it to shreds.

'You are in love?' I whispered, delighted.

'Yes, darling,' she confided, 'but don't tell Ma or Dolly-kaakima. Only Beejeepishi knows. And she's very, very pleased.'

'I'm so happy for you, Bordi! You've finally found your dream prince,' I said. 'But how do you know you're in love?'

'Oh, it's very easy! Very, very easy! When you know there's the right amount of sunlight in a room, or the right amount of blood in rambling roses, or why there are stars in the sky, you also know that you're in love!'

'And who's the lucky man?'

Shubha hid her face with her palms. 'Promise you won't tattle?' she demanded.

'Promise!'

'It's Krishno.'

'Krishno? Krishno, as in Krishno Thakur?' I said, stunned. 'What do you mean?'

'I want to marry Him, don't you understand...?'

'Oh Bordi, but He's...'

'He is?'

'A bloody god!' I blurted out.

'So? What difference does that make?'

'No. Not to you. Because I think you're mad!'

Over Shubha's laughter I jumped up and ran across the falling shadows, too enraged to realise that my sister sat poised on the cusp of sanity and lunacy, helplessly slipping from one to the other for no fault of hers.

I was too young then, too self-absorbed to understand that it is only through love that we fulfill or destroy ourselves. I couldn't believe that Shubha had deliberately sunk into the treacle of her preoccupation with Krishno, to escape the insults heaped on her almost every day. Krishno Thakur won her over only because he was invisible. Under his spell, she slammed the door on the faces of those who had hurt her. It was easier to remain Krishno-intoxicated, quietly lying in his cerulean arms when nobody was looking, than get up and face the world. Poor Shubha! Lost in some fragmented universe, all jumbled up in the fragrance of jasmine and the sound of the celestial flute and Raag Mollhaar, she let herself be seduced at last.

What was I to do? How was I to save her? Inevitably, I had to tell Sylvia.

In Sylvia D'Silva I had always found a spirited ally from my first day at school. She had been Hyde to my Jekyll all along. We had come from disparate worlds but our rebellion was similar. Her life had such speed, such excitement, such music; mine, in comparison, was almost cloistered like the nuns. There were too many 'ifs' and 'buts' that I had to take into account, too many rules that I had to remember. Sylvia's carefree, impertinent attitude was a direct contrast to my measured gait, but I learnt to loosen up as we went up to higher classes, finding fleeting opportunities to run free in Sylvia's boisterous company. Sylvia always remained a scourge, a vociferous campaigner against hateful convent regulations. She was always the rowdy leader and I, her meek accomplice. Street-smart Sylvia had, over the last few months, lured me firmly into her pen. Severe warnings from Mother Bernadette fell on deaf ears. I absolutely refused to brook all intimidation that could prevent me from following my confidant at break-time all over the basketball court like Mary's little lamb.

Our woes would usually start at morning assembly, led by the Mother Superior and watched over with a hawk's eye by the holy Sisters floating in their black habits and reciting their rosaries. Underneath her wimple, Mother Bernadette was a tough old bird, repressive by instinct and full of advice. The older girls used to secretly call her 'Juliet's nurse,' as she'd shepherd her younger charges into the big hall for prayers, always suspicious of their impulses. If Sylvia happened to chatter away or let a frog slip out of her tunic pocket, unmindful of the novenas, the nuns would punish her after school. Not that Sylvia cared. Her disappointment arose more from the fact that she wouldn't be able to meet Michael Barnes, her boyfriend, in time for the four o'clock jam sessions at Trincas and jive to '*Lipstick on your collar*' or '*Speedy Gonzalves*.'

Sylvia was my best bet for seeking advice.

'Shubha has fallen in love,' I confided, bouncing a ball at the basketball court during short break.

'Oh good!' Sylvia laughed, dodging it away from me. 'With whom?'

'With Krishno,' I said, chasing her down the court.

'Where does the guy live?' Sylvia asked, aiming the ball into the net.

'In heaven,' I sighed, watching Sylvia score once more.

'That's cool!' Sylvia yelled, wiping her sweaty brow with the crook of her arm.

'She's fallen hook, line and sinker for a god,' I revealed, looking into her eyes without blinking.

'The bloody bugger! Is he *that* good-looking? What's he gone and done now, haan? Made her jerk him off or what?'

'I've no idea,' I whimpered, turning away.

Sylvia thoughtfully chewed on her bubble-gum and was amazed to see tears in my eyes.

'Stop being a ninny. Or do you too want to go batty like your sister?' she scolded.

'How can we help Shubha?'

'Simple, my dear Watson! Let's find her a proper boyfriend.'

'Don't be daft!'

'You must get her over to my birthday bash,' Sylvia whispered, confident. 'I'll get Eddie Jones to sort her out.'

'That guy who looks like Tony Curtis?' I exclaimed. 'You mean he'll actually date Shubha?'

'Yes, my darling Mohini, yes,' Sylvia grinned, playfully smacking my bottom.

'And Mini?'

'Keep her miles away.'

'Damn Krishno,' I hissed under my breath. 'Why can't he leave my poor Bordi alone?'

It was a stroke of incredible luck that Dolly-kaakima and Ma decided to visit Akaash Baba the very evening Sylvia D'Silva threw her birthday party. Baba was in an expansive mood. He not only allowed Shubha and me to go to the get-together, but decided to play our escort as well. On his way to the Calcutta Club he'd drop us off at Sylvia's, he promised, and collect us on his way back home. It was that simple!

Giving Mini the slip, I managed to convince Shubha to come along.

I didn't care that Dolly-kaakima would lash out later; that Ma would helplessly wring her hands and get Beejeepishi to splash Gongajol mixed with cow dung all over us. I just didn't have the energy to think about the consequences. I didn't want the fun to end before it had begun. Nat King Cole's '*When I fall in love, it will be forever...*' kept playing over and over in my head. Our escape was all that I could think of.

It had been a while since Shubha had left home. She chuckled softly, looking out of the car as if she had never seen the Calcutta pavements before. Freshly washed by the bishti who went around sprinkling water from his leather bag every morning and evening, they stretched before our eyes, almost deserted. The setting sun burnt huge bonfires in the sky. The tram wires spun a web against the flames. Some rooks flew by, lost in a muddle of factory chimneys. The road sped past many angular, misshapen houses, standing silently with their soot-ridden façades. Here and there, through the cracked bricks, a tree, shimmering with leaves, tried pushing forth its branches. Billboards were stuck on many building rooftops advertising a variety of products from Kolynos toothpaste to Himalaya Bouquet talc. Film posters were plastered on crumbling walls. I could see Vyjayanthimala, in red stretch pants, clutching a bilious green hat and sticking out her obscene behind into Raj Kapoor's yellow face, grinning and enticing audiences to shows of *Sangam* at Ganesh Talkies. Suchitra Sen, in a diaphanous pink sari, with no behind to boast of, clung to Uttam Kumar, beckoning their diehard fans to a rerun of *Pothey Holo Deri* at Uttora, Purobi and Ujjola. A pie-dog kicked up its leg, urinated on the bulwark and limped away. The city wore the mysteries of the commonplace but Shubha's eyes sparkled. Escaping from Amherst Street, she seemed to have become a different person and I couldn't but help give her a friendly hug.

Perhaps Eddie Jones would finally jounce her out of her Krishno trance!

The more I thought about the little interlude I had planned for Shubha, the more restless I became till we were deposited at Sylvia's doorstep on Ripon Street. The faint faecal odour of inadequate drains and the blaring radiogram shook me out of my daydreams. Sylvia appeared at the main door and swept us in. Suddenly, without prior warning, Krishno Thakur miraculously disappeared with the same speed at which the paper roses spilling from ornate Muradabad vases had begun vanishing at the party. Shubha seemed to be enjoying herself hugely. The magician, who was the star of the show, kept bowing and preening. He was a short, square man with a funny little moustache and ginger hair. The sheer merriment of the atmosphere reeking of cigarette smoke, loud music, the pungency of vindaloo, alcohol and heavy perfume swallowed us up.

A fat lady in a floral-patterned dress kept repeating, 'Welcome, my children. Welcome! Welcome!' over Connie Francis crooning, *'Everybody's somebody's fool! Everybody's somebody's plaything...'* on the huge radiogram that took pride of place at the far end of the hall. We smiled at her shyly. Sylvia introduced us to her mother who patted my cheek and insisted we call her 'Auntie Nellie'. Then the magician began chasing Shubha all around the room. He made her laugh and clap, melting her out of the curtains. Before she could get away, he had fished out hard-boiled eggs from her blouse and the King of Hearts from the folds of her sari. Shubha giggled helplessly and covered her face with her palms. The crowd hooted with laughter. Ian, Sylvia's elder brother, came around to hand us glasses of rum punch. Just then, a woman with bright red, bee-stung lips and wearing enormous high-heels, sashayed across and thrust slices of birthday cake into our mouths. Ian pinched her bottom and she giggled and slapped his hand, almost toppling over and dropping the plate she carried. A balloon burst in the middle of the commotion. I stood mesmerised, watching Michael Barnes kiss Sylvia smack on the lips under some coloured streamers. His friend, Eddie Jones, now sauntered up to Shubha and led her to the makeshift dance floor. But for a stubborn cowlick that fell over his brow, he had slicked back the rest of his hair with brilliantine. His exceptionally good teeth kept flashing as he smiled. He looked so thin in his tight-fitting jeans that Shubha could have touched his spine by merely pressing his bellybutton. But, behind the slim façade, his arms rippled with solid muscles. He wore his sleeves rolled up high, showing-off his biceps as he started to dance.

Shubha happily wafted where Eddie Jones chose to lead her. The thumping success of his band that played three nights at the Blue Fox made him bold. His asides to Shubha, as they swayed and sashayed together, must have been dribblingly wonderful and perfectly emulsified for she couldn't help breaking into fits of laughter every few minutes. There was clapping and whooping as he spun her round and round. No one was quite sure what he'd do next till he hurled her right off the floor.

'Put her down, you crazy cheapskate,' yelled Ian, as Sinatra's boots meant for walking came to a grinding halt.

'Relax! I like you,' Eddie whispered to Shubha. 'I'm not going to stitch you up!'

Shubha blushed, watching Eddie sink on his knee and peck her hand over and over.

'My goddess, oh my pagan, sexy goddess,' he purred, winking at the guests. 'What would I do without you? Don't make me faint! Don't make me die! Don't break my heart and go away!'

Jimmy, Sylvia's younger brother, catcalled over the music. A piercing whistle followed. And in a grand finale the guests raised a toast to the most popular dancers of the evening.

The Great Escape was disclosed to Ma as soon as she returned from Baghbazaar. Mini let the cat out of the bag even before she could enter the house, accosting her at the gate and telling her, between sobs, how we had run away with Baba.

'Hai Bhogobaan!' Ma shrieked. 'Now they'll meet shameless half-castes! Hai Bhogobaan, they'll bump and grind and dance like cheap whores to English music! Hai Bhogobaan, they'll eat beef – they'll eat *beef* – and defile forever the names of their forefathers!'

Dolly-kaakima, of course, aimed all her accusations at our karma. She drew to the fore her past talent and displayed once again how brilliant she could have been at creating a rip-roaring song-and-dance had she had the opportunity to participate in a high-voltage melodrama in one of north Calcutta's commercial theatres. The salver in her hand, laden with a jasmine garland and some proshaad, came crashing to the floor. Over her hollers, Ma disappeared into her bedroom and banged the door shut.

We returned to Amherst Street with Baba well past midnight, basking in the afterglow of Ian D'Silva's rum punch. Ma watched us silently from her bedroom window. She knew that the whisky inside Baba's belly was still warm. But she hadn't guessed about us. Disgusted at his inebriation, Ma tugged at the manacles of her marriage and rushed to the top of the stairs, waiting to catch us red-handed. Beejeepishi opened the main door and let us in.

'*Stop!*' Ma bellowed as soon as we entered the foyer.

Baba was startled by her outburst. We cowered behind him in

fright. The intensity of the moment magnified like the sound of a pin dropping in a vast and empty hall.

'Don't you dare send up the girls without having them wash up!' Ma screamed, turning into a snarling, disputatious bitch. 'I can't take this any longer! Year in and year out I have tried to hold this family together! But *you*,' she pointed an accusing finger at her husband as he stepped back. '*You!* What have you done to make me happy? Answer me! Now you want to ruin your daughters as well, do you?'

'What do we do with her?' Baba whispered, clutching the fanfold of his dhuti. I started to giggle. But Shubha would have none of it.

'Give her vindaloo,' she pronounced, tipsily swaying from side to side. 'Give her pork vindaloo fired with lots of bloody chillis! That will take care of her righteousness! Burn her twice! Once going in! Then going out! She'll be fine in a jiffy!'

In the silence that followed Ma came tearing down the stairs, ignoring her sciatica. I only saw streaks of lightning and thunder like those she had witnessed in her dreams. And then I heard the sound of a stunning slap, rapidly followed by others. Once the fury died, she returned to her bedroom, limping and exhausted. The inclemency of her rage left streaks across our cheeks. But, worse, my best friend, Sylvia, was forever forbidden from entering 189/A Amherst Street.

The ban didn't work though Ma tried her best to ensure that Sylvia and I were kept apart. But that was not to be.

The Senior Cambridge exams were over and I was now in college, again at Loreto on Middleton Row. Sylvia had scraped through and mercifully found place at Mrs Dunford's, not too far from the convent, to do a course in typing and shorthand. We'd try and meet in the afternoons, whenever I could make excuses to go to New Market to buy some trinket from Chamba Lama or Baba's favourite cupcakes and Baklava from Nahoum's or catch up for a spot of lunch at Bar-B-Q on Park Street. Some days we'd even disappear to watch an English movie at Lighthouse or New Empire. Ma never found out. And our rendezvous never stopped.

Then, from nowhere, I discovered Mini's secret.

Always cagey and furtive, Mini had slowly built around herself a wall so impregnable that we now had very little to share. Her unexpressed bitterness had driven a wedge between us and it never allowed for concessions, for forgiveness, especially after I had whisked Shubha off to Sylvia's birthday bash. That grudge festered over time, mounting to proportions beyond my control. I became the evil witch and her arch rival. She blamed me initially for my looks that always won for me – 'most unfairly' as she put it – Baba's partiality and, later, a hundred different things she liked to imagine as impediments. She called me manipulative and selfish but my instinct always told me, even in those early days, that there was something more disquieting than what met the eye.

A small, demanding demon had taken possession of Mini – a green-eyed monster that mercilessly reduced her emotions to burn helplessly in the fire of jealousy. And by now poor Shubha was too far gone in her affair with Krishno to allow for others' confidences. Seasons had passed with a harsh emptiness for her. She took to spending most of her time in Ma's prayer room, irritating the hell out of me and pulling at my heartstrings by turns.

A year senior to me in college, Mini's new set of friends were an exasperating bunch of girls who had money to burn – offspring of nouveau riche Bengali merchants trying to make memsahibs out of their daughters through Western education. Mini began using makeup on the sly and seemed more worried about the size of her bra than her studies. Her mind, cluttered with foolishness and tied up in pink ribbons, was easily browbeaten by all that glittered. And to my annoyance, she always went missing at home once we returned from college. One day I bumped into Beejeepishi in the courtyard and confronted her.

'Have you seen Mini?' I asked. 'I can't for the life of me ever find her in the house.'

'And you never will,' Beejeepishi murmured, sweeping the floor with her battered broom. 'Your mother ought to look into her sudden disappearances. But who am I to open my mouth?'

'What do you mean?'

'Your mother's gone to the theatre again, with your kaka and kaakima,' Beejeepishi complained, adjusting the stark white thaan she wore over her shorn, salt-and-pepper hair. 'Baap-re-baap, what is so enticing about the theatre I'd like to know? One would think Noti Binodini has made a stunning comeback!'

'I know Ma's gone to see the new play at Rongmohol,' I said with impatience. 'But where's Mini?'

Beejeepishi only twisted her mouth and remained silent. I set off in the direction of the garden. Beyond the pond there was a tiny room used by the gardener to keep his implements. I saw a few stray pigeons roosting on its roof. A soft breeze rustled the leaves of the jamrul tree that sheltered it. Then I heard voices. My curiosity aroused, I walked quietly towards the outhouse and was startled by Mini's smothered laughter.

'Not here, not here, you fool. I want it here,' Mini's voice was fierce. 'Oh don't stop now! Don't stop!'

Unable to arrest myself, I put my eye to a crack on the door.

In a haze of shifting light, as if between sleep and waking, I saw Mini leaning against a stack of gunny bags piled up against the wall, her blouse undone. Dibaakor-da kept kissing her neck before sliding his mouth down to take a nipple between his teeth and impatiently suckle her breast. Mini clung to him with unbearable hunger, clamorous with small moans. Yet, she seemed content in the knowledge that he knew her body better than she did. And as he held her in his arms, exorcising whatever withholding there may have been, Mini's breathing started to come in short bursts – a strong and cunning beast that had overpowered its victim – and she clutched at his hair at the nape of his neck, setting off a constant, low litany. 'Bite! Dibaakor-da, I love it when you bite!'

I was petrified. The ferocity of Mini's passion made me sick. Without warning, my legs gave way. I couldn't believe what I was seeing! I was furious and utterly helpless. Mini and Dibaakor-da were lovers! I should have guessed it long ago! I should have guessed it the day they went off to the movies without informing Ma! The day he pulled at her pigtails and said that he was in love with her! There had always been something surreptitious in the way they stole glances, smiled at each other when no one was looking or accosted each other on the first floor corridor. Oh, I should have guessed! But fool that I was – a blind, idiotic, damned fool – I kept my eyes shut! My sister could do no wrong! Mini could never be a cheap little sexually frustrated minx!

With great effort I fled to our bedroom and lay down, willing my heart to stop beating so wildly. Then I rose and went to the bathroom, splashed my face with water and looked into the mirror. A slow, grey misery descended on my thoughts. I felt emptied of all reaction, sunk in a heap of broken images. Too horrified to make sense of Mini's suffering and inevitable doom, I kept groping for a pattern of words that would relieve my outrage. What was I searching for in that haphazard rubble of guilt? What would Mini do if Ma found out? Did Dolly-kaakima already know? Oh God, oh God, Baba would kill Mini!

Incest!

Did Mini realise she was playing with fire? The little slut! The little whore! Mini, Mini, Mini – my poor, neglected sister! Should I just go back and slap her till she came to her senses? What could I do to put Mini out of her misery? Didn't Dibaakor-da know what he was doing? Didn't he realise the enormity of such unbidden passion? The selfish bastard!

In my utter helplessness I wanted to shout; I wanted to reach out and rally round. But I remained miserably paralysed by my discovery, stuck in front of the mirror with beads of water dripping down my face.

Next afternoon, I rushed to Mrs Dunford's after class. Sylvia was waiting for me. Her skills at shorthand and typing were average and she was often bored. Now she poured forth her woes before I could express mine.

'You know how frightened I am of chipping my nails on the bloody keyboard,' she cried, fuming, as we walked to Flurys for a quick cup of coffee. 'So I tried typing carefully. But it only managed to slow down my speed. And bloody Mrs Dunford! None of my excuses worked! She said she couldn't accept my "slackness", the bloody bitch! Slackness, indeed! I was only doing it to save my poor, beautiful nails!'

'Darling, we all have to bear our crosses!' I tried to laugh. But Sylvia was in no mood for my placations.

'Now don't you bloody start off too! I told her I had a terrible headache, but do you think she'd listen?' Sylvia ranted. 'When I asked if I could be excused, she shouted "Certainly not! Don't you know the uses of an Aspro and half a glass of water?" Just imagine! Insulting me in front of the whole bloody class!'

Ignoring her tirade, and as soon as we had settled into our seats, I couldn't help blurting out, 'Damn your nails, Sylvia! Something terrible has happened at home.'

'What?' she said, casting me a worried look. 'Is your father unwell?'

'No. It's Mini,' I whispered, fidgeting with the strap of my hand bag.

'She's shagging that cousin of yours, isn't she?' came Sylvia's prompt response.

'How did you know?' I inquired, taken aback.

'One look at old Dibbie, and I knew it two years ago!' she laughed.

'Why didn't you tell me?' I accused.

'You never asked!' she retorted.

'What do I do? Should I talk to Dibaakor-da?'

'You could try, but I don't think it'll work! My advice is – do nothing! They'll have to work it through, silly. You stay out of it.'

'Should I tell Ma?'

'Are you daft, my darling girl? If I know her, she'll have an instant bloody heart attack! Have you forgotten what happened after my birthday party? Baap re! I'll never forget the mouthful I got from her, by God! You just stay calm, understand? I might be out of old Dunford's clutches after next Friday's tests. And if I get a job, come to my office, in case there's further trouble. We'll try and see how Madam Mini can be sorted out without your Mom having a fit.'

So I let sleeping dogs lie. I accepted Mini's affair – as I was to accept a hundred other injustices later, with my eyes closed and my lips sealed, only because girls from good families never talk about these things. Foolishly, I had hoped a sudden gust of magical, benign wind would blow the aberrations away. But Mini remained secretive and distant.

In the meanwhile, Sylvia, true to her words, landed a plum assignment.

Mrs Dunford had certainly worked Sylvia to the bones till she was fit for a certificate. And before the week was out, she found herself a cushy job, sashaying down the corridors of the British Council as Peter Hammond's secretary.

Peter's wife, Henrietta, was an emaciated violinist. I had met her once when I had gone to fetch Sylvia from her office to go to the movies. And, quite honestly, I hadn't liked what I had seen. She had a mean little mouth and hated India and everything Indian. Her loud complaints were ridiculous. Nothing about Calcutta seemed to please her – not the biryani from Aminia that made her burp through the night, nor the scented fennel seeds she was forced to chew as a digestive after dinner that invariably went and wedged between her teeth. Sylvia whispered that Henrietta had even complained about the local loo paper that only managed to aggravate her haemorrhoids!

With a bleeding arse and a runny tummy, Henrietta was having a tough time trying to cope with Calcutta. And Peter Hammond was hard pressed to make her see sense; to make her understand that no civilised life was complete without a dose of amoebic dysentery by the time you were twenty and living in exotic India. The more he tried distracting her, the bitterer she became with his colleagues and the local guests Peter had to officially entertain. Initially Henrietta did try and give a handful of concerts by arm-twisting the Calcutta School of Music. But the audience had better respect for Mahler's symphony No. 5, worried that poor Gustav would turn in his grave listening to her renditions. Henrietta, in turn, could only throw a tantrum to salvage her reputation and blame her failure to bad acoustics and illiterate listeners. It was left to a meek and an unusually mild clerk in Peter Hammond's office to set the high and mighty Bara Mem right.

Sylvia took great delight in telling me about Henrietta's downfall.

She had confided to Khirod-babu, head clerk at the library, about Henrietta's woes, remembering that he practiced naturopathy in his spare time. Khirod-babu had gathered enough courage to clutch at the folds of his dhuti and suggest that, perhaps, he might be able to help the Bara Mem. Sylvia wasted no time passing the information to Peter Hammond. Peter immediately conveyed Sylvia's message to Henrietta. And with great alacrity Henrietta decided to drop in on Khirod-babu.

A firm tap on the clerk's shoulder the following morning made him start. He jumped up from his seat, turned around and was delighted when he realised who the visitor was hidden under the brim of a large panama.

'Oh, bhot an honour, Mrs Henrietta,' he gurgled. 'But why for you are creeping up my backside, Madam? Come to my frontside! Not to worry! And do shit and be comphortable; do shit down! Shit down and relask!'

Henrietta raised an eyebrow but, nevertheless, walked up to the two chairs meant for visitors and lowered herself onto one of them.

'I understand you dabble in alternative cures?' she trilled in her best Oxonian accent, sitting opposite the clerk.

'I leave it all in Bhogobaan's hand, Madam. Like your great Pope-da in Rome. Bhogobaan is great! Radhey-Gobindo! Radhey-Gobindo!' Khirod-babu grinned brightly, stealing a glance at his patient over the rim of his glasses. 'Just little bit here, little bit there. Putting finger in and out. Sometimes slowly. Sometimes fast-fast. On the pulse. That's all. No big deal.'

'Has Peter told you that I haven't been keeping too well?' Henrietta inquired in her superior contralto, still recovering from the clerk's attempt to mollify her.

'Oh yes, Madam, oh yes,' Khirod-babu affirmed, vigorously nodding his head.

'So what do you suggest I do?' asked Henrietta, slowly losing her patience.

Khirod-babu grabbed Henrietta's wrist before she could withdraw, pressing his thumb on a nerve that commenced beating in erratic fits and starts. He cocked his head to one side, squeezed his eyes shut and concentrated on its intermittent thumping for a few seconds before pronouncing his recommendation.

'Gibh up sholt and soo-gar at once, Madam,' Khirod-babu advised, urging his knees to dance in exhilaration for having found such a perfect diagnosis. 'No tea. No cophee. You are having too much pitta, too much bile and bitterness that is making your paikhaana – I mean stool, Madam, stool – run like Howrah Mail-gaari. Don't you understand, Madam? I am also suggesting you may please drink one fresh glass of your own ureeeeen first thing in the morning. Like Morarji Desai!'

Astonishment loosened the hinges of Henritetta's jaw and it started to drop in horror.

'*What?*' she shouted. 'What did you say?'

'Myself suggesting auto urine-therapy for you, Madam,' smiled Khirod-babu, extremely chuffed at his judgment. 'It will get rid of your irregular bowels at once, make your marriage happy and stop all bleeding from your bum.'

Henrietta drew herself out of her seat, rose to tower over the docile little clerk and threw a dizzy fit.

At Peter's next dinner party Henrietta donned the characteristic fashion-blinkers of the successfully opinionated and barked, flicking at her hair obsessively, 'What a country! Even piss here is poshed up as aqua!'

Peter Hammond's friends tried ignoring her till Henrietta rubbed RajRani Sunanda Devi of Natore the wrong end. As the fairy lights blinked on the low hedge circling the lawn, the princess, thoroughly put out by Henrietta's harangues, bared her fangs and snarled, 'You snotty little punk! You think it's your divine right to be racist and white? You make my teeth grind!'

To her utter horror, Henrietta Hammond noticed Sunanda Devi's evil-looking molars and almost fainted. Without much ado, she caught the next available flight to London and preferred spending the rest of her days with her sister Clementina and her two fluffy cats in a little cottage in the countryside near Stoke-on-Trent. Peter may have been proud of his verbal swagger and sexual loquacity; his wife fancied cultivating sweet williams to sex.

Peter Hammond grew lonely but refused to give up. Many 'arty-farty kaala buggers' (Sylvia's epithet for all those so-called avant-garde theatre freaks and art-house film makers and local musicians) rolled out the red carpet to seek his favours or let their wives and girlfriends whirr around him like foolish humming birds in the hope of getting arts fellowships to England. His home on Theatre Road resembled a castle. He couldn't have ever dreamt it up in his wildest dreams in London. Here, there were no miserable loos with creaky floorboards and leaking faucets – only grand washrooms that made him lower himself on the toilet bowl with unprejudiced awe. Here, unlike his tiny apartment at Elephant and Castle, he didn't have to succumb to the banality of pasta or, worse, Tesco sandwiches washed down with some beer most nights, after returning, exhausted, on the Bakerloo line from having run around all day, trying to finish a hundred different chores all over the city. His job at the British Council in Calcutta came with a retinue of minions and a solid snooze after lunch. What more could he ask for?

Peter Hammond was pleasantly surprised when he stopped missing Henrietta and hardly read her self-righteous missives that arrived at sporadic intervals. Those that did manage to find their way into his office were left on the table, weighed down by a miniature brass toad gaping at the world passing by. There was something so reassuring, he said to himself, about unanswered letters.

In this happy state of abandon, one sultry afternoon he noticed Sylvia's generous shoulders. He had a good cry upon them that evening, seeking courage from the round of pink gins he had knocked back at lunch and then proceeded to ask her to stay back after office hours on the pretext of some urgent work. Within weeks he discovered that his secretary also had taut bosoms and rather shapely legs.

'His views about my tits and ass were well founded,' Sylvia giggled, 'though slightly asymmetrical like his tie. And when he finally brought me home to dinner, the setting had been perfectly organised. The napery was thick and crisp, the chef had not cried into the custard and the meal was beguilingly cooked. But through the entire feast the poor chicken remained undressed! It was past midnight when I decided to do what the chicken should have done at supper. Darling, if only the carpet in his living room could talk! The very next afternoon Peter called his lawyers at Holborn and filed for divorce!'

I couldn't attend Sylvia's wedding because Dolly-kaakima decided to go to Nepal that same week to worship at the feet of Lord Poshupotinath.

All these years later, I'm still not sure whether she had nosed out Mini and Dibaakor-da's affair and was looking for some kind of atonement. She never did confront Mini, not quite admitting the possibility of her own cowardice. Her trick was ingenious. She started treating Mini like a princess and a pariah by turns. Given her high-strung disposition, why Mini need have bothered to please Dolly-kaakima I do not know. But I grew apprehensive about the situation and couldn't abide her temperamental trickeries even as Mini turned stoic. There was no question of Mini accompanying us as she was about to take her final graduation exams. Dibaakor-da looked totally clapped-out and went around for days with a hangdog expression. Mini, of course, was heart-broken but kept her mouth shut.

There was little Dibaakor-da could do to rectify the situation. His love affair was conducted on his own, lopsided terms. He was a typical Scorpio. And even if he and Mini had great sex, he remained sly and secretive and avoided talking to her about the trip, afraid of his mother's reaction. Mini started sleeping badly and coming down for breakfast later than her usual time. Every third day she claimed to be ill and in the end, before we finally departed, she subsided into a sort of sulky acquiescence. Ma was more than willing to drag her away to some esoteric Tantric who'd make her sit cross-legged on the floor and turn on her chakras. But Mini wouldn't budge. Overnight, she transformed into a tragedy queen, licking her wounds and wondering why she was so hopelessly misunderstood. Baba, of course, was indifferent. Ma seemed much relieved when we finally left for Kathmandu.

Little did I know then that this trip was to drastically change my life.

I find it difficult, sunning again those accumulated reminiscences, to pinpoint whether all that happened later was also plotted by Dolly-kaakima. I was relieved that for a week at least Dibaakor-da wouldn't lay his dirty paws on my poor sister. Was I naïve in placing all the blame squarely at his doorstep? Was Mini not equally guilty? Yet, foolishly, I refused to accept that the dilemma actually lay in our collective repression, where desire died in the tightly woven net of social subterfuge, struggling like a fish hauled out of water. As we grew up we were neither made to feel comfortable with the outpourings of our emotions nor with the awkward stirrings of our bodies. For girls like me, the humbug of life began and ended in the canticle that endlessly chanted time-tested rules of solid 'middle-class morality'. The raw hungers – all sap and swelling buds – were frowned upon with oppressive authority. Matrimony was altogether the great redeemer; the solver of every problem.

Marked today by a slash of sindur in my hair and shackled to my noa-bangle, I still wonder if life is merely an inventory of things we inevitably lose on the way – an innocuous bunch of keys, a sheaf of love letters, a child we may have nurtured but not entirely understood, parents whom we took for granted, virginity, individuality, the ability to laugh, and, more important, the ability to forgive. It is a terrible conditioning so that even now, in an attempt to find some reprieve from pain, there are times when I feel I've put an end to all the bother of loving. And then, suddenly – rebelliously – memories impinge my privacy, and there comes a burst of sweet rain laden with recollections...

Dibaakor-da ran down the creaky wooden steps of the hotel lobby, adjusting his muffler and monkey cap, and said, 'The rooms are good.

They have a wonderful view of the mountains, and you can even glimpse the pagodas at Honumaan Dhoka.'

I was still recovering from hopeless disappointment. My lofty vision of Kathmandu had disappeared the minute the bus pulled in, after a backbreaking ride from Benares. We had driven, almost non-stop, past treacherous and hilly terrain dotted with fresh mustard fields, timorous in the breeze and bathed in a yellow haze, and later, as we climbed higher, through wild stretches of rhododendron forests. The vehicle had been overloaded with luggage, baskets of cackling duck and chicken, and strangers with tired eyes. The driver furiously swerved around hairpin bends, cursing. Perhaps he was high on toddy. But nobody dared to confront him. And then, after hours of being jostled in nerve-racking tension, he charged into the bus station, jamming the brakes and lurching us out into the squalor and filth of Kathmandu.

I wondered where the fabled towers had disappeared – the golden shrines every tourist pamphlet eulogised. We had tumbled right into a nightmare a month before the Dasain festival. The air was still, pregnant with humidity. I had yet to discover the vigorous jumble of shops, temples, myths and mementos. What I fell upon, alighting from the taxi we had taken from the bus station into town, was the eccentric assault of odours – rotting peel and jalebees being fried, sandalwood and urine, dung and marigolds, spices and the overriding stink of open drains and garbage.

Kathmandu was such a let-down! Men in loincloth vended overripe bananas swarming with flies. There were backpackers everywhere, bent with their load, trudging up and down the lanes. Second-hand bookstalls sold anything from Proust and Mrs Henry Wood to A.J. Cronin, Denise Robbins, Hermina Black and hardcore pornography. A string of shops spilled over with sleeping bags and down jackets to remind visitors of their proximity to the Himalayas.

Some scrawny porters, with wicker baskets slung across their heads, darted sly glances at our direction, hoping to be hired. A bunch of local urchins, with chapped cheeks, ran after us, rolling steel hoops and shouting, 'Tourists, tourists! Bangaali tourists! Want to change money?'

It was a huge relief to finally find a hotel that suited our budget. Over the dusty counter, the king in his trademark dark glasses and his placid-looking queen in her trademark bouffant peered at us from a framed photograph. And beyond the frayed carpet, where the staircase ended, stood a lone erica palm in a brass jardinière, punished in a corner.

'I think this place will do nicely. We are only here for a week,' I murmured, adjusting my kantha stole and trying to convince my aching feet that we needed to stop wandering. 'And it has an interesting name. *Hotel Nirvana*. What else do we want?'

'Have you checked the bathrooms?' Dolly-kaakima hissed urgently. 'I hope they're not Western styled. I have a fear of sitting on a pot, feeling like Rani Bhiktoria!'

The receptionist's catlike expression didn't change. Over the phone he called the manager who arrived in a short while, breathless, his tired face sunk in a bed of wrinkles. His black cap was typically Nepalese, with a miniature khukri clipped to the front.

'How many rooms?' he asked, impatient and prone to a short fuse.

'We'll take the big one with the three beds,' said Dibaakor-da quickly, before the old man could change his mind. 'And the single one down the corridor on the second floor. Can you manage on your own, Mohini?'

'Oh yes,' I replied. 'Unless you want it for yourself.'

'No, no,' said Dolly-kaakima, collapsing into a creaky sofa. 'Bachchoo will stay with us. His father goes to the bathroom a hundred times at night, and you'll be disturbed.' Then turning to her son she moaned, 'My knees, oh my knees!'

A loud knock on my door the following morning woke me with a start.

'Who's there?' I shouted, irritated.

'Mohini,' Dibaakor-da called urgently. 'Ma's unwell. Can you come and help?'

'What's happened?' I asked, opening the door.

'An attack of colitis,' said Dibaakor-da, standing before me in a tousled daze. 'What a way to begin our holiday!'

'Is she in pain?'

'You know Ma. She loves making mountains out of molehills.'

'Where's Bijoy-kaka?'

'Disappeared, as usual. Can't blame Baba for his vanishing act!'

'Then I better come and calm her down.'

Dolly-kaakima was, indeed, in 'one of her states'. She blundered about the room, heaving her bosom and clutching her stomach, calling out to all the gods whose names she could muster to relieve her pain. But, hard as Dibaakor-da tried, she didn't let up on cursing Bijoy-kaka, having thrown herself into her role as the dying, deserted wife with gusto.

My smile submerged in politeness, I tried coaxing her back into bed and pacifying her. But ducking my overtures, as if warding off invisible blows, she kept screaming that her troubles had started at the crack of dawn when she discovered a bird on her window sill drop dead in a paroxysm of flutters. It was a terrible, maleficent omen that heralded her sudden illness. Couldn't I put two and two together? Was I that stupid? I turned helplessly to Dibaakor-da who had gone up to the open window and stood slouching there, his hands dug deeply into his pockets. There was no sign of the dead bird, leave alone a heap of forlorn feathers – no tell-tale indictments; no portents.

Dolly-kaakima's need to match and pair events into the thinnest fabric of meaning started to get on my nerves. Leaving her to her son's care, I went down to the reception in search of a doctor. The receptionist kept digging wax out of his ear with a gem clip, wincing and winking, before he condescended to tell me that there was a dispensary at the top of the street. I stepped out into the bright daylight, unsure how long Dolly-kaakima's endless theatrics would carry on, or what new turn her performance would take as the day wore on.

My search proved futile. Unable to locate the dispensary I walked into a makeshift bistro instead, beyond the two-dollar lodges. The eatery had about it a greasy feel, smelling of coffee and fried omelettes. The shopkeeper was indifferent, though I kept asking for directions in Hindi. Frustrated, I was about to leave, when a distinct American accent from the shadows asked, 'Hey! Need help?'

I turned to see a foreigner sipping tea from a thick glass tumbler at a wooden table. He smiled at me, getting up from the bench. He was unusually slender and his skin seemed pale and delicate. His blond hair, parted at the centre, hung loosely down to his shoulders. Strings of coloured glass beads crowded his neck and a scraggly moustache ran along his upper lip. Garbed in baggy pyjamas caught at the ankles and a loose printed shirt with two missing buttons, he looked the archetypal hippie on the run. But I was struck by his face and his height. He was far too handsome, despite a spray of freckles, to be just another useless junkie crowding the streets of Kathmandu.

'Are you a doctor?'

'No,' said the stranger. 'But I've lived here long enough to figure out how to combat dysentery!'

'It's my aunt. She's unwell.'

Collecting his shan bag, he turned to pay up. And then, without preamble, grabbed my hand. 'Let's go,' he said, grinning.

I was completely thrown, caught in a mesh of contrary feelings. Never had a stranger seized my wrist with such familiarity. I hesitated at the door, not knowing what to do, feeling the blood rushing to my face.

He turned to look at me and said, 'What's up?'

'What's your name?' I asked quickly, lowering my eyes and drawing my hand away, trying to cover up for my discomfiture.

'Morrison. Paul Morrison,' he said, stepping into the street.

'Where are you from?'

'Chicago.'

'And what are you doing in Nepal?'

'Searching. I guess...'

'Oh! Have you lost something?'

He raised an eyebrow and started to laugh, tangling my thoughts further and leaving me all tongue-tied and nervous.

'I'm not too sure,' he said, at last. 'Perhaps, myself. Who knows?'

It was a chance encounter but his mirth was infectious. My heart, baked hard from months of trying to live with Mini's secret, instantly melted. As we left the bistro, it seemed as if I had known him all my life. Who was he, walking by my side, risen from the hills, like the chime of prayer bells calling the deities to notice? A flock of pigeons descended on the road, circled in a beam of sunlight. Was this a premonition too? Did winged creatures, after all, have the power to predict?

When I introduced Paul to Dibaakor-da and Dolly-kaakima, she asked, irritated, in Bengali, 'Couldn't find a better quack, could you?'

'Ma!' admonished Dibaakor-da in a fierce low voice. 'He has been kind enough to come and help!'

'Your mother obviously doesn't trust me, but I ain't complaining!

I'll leave behind medicines that may relieve her pain,' grinned Paul. He dug into his shan bag and fished out a small cloth pouch. Loosening its puckered mouth, he pulled out some tablets.

'Give her two of these after she's had something to eat. And then follow it up with a single dose every three hours,' he instructed. 'The water here can be quite treacherous. How long do you intend to hang out in Kathmandu?'

'Oh, for just a week,' I informed.

'I think she'll have more faith once the medicines work,' Paul grinned, looking me directly in the eyes. 'Would you mind if I came by later? Perhaps in the evening?'

'Of course not,' I blurted out before Dibaakor-da could intervene. 'How can I thank you for all that you've done?'

'Buy me a cup of tea tomorrow!'

By the afternoon Dolly-kaakima had changed her tune. She was back to being her old, belligerent, gossipy self. When Paul returned that evening, he was promptly offered not only a cup of tea but also hot samosas that Bijoy-kaka had brought to appease his wife and calm her nerves.

'*Ki bhaalo chheley!*' Dolly-kaakima pronounced and turned to ask Dibaakor-da in Bengali. 'Why has he left home, the poor boy, aha rey? Why has he come miles away from his kith and kin?'

Paul had us in stitches with his funny stories about Americans. Bijoy-kaka was fascinated when he expressed an interest in Indian music. Then, quietly, he drew out a bamboo flute from his shan bag and played the prelude to a Nepalese folk song.

'You coming to Calcutta? You must bhisit us,' Bijoy-kaka exclaimed, delighted. 'My wife, she is bhery good cook of Bengali phood. Shukto, mochaar ghonto, phish curry, what not! Best in the waarld! You come and try.'

Paul laughed and made some light comment. He was so comfortable with us that I wondered if we had not met him before. Was it in a dream? In another lifetime? Who was this strange white god with the bluest of eyes? Had he ever descended from the Himalayas to sit inconspicuously in Ma's pujo room? I, who had scorned Shubha's infatuation for Krishno, I, who had been shocked by Mini's aberrant yearnings, now succumbed, without reserve, to the call of the flute!

What was wrong with me?

A thick knot of guilt suffocated my feelings as night stole upon the sky and Paul finally told us about his escape from the war in Vietnam. Initially, he had been too far south to get involved at the fire support bases. But later, hiding in the village of Phu Hoa Dong, surrounded by a sea of swaying green rice paddies and booby traps, he had grasped the meaning of death and how cheap it came in the wilderness of 'Nam. His memories bled afresh and the raw wounds surfaced again in his voice, torn asunder like the lip of a bomb crater.

'Saigon,' Paul said, 'was teeming with little blue Renault taxis, bicycles, motorcycles and pedicabs. The huge amount of military traffic complicated matters. And then, there were the pubs and the bar-girls with ebony hair fluffing around their perfectly made up faces, simpering and encouraging lonely soldiers to buy them a drink.'

'Oh, you bhent there often?' laughed Bijoy-kaka, rather more assured than he could ever hope to be in his wife's presence.

'As often as we could,' Paul laughed back, keeping an eye on Dolly-kaakima.

'And the gaarls?' Bijoy-kaka egged him on, a great, shaggy animal wagging his tail in furious little pleasures.

'Oh, they were always there, waiting,' informed Paul, once he had stopped chuckling. 'They were a sweet, painted lot. "You buy me 'tea', GI?" they'd pout and, without warning, land on our laps like a chattering flock of parakeets.'

'Then?' asked Bijoy-kaka, guffawing and rubbing his hands together. 'Then bhot you did, haan?'

'That depended entirely on our mood,' Paul winked. 'If we had money, they'd come with us. But if they were unceremoniously dumped, they'd take off their high-heeled shoes, slipper us good and proper and scream, "You Numbah Ten Cheap Charlie, you dirty little bah-sturd!" and walk off in a huff.'

In our mirth we had forgotten that Paul had seen death in every shape – sliced, charred, throttled, blasted, strangled. He had stayed awake several nights, shivering in his bunker. Memories of his grandmother's garden in New England had overtaken his nightmares riddled with the twelve thousand pound daisy cutters, guava and pineapple bombs and Willie Peters. Where had that invincible little world of summer roses and winter carnations disappeared? Did he now deserve to have his neck snapped without notice? Beyond the boom of guns lay another world, always beckoning, always begging him to run back to. A world away from hatred and petty games played in the name of power and honour. A world of equality where the only mantra was compassion and love, aided, perhaps, by a little bit of marijuana. At the first opportunity, he deserted the army and escaped to Kathmandu.

'Have you found a reason to live again?' I asked him, as he was leaving and I could steal but a moment in his company.

'Yes,' said Paul, stretching out to hold my hand. 'Would you believe me if I said that you are reason enough?'

That night I couldn't sleep. There was too much moonlight. And I didn't for the life of me want to get up and draw the curtains. A dog howled in the distance; a few leaves on the bo tree outside my window dared to rasp. Then utter silence.

Did love always steal into our lives without warning, clumsily leaping across our threshold when we least expected it? Could love ever be perfect? Could the search for perfection be a dangerous ideal, after all? I thought of Mini and wondered – lying in this unfamiliar room, in an unknown hotel and isolated from all denial or dismissal – whether it was her fault that she had fallen for Dibaakor-da? Poor Mini! Was she really in love? Or was it just defiance that made her look for a little danger; for an inept hand to slide up her thighs and awaken new mysteries? Was Dibaakor-da only a physical need like substance abuse – a compulsion she couldn't break – or did she see in him a greater desire to be understood and cherished? And what about my feelings for Paul whom I hardly knew? Why did my limbs break into sweet pain as I willed myself to sleep? Did Mini too ache thus, wanting to gather Dibaakor-da so close to her heart that she suffocated, like me, with longing?

Paul! Paul! *Paul!*

What was it about Paul's name that filled me with freedom and, all at once, enslaved me? Why did he flit in and out of my thoughts, making me follow him wherever he went? I was totally unprepared for this extraordinary surge of emotions and kept marvelling at love's validity without any guilt. Because all loves, I realised now, were insecure. All loves were binding. And hopelessly imperfect. I dreamed of him so vividly, so compellingly, that had I stretched out I could have touched Paul over and over again. He was everywhere and all I needed to do was summon him to lie beside me.

There he stood, in a narrow strip of moonlight, holding my hand and laughing, and there again, looking deep into my eyes, not bothered by Dolly-kaakima's frowns. And as I slept fitfully, I let my love for Paul rest upon my heart no heavier than those fragile alpona patterns painted on the wings of a butterfly. The weight made me inordinately shy. But, somehow, I didn't care. It was such a relief after my regimented life in Amherst Street; the oppressive scab of its shelter. I picked at it and let the blood flow, happy to know that I belonged at last – not as a sister or a daughter or a friend – but simply as Mohini, freed from all fetters.

Next morning, encouraged by Dolly-kaakima, I decided to explore the nearby marketplace. Dibaakor-da volunteered to stay back with his mother. Bijoy-kaka, of course, had already escaped in search of breakfast.

I hurried out, past the geranium blossoms nurtured in earthen pots in the hotel veranda, and picked my way down a narrow, cobbled street. I had a sudden longing to feel the Himalayan wind on my face. But the lane I crossed was anything but nourishing, clucking with a brood of hysterical hens being bullied by a handsome rooster. An assault of curious smells made me involuntarily cover my nose with the loose end of my sari. On either side stood a variety of open stalls, mostly run by garrulous women with copper skins and slender hands adept at counting wads of paper notes with a flourish. They wore flowers and slender stalks of fresh paddy in their hair. Tikas daubed with grains of broken rice adorned their foreheads and huge silver earrings encrusted with turquoise and opal dangled from their elongated lobes. They kept up a constant chatter, giggling and talking in high-pitched, musical voices, moving away now and then from soft Nepalese syllables to break into Hindi for tourists like me.

The atmosphere stirred with the flutter of prayer flags and a supple agglomeration of commerce and crookery; of Nepalese traders and Lepcha porters; Newari money changers and Buddhist monks wending their way through the bustle. All around me were latticed balconies of wood cascading with garlands of red chillies set out to dry in the sun or hung out with the washing – saris in bright prints, petticoats and blouses, children's garments and patchworked sheets and an ungainly bra or two. Most of the homes boasted curiously carved doors, moist with age. Little alcoves, carved above the wooden beading, sported images of gods smothered with orange paint to chase away evil.

I strayed past a tiny shrine where Bhoirob's phallus had turned bloody, liberally smeared with vermilion and choked with scarlet hibiscus flowers. Temples in different shapes and sizes seemed to spring out of nowhere, replete with an assortment of sinners bearing baskets of offerings to try and appease the gods. Ahead lay the main road, congested with traffic. And as I hesitated, not knowing if I should venture further into that miasma of diesel fumes, Paul appeared seemingly from nowhere, grinning through his beautiful, blue eyes. 'Hey, you look gorgeous,' he shouted with startling familiarity, raising his voice that wee bit above the roar of the Mercedes Benz taxis and private cars in the distance, as he stretched out his hand to take mine. The gesture seemed so natural that I managed to smile and let him lead me, not caring where I went.

Without any warning, the schizophrenia of Kathmandu took over. I slipped into an enchanted trance and could barely pay attention to Paul as he pointed out the city's many landmarks till we found ourselves in the vicinity of Honumaan Dhoka. Transported most magically into another century, replete with palaces and pagodas and elaborate friezes, it seemed we were walking through a dream. Wherever I looked, frozen and staring back at me in carven stone or blocks of wood were Shib Thakur's bull, the bird-god Goruda, the steeds of Bishnu and countless elephants, rams and snakes. There were naked sadhus by the roadside smothered in ashes, adorned with rudraksha beads. They squatted on deer skins, smoking bhang or contorting their bodies into yogic positions like circus tricks for the pleasure of curious Japanese and European tourists, hoping a few dollars would roll their way.

Bhoirob's lingam sprouted like wild shrubs at every street corner, enticing devotees to circumambulate its erect arrogance. Many pilgrims prostrated their bodies, forearms extended, rubbing away the skin of their foreheads in repeated abrasions against the cold stone in the hope of remaining forever fertile. The smell of dung, the sudden clash of cymbals, the roar of traffic – where was I? In a medieval market soaked with the scent of incense and marijuana? Or in the hustle and bustle of the twentieth century where cinema posters of *Gone With The Wind* and *Mughal-e-Azam* stuck to ancient walls confused me so thoroughly that I lost the ability to fathom in which epoch Paul and I were walking? Porticos and pillars sorrowed over rundown fountains that had stopped playing. The atmosphere was unreal, thick with legends of the Ranas and the Malla kings. In the midst of the overwhelming chaos, I managed to hear some temple bells chime clearly. And, jostling with the crowds, I turned to look at Paul, amazed that what was happening to us was, after all, true!

Everything became a hopeless tangle of frozen wings, arrested lions, immobile creepers and petrified couples halted in their game of love. I only witnessed fragments engraved in bronze and copper and stone. Then, down a side alley, divinity accosted us, breathless, as we went past the seat of a living goddess of the Sakya tribe married off to Narayon in the form of a wood-apple tree. She was not even knee-high, the poor mite, dressed up and painted for display – a child with a face as ancient as the mountains, dotted with sandalwood paste – a Kumari Debi who would soon lose her virginity and her mystic powers and transform into a mere mortal, trapped in the throes of early puberty. There she was now, ignorant of her cursed future, smiling through her glimmering jewels and silks at cautious Americans in Bermuda shorts adjusting their dark glasses and cameras before clicking her pictures. Beyond her shrine were chattering monkeys and pestering beggars. And a plethora of curio stalls, waiting for business to begin as usual.

Paul stopped to browse through some inconsequential bric-a-brac. And then, out of the blue, he lifted his head and said, 'Can I call you Moh? Moh of the mountains? Mohini is too complicated. For me you'll always be Moh. Do you mind?'

I didn't know how to react. In the midst of so much noise and confusion, he gave my cloistered life fresh meaning and chose to christen me with a new name that was like a magic spell. In that space between us, stronger than any bond of touching and union – without the blister of words – I suddenly found myself staring at Kaal Bhoirob, my lips moving inaudibly in supplication, begging the God of Destruction to restore me and make me whole once more.

Oh, to be anonymous and unfettered! To be an errant cloud dragging its shadow across the face of the mountains! To be in the presence of the beloved always!

Grant that I be with Paul, O King of the Dead and the Living! Grant that I may let my love flower like the fragrant petals at your feet!

And as if in answer to my prayers, Paul took out his flute and began playing a tender raga.

In a sudden blaze of extravagant sunlight spilling henna on the soft palms of morning, I was born again. It hurt to be so near to each other. I realised that love had its own silent language, its own crazy idioms and hidden meanings. And it held no fears, no unknown devils. Love was courage. Love was freedom. Love was life and all reckless giving.

'Hey, say something!' Paul grinned at last and I could only nod my acquiescence, acknowledging that this is how it should have been, always.

And miraculously, unprotected, I became Paul's Moh.

That night Paul's blue eyes came to haunt me and suck sleep from my own. I couldn't forget his slender neck, slightly tilted, and his animated fingers dancing on the flute, releasing, shutting, quivering and tempting out the notes. I wanted to cry and laugh and forget the cause of my despair. Shubha's intoxicated madness became a dream. Mini's troubled life seemed lost in some perverted void. And I so wanted to talk to Sylvia and tell her, wrapping my arms around her waist, that I too was in love. That I too had the capacity to give away my heart. To revel in myriad nuances of feelings I had never known before. The dazzle of the stars was that much brighter, the consistency of shadows that much thicker and the profuse velvet of the night, that much sweeter with unspoken longing. Every pore in my body was suddenly filled with new life.

I rose and went to face the mirror. Deliberately, I flung away the anchol of my sari. Then I undid my blouse. I couldn't believe what I saw – in my nudity I was like a goddess, proud and unvanquished. My nipples stood gratified, swollen like unplucked buds; my ribs stretched below their weight – my beautiful body, impatient, impermanent but, alas, my only refuge. Floundering through the drawers, I found a pair of earrings and dangled them from my lobes. The precious stones emitted tiny sparks. In the parting of my hair I hung a lapis lazuli pendant. Then, tentatively, I caressed my breasts. It was a sensation I would long remember – sensuous, inculpable and wholly my own, hinting at everlasting fires.

Slowly, I became aware of the flute again. Paul's enchanted flute. Was I dreaming? Was I going mad in this small room in Hotel Nirvana, with not a drop of salvation and just two large windows and whitewashed walls that seemed hopelessly possessed by moon madness?

In a thickly woven mesh, the alaap climaxed slowly. Each set of musical confessions tore apart the distance separating us. When the melody had continued for a good ten minutes, I hurried to the window. Impulsively, I leaned out and was amazed to see Paul sitting beneath the bo tree, distinctly visible, playing his flute. Gradually, the scale faltered. He rose and stepped out of the shadows. And, without warning, in a gesture that said it all, he threw back his head and stretched wide his arms, bathed in a flood of moonlight, asking me to come to him. I drew back in a hurry, suddenly mortified. And creeping back into bed I let the tears come at last, pouring in sluggish trickles down my cheeks.

Next day I noticed Paul's eyes once more. How blue they were – like the vast expanse of the sea – and I was their empress, crowned with negation!

'Don't tempt me, Paul, like you did last night,' I smiled, walking ahead of him in the market. 'My father may forgive you. My mother won't. She's too old-fashioned and set in her ways.'

'Oh hell, Moh, I don't ever want to lose you,' he said, catching up.

'But I have to go away,' I teased.

'Only to return. To me,' Paul countered.

And everything became so simple and right and beautiful. Our little world of trust and tenderness and make-belief bridged by our common love for Shakespeare, Edna St Vincent Millay and

Tchaikovsky's *Waltz Of The Snowflakes*. Paul drew out a battered little book of poetry from his pocket as we sat sipping tea in a makeshift stall and read softly, '*I am not resigned to the shutting away of loving hearts in the hard ground/ So it is, and so it will be, for so it has been, time out of mind:/ Into the darkness they go, the wise and the lovely. Crowned/ With lilies and with laurels they go; but I am not resigned...*' In a trance, I picked up the lines when his voice faltered and continued from memory, '*The answers quick and keen, the honest look, the laughter, the love,/ They are gone. They have gone to feed the roses. Elegant and curled/ Is the blossom. Fragrant is the blossom. I know. But I do not approve./ More precious was the light in your eyes than all the roses in the world...*'

How true! The light in Paul's eyes filled me with utter joy as I descended time and again into their aquamarine pools and happily drowned, hoping I'd never have to swim back to reality's mundane shore! We refused to think of the future. I hated the idea of returning to Calcutta and the claustrophobia of Loreto College, and Paul was reluctant to disappear again into the lonely mountains with a gang of Bouda Bums he had found hanging out at the Rum Doodle Bar. I didn't want the routine of books and exams and Ma's nagging. And he was chary of sitting with the Happy Skeletons at Swayambhu, filling opium into his chillum. We talked of inconsequential things, fragile like my longings. In and out, in and out we wove through the narrow lanes, past sadhus and pilgrims and touts and sightseers and local boys in tight drain-pipe trousers zooming past on motorbikes. Paul must have read my thoughts. He turned to tightly clutch my wrist, and under the pressure of his fingers, some of the glass bangles cracked.

'Oh, I'm terribly, terribly sorry,' he apologised, flustered. 'Are you hurt? What do you want me to do now?'

'Help me break all laws like these glass bangles,' I laughed, taking the broken pieces past the bruise and folding them carefully into my handkerchief.

'Always?' asked Paul, smiling into my eyes as he lifted my hand and blew into my wrist to soothe the soreness.

'Always,' I assured him. 'I'll always wait for you.'

In that short span of seven days, Kathmandu filled me with a lifetime of joy. The silence in Paul's eyes constantly spoke to me. I didn't realise that falling in love could be so simple. Paul granted me wings and set me free. And then, before I knew it, it was time again to return to Amherst Street.

Well past midnight, the day before we were to leave, I was aroused by a persistent knock on my door. Trembling with fear, I sat up and heard the rap-rap-rap again.

'Moh, it's me,' whispered Paul, pleading, urgent, unrelenting. 'I know you're in… Moh, it's me… Please open the door. It's me, Moh… It's me!'

In a daze I lifted the latch. Paul stood silhouetted at the doorway.

'You'll write to me, won't you?' I asked.

'Every single day! Till we meet again,' he promised, drawing me into his arms. 'Moh, I want you, Moh…'

'Paul, please, if you love me, go away… *please* go away!' I begged, my eyes brimming, as I tried to push him aside.

'Are you afraid?' he challenged, holding me tighter.

'Yes, for both of us,' I confessed, looking into his eyes.

I could feel his hard, slim thighs pressing against mine. He took his own sweet time to impress my face upon his memory. Anything could have happened, but the moment passed. Yet I knew what it meant to be hopelessly, utterly in love. There was so much that remained unspoken, so much I should have said, till gently, very gently, he smiled and wiped my wet and clammy face. Then, escaping from the need for words, he lowered his lips on mine, his tongue urgently seeking, and all the telling was done in a kiss.

Paul didn't come to see us off.

Dibaakor-da tried to find him but his room at the guesthouse in Thamel was locked. Bijoy-kaka was disappointed but soon it became a mad rush, trying to get our packing done; trying to stop Dolly-kaakima from visiting yet another temple; trying to cram all that we had bought into various suitcases and bags. Nobody noticed that I had been crying. Then, at last, we boarded the bus.

Just as it started to pull out, I saw Paul hurrying towards me.

Too late! Too late! Paul was too late!

We could only utter inconsequential sentences as the vehicle gathered speed.

'Where had you gone?' I murmured, trying not choke.

'To get you these...'

He handed me a newspaper packet and ran alongside the vehicle. It contained a bunch of cheap green glass bangles.

'Wear them. For me,' Paul said.

'I will. And I'll wait,' I said. 'You'll come, won't you?'

'As soon as I can,' he promised.

I took one long, last look at him, not knowing what the future held.

'Will you break them the day I arrive?' he asked.

'The bangles?' I enquired.

'And your father's rigid laws,' he said, trying to smile.

'Yes.'

'Moh, I love you...'

'Paul...'

I couldn't see too well. Everything was swimming in front of my eyes.

'Moh...'

Paul's blue eyes, sad lakes, rippled on and on.

'Moh, don't forget me...'

Paul did not come to Calcutta. But within a few weeks his letters started arriving, full of engaging promises, till they were intercepted by Dolly-kaakima.

I was trapped. Dolly-kaakima had cleverly set her snare in Kathmandu, persuading me to go out alone. Now she held an invisible gun against my head. It was her revenge for what she supposed was my betrayal – I knew Mini and Dibaakor-da's secret; and she knew that I knew, without ever daring to confront me. In one abrupt move she turned the tables. As soon as she laid her hands upon one of Paul's letters, she wasted no time flourishing it in Ma's horrified face, goading her to prudently marry me off before the situation skidded out of control. Her parched voice cracked like flames that burst in furious leaps to settle scores. The following months turned into a haze of frustration. Ma said I had disgraced the family; heaped shame upon her head. Was I a common tart or a pariah bitch on heat, chasing some unkempt, filthy firaghee? Did I think he'd whisk me away to America? Offer me a life that my parents couldn't afford? And, inevitably, as her temper soared, fingers were again pointed at Baba's foolish insistence that his girls be educated at a convent.

There was nothing I could do save retreat into a shell. But Dolly-kaakima wouldn't relent. To add salt to Ma's wounds, she sprinkled the kitchen with insalubrious gossip about Paul and me like pungent chillies that exploded with sly allegations. With every scrap of the spatula, she made me out to be an unholy siren who had taken advantage of her illness. Mini remained strangely unmoved. Dibaakor-da cunningly abetted the scandal. And as I tried to argue and overcome Ma's constant harangues, Pansy Pishimoni, my future husband's aunt, got wind of the fact that I was available in the marriage market through one of Baba's clients. She quickly fixed an appointment and dragged her sister, Petunia Pishimoni, to come and suss me out.

Before Bobby and his aunts bought me off the shelf, many others had come to appraise my worth after that doomed holiday in Kathmandu. The prospective mothers-in-law often coaxed me to walk the length of the room. They made me pour out tea precisely; talk like a parrot. I'd be dressed in fine clothes and jewels and I'd sit through the torture with my eyes downcast, hating every moment of this cattle bazaar. Ma made light-hearted conversation, hoping that I'd be chosen, so that the shame of my past would never again surface. Dolly-kaakima bustled about, amusing the guests with her ample fund of chitchat and vigorously slicing shupuri nuts on her nutcracker and offering a fresh round of betel leaves. Ma forced upon them some more payesh and lied that I had made it, and Beejeepishi found some excuse to come and gawk at the prospective groom.

Some of the visitors praised my looks. Others commented on my convent education. Some gently laughed at my silence and mistook it for shyness. They coaxed me to speak in English and recite a few lines from Shakespeare or Wordsworth, as if I were a prized cockatoo on display.

'William Wordsworth was the best Romantic poet, after all. Did you study him? "*My heart leaps up when I behold a rainbow in the sky?*" You do know the lines, don't you?'

Some loftily remarked, 'Have you read the Lucy poems? "*She lived unknown and few could know when Lucy ceased to be; but she is in her grave, and, oh, the difference to me?*"' And yet others just chose to merely ogle and titter. I sat through it all, sat through the deceit and humiliation without protest, blind with rage and trying to look presentable. And in his chamber my father waited to drive the last nail into my coffin; waited impatiently to give away his youngest daughter who had brought him untold disgrace.

What I had taken for granted in Kathmandu now ricocheted with vicious ferocity. My father, swimming through a labyrinth of Ma's incessant ranting, became impatient. And the minute Pansy Pishimoni laughed and sipped her tea and exclaimed, 'We are *sooooo* pleased; *sooooo* pleased! Our Bobby will fall in love with Mohini as soon as he sees her,' my wedding was hurriedly fixed. No one cared for my feelings. The honour of the family had been vindicated. That was all that mattered.

I came to realise how every ounce of western education that my father flaunted only contributed to harden a foolish mask. All of us were marionettes drawn by invisible strings, as he sat with his legs crossed and in complete authority in his chamber, smiling his half-mocking smile. Of course we sisters were educated in Calcutta's best convent. Of course we could speak our lines in flawless English. *How now, brown cow!* But we couldn't, even if we tried, ask for some reprieve, some self-worth.

It soon became Beejeepishi's turn to plaster my hair with coconut oil every morning. She rubbed gram-flour thinned down with milk all over my body and scented my bath with the essence of roses. But no fragrance lingered in my soul. I felt abandoned, empty. I had no strength to confront Dolly-kaakima. I felt futile and drained, yet hoped for a miracle till I knew it was no longer coming. The delirium abated; the fluttering heartbeats died. Paul and I lay awake in different cities, beyond the possibility of words. And it was no use trying to make my parents understand. They had, in all their indignation and pique, chosen to forget even Shubha's constant suffering and Mini's increasing belligerence.

Was it out of some sense of guilt that my ears now filled with the storm of what I had done? Or was I trapped again in the reality of my social status, where I dared not seek what my heart desired? I couldn't even walk out of the house because there were no signs of Paul to walk to. In desperation I wrote to him, asking him to immediately write back to me at Sylvia's address and tell me what to do. But there was no reply. Frustrated, I blamed him for playing with my emotions. It was because of him, I cried to Sylvia, that I was imprisoned in my current predicament. Kathmandu vanished like a delusion blanched in shocking moonlight. And before I could come to any sort of decision, the dhaaks started to play, beating out fresh notes, and it was time again to worship Durga.

Like previous years, I should have been dressed in a new sari for the festival. I should have been rushing out to the decorated courtyard, laughing and chopping fruit for the proshaad, offering onjoli and lining my eyes with kajol. I should have been running up and down the staircase in a whirl, calling out to Beejeepishi to iron my blouse or yelling at Mini for stealing my nose-pin. But, in league with the goddess, I waited to be taken in a boat after the festivities and sunk in the river.

Every autumn Dibaakor-da and his friends brought Durga home from her thatch at Kumortuli, riding on a small truck festooned with balloons and flowers. It didn't matter that the rickshaw-pullers and local drunks had urinated all over our boundary wall. The revellers pressed handkerchiefs to their noses, shouted 'Durga Mai ki jai!' and welcomed the goddess to the newly refurbished thakurdalaan.

The courtyard had been dusted and swept and given a fresh coat of paint; the chandelier cleared of cobwebs. New candles were fitted and glowed gold in their pretty glass chimneys. The drummers came from the village and played maddening rhythms. The cooks pored over huge cauldrons. And on the night of Mohashtomi, Bijoy-kaka, as usual, organised a lively musical soiree with the help of his old Benares connections.

The women in our home rose at the crack of dawn and bathed before coming to pamper the goddess. They wove her garlands, lit incense at her feet and cajoled her to fulfill their wishes. Her elephant-headed son, Shiddhidaata Gonesh, was invoked to remove all obstacles. His brother, Skondo Kartik, was eyed for his good looks. Bijoylokkhi, the elder daughter, was worshipped for her wealth and her younger sister, Shoroshwoti Binaapaani, urged to part with her wisdom and knowledge. Everybody enjoyed the rituals. Neighbours arrived in hordes in the evening when the brass lamps were lit and the aroti performed. Durga smiled at her devotees through a haze of blue smoke, and they all fell at her feet, humbled by her power.

On the morning of Oshtomi I rose early. Clouds had thickened outside my window. After a night's revelry, the goddess seemed to be snoring peacefully, oblivious of the impending squall; of the air thick with the scent of wet earth. I sat huddled in bed, restless and waiting for the downpour. It came at last in persistent, sharp rapiers, waking the rest of the house and taking them by surprise. The servants ran to the courtyard, afraid that Ma Durga and her children would get drenched. Beejeepishi flew across the veranda to salvage the feast she had prepared. Bijoy-kaka managed to tackle the thick bamboo curtains and draw them around the sanctum. Dibaakor-da stood supervising, calling out to Joga-kaka, the family chauffeur, and rapping out crisp instructions. In all that rush and frenzy, nobody noticed me.

I leaned against a pillar, unprotected, not having bothered to tie back my hair. My sari fell about me in untidy folds. Water dripped down my face and smudged the kajol in my eyes. Alone and in sudden defiance, I faced Ma Durga, asking her all those harrowing questions that had been hammering in my heart. But Ma Durga was indifferent; she didn't bother to respond. I begged and pleaded, yet she chose to remain silent, too sleepy and drained by my incessant demands. Thoroughly rejected, I returned to my room, mocking the lazy goddess. I realised I'd have to rely on my own strength now.

Henceforth, I'd have to take my own decisions.

The nuns at the convent, the relatives at home – they were all part of a pact that wanted to pull me down. Yet, foolishly, I clung to some stray memories.

'Moh, it's me. Please open the door. It's me, Moh. It's me!'

What would have happened had I succumbed or run away with Paul that night? In a fit of temper I took out the letters I had managed to save and tore them into shreds. I'd remember little things afterwards when the hurting was over. But now they were of no use.

Once the initial tantrums died, I was forced to meet my would-be husband at the Coffee Shop at Grand Hotel so that he could check me out before casting the die. I arrived, chaperoned by Dibaakor-da, terribly self-conscious in a Dhaakai sari and stilettos that hurt. Bobby was too much of an egotist to notice the silence in my eyes, the utter stillness of my feelings. Paul had come to me with the confidence of a moonbeam. And the man who now sat before me, drinking coffee and making small talk, offered me nothing beyond the legitimacy of his bed. His arrogance and the stink of his successful career made me feel sick.

Yet I had to choose. And choose quickly.

Only once, before my formal engagement, I went to confront my father in his chamber. Without bothering to knock, I barged into his library and asked, 'Baba, do you think what you are doing is fair?'

He looked up from a sheaf of papers, visibly tired, and said, 'My opinion is of no consequence, Mohini. Your mother knows what's best for you.'

'What's best for *me*? How can somebody else decide what's best for me?'

'Mohini, a girl has to, I'm afraid, be the keeper of her family's honour.'

'But that's ridiculous!' I wept. 'I know I've done nothing wrong, nothing at all! Baba, what's my fault? Is falling in love a crime? Defend me! Fight for me, I beg of you! Why have you deserted me?'

'Because in this house you were born a woman,' Barrister Bidhushekhor Dotto pronounced, looking at me through careworn eyes.

Book Two

TODAY

Bobby Shaftoe's gone to sea,
With silver buckles on his knee.
He'll come back and marry me,
Pretty Bobby Shaftoe!
Bobby Shaftoe's fine and fair,
Combing down his auburn hair.
He's my love for evermore,
Pretty Bobby Shaftoe!

—FROM MOTHER GOOSE

My husband's family had adopted Western manners in the wake of Bobby's grandfather leaving his village in distant Borishaal and coming to Calcutta a la Dick Whittington, wondering if the city's pavements were, after all, paved in gold. Enduring months of starvation and finding odd jobs to keep body and soul together – initially as an assistant to a prosperous fishmonger in the Sealdah market, and later as a helper in the dispensary of an apothecary in the Borobajaar area – he encountered a close brush with death that, ironically, changed his luck.

He was waiting to cross the road at Chowringhee, trying to run an errand for the ill-tempered Kobiraaj, when a reprehensible memsahib's speeding brougham knocked him down and drove over his ribs. Destiny had probably planned the accident with great care. Grandfather Sen rose from his hospital bed two months later and stood on the brink of shattering transformation. The memsahib's husband, a famous gora doctor, out of Christian compassion and guilt, took the responsibility of putting him back on his feet once his ribs had healed. He offered him a job as his personal compounder and even agreed to pay for his conversion. Grandfather Sen accepted the job but, with equal alacrity, rejected the call to baptism. A compromise was reached whereby he'd accompany his employer, riding a tom-tom, to St John's Church every Sunday morning and slink into the last row of the pews. The King Of Love smiled benignly at him, nailed to his Cross, even as the adolescent stubbornly muttered Sanskrit mantras to counter the choir that burst into, '*Be Thou my guardian and my guide and hear me when I call...*'

Indeed, the omnipotent 'call' never failed Grandfather Sen though he did not have to change his religion and become a renegade. In the days to come, he refused to look back on either his early years spent in utter penury or his native origins that proclaimed the adage, '*Aitey shaal jaaitey shaal, taarey koy Borishaal.*'

Now, all these years later, his progeny showed their true colours. Having assiduously 'shaal-ed' or – as the vast tribe of wily clerks in various Bengal offices put it – 'bambooed' their way into high society, they quickly learned to eat their meals with forks and knives off Royal Doulton dinner services and often spoke to each other in affected English. They wore western clothes and laughed and shared anecdotes about foreign holidays. Some cousins even adopted names that were decidedly 'British.' There was Noel-da, happily married to the English missionary's daughter, Priscilla Knightly, and living on Camac Street. There was Cousin George, still trying to speak in a fake, 'haw-haw' accent and selling fake Bengal renaissance artists to unsuspecting Marwaris. And there was, of course, Sister Ivy, the daughter of a vagabond aunt, who had converted and fled to a nunnery in Kerala, out of the clutches of an abusive stepfather.

At the time his family asked for my hand, Bhobotosh, alias Bobby Sen, was a marketing executive in a British company working under an affable Parsee boss and selling a variety of teas. Bobby's flat at King Edward's Court was the focal point of his pride. His widowed mother, Shadhona Sen, had gone to live with her elder brother in a comfortable apartment in Rayner's Lane in north London, visiting relatives rather infrequently in Calcutta. And the roar of Bobby's car and the smell of his pay packet turned many of my relatives green with envy.

Did someone as impulsive and willful as me deserve this handsome god?

If only they had known that Bobby's real mother had died when he was struggling in an incubator, barely five days old!

Bobby's father, Dr Haradhon Sen – Harry for short – a well-known surgeon, could spare little time from the demands of his curette and his scalpel to either grieve the loss of a spouse or bring up a whimpering baby. His sisters, Bara Missy and Chhota Missy – Pansy and Petunia – stepped in to help. Bobby was spoilt silly by his spinster aunts. They'd pour tea for him out of an elaborate three-piece Queen Anne silver service on the dot of three-thirty in the afternoon at their sprawling family home in North Calcutta's Jhamaapukur Lane, accompanied by wafer-thin tomato and cucumber sandwiches. They'd take him to Firpo's for Sunday lunches, arrange picnics at the Botanical Gardens and visits to the zoo, and encourage him to sing: '*Oh Danny Boy the pipes the pipes are calling from glen to glen and down the mountain-side...*' as they accompanied their precocious little nephew on the piano.

The pishimas did a fine job of bringing up Bobby till, thirteen years later, a fistula in a rather upsetting spot on Harry Sen's posterior changed family fortunes forever. According to the pishimas, a third class, 'paatee-kichchan' nurse, with all the guile of Cleopatra, came to look after Harry and irrevocably disrupted their lives. The nurse's family had originally belonged to the refugee colonies housed in the back of beyond at Ranaghat, but she pretended they'd just stepped off a royal barge on the Nile with sails soaked in perfume.

Once Harry returned from Nil Roton Shorkaar Hospital, after a complicated operation, he badly needed rest. The nurse, provided to take care of him, often overstepped her limits. From putting him on and off the bedpan – an embodiment of starched efficiency – soon she started to get on and off his phallus, happy to ride her patient and undo sundry pieces of her garments and antiseptically challenging ways. Harry was thrilled. However, walls for once not only had ears but also salacious tongues. The nurse's sexual improprieties, alas, unhinged the poor spinster aunts.

Nurse Shadhona's father – if Pansy Pishimoni was to be believed – had converted years ago so that he could follow Jesus out of poverty's wilderness and stray into the heavenly riches of pulpit-thumping priesthood. But, according to Petunia Pishimoni, Shadhona had been born with the predisposition to transform into an asp hidden in a pretty pile of figs. The serpent, soon enough, scotched all speculation and cheerfully emerged as Harry's second wife from the rubble of scandal's edifice. Not once did the lucky girl look back at the muddle left in its wake. The aunts threw up their hands in horror. What would become of the son, they asked? The stepmother would surely convert him too!

Bobby, though, never fell into Shadhona's trap. He loved his pishimonis too dearly to be distracted by his stepmother's cunning. Years later, he even plotted with them to throw her out from his father's fortunes. In the end, once Dr Harry Sen died, Shadhona was given a pittance. The crafty vixen, however, was by no means finished. She proceeded to revile the family and even threatened to sue before her brother offered her shelter at his home in London. Shadhona fled the country, promising as her parting shot that she would return to ruin Bobby and his aunts for the shoddy way they had cheated her. But her new life in England, peppered with private parties, At Homes, visits to the theatre at Shaftsbury Avenue and shopping sprees in Knightsbridge, turned into a great distraction. Miraculously for Bobby – who wasted no time in elaborating a thrilling alternative to the truth – his stepmother's foreign address added to his own rising status in Calcutta.

Bobby remained an unalloyed snob, falling for all things 'foreign'. He typified what Calcutta society called a quintessential 'Ingo-Bongo' who could just about tolerate, for the sake of hedonistic pleasure, PomPom, one of his numerous starry-eyed girlfriends, singing ghazals at his parties.

Soon after the wedding, Bobby took me along with some of his close friends to Trinca's to listen to a new South Indian crooner who had recently hit the showbiz trail. Overnight almost, she had become a rage, swaying into the spotlight every evening in her shimmering Kanjeevarams, armed with a flourish of risqué jokes, and letting her unusual appearance take the diners by utter surprise. The media declared Miss Parvathi Bhaskaran the eighth wonder on Park Street, with a tambourine and two adorable dimples and non-stop patter that kept audiences enthralled.

'Wife, come dance with me,' Bobby commanded, after the first round of drinks, letting PomPom, who was evidently frightfully gone on him, grind her teeth. To suppress her disappointment, she whipped out a compact attached with a small mirror from her snakeskin bag. Carelessly, she proceeded to dust her freckles with a small puff to hide as best she could her displeasure at losing out on the first foxtrot with Bobby.

The lights dimmed. Parvathi Bhaskaran strummed the romantic prelude on the guitar and sexily shut her eyes. Pulling the mike close to her lips, she threw herself into crooning '*Besame Mucho*' in a low, libidinous drawl. Much to my unease, Bobby drew me to his chest and winked at PomPom from across the dance floor. Moving cheek to cheek, I was unable to see PomPom brighten up at once and mouth Bobby a kiss. It took me years to decipher PomPom's constant charades.

In Bobby's company I was thrown, without sufficient notice, into a world so different, so fast-paced and so selfish that I slowly began to realise how unprepared I had been to handle his crowd. And much to the amusement of PomPom, Bobby handed me over to Shireen Readymoney and her tribe to 'spruce and polish' me up. Bobby's insensitive remark, meant as a joke, cut me to the quick. I was deeply hurt as much by his thoughtlessness as by the insinuations against my innate gaucherie. But the vultures, given the green signal, immediately sensed that the fruit was ripe for picking.

I hated their patronising veneer, their painted, doleful expressions and their studied slouch that must have come from years of spending their husbands' money and cultivating a clever indifference in the dog-eat-dog corporate world. Bobby's bride was sweet but, alas, too raw, too simple, they laughed. And to set things right, they began their act of 'sprucing and polishing' in right earnest.

A few days after the reception, Shireen Readymoney and Shobeeta Mitra trotted me off to PomPom's beauty parlour, as if I were an untested filly in urgent need of being shoed and saddled. While PomPom got to work, the others fluttered around with the insouciance of faux fairy godmothers splattered with tinsel. Soon they were trimming away at my cuticles, buffing and painting my nails, pedicuring my feet, yanking at superfluous hairs and plucking and pencilling me into shape so that I could become sleek and smooth to the touch.

They giggled and told me that I was being prettied up so that my sex life dazzled like their diamonds. I blushed. All this cleaning and scouring was going to be part of the deal, whether I liked it or not. Babies were necessary for holding on to men who were apt to stray.

A virtuous wife by day had to be a filthy little slut by night. Didn't I know? Was I *that* naïve? Where had I lived before? On the moon?

'When he mentions sex, for heaven's sake, don't cringe. Pretend you have better things to do. With studied indifference comes style. Thwart his moves. Frustrate him with half-an-hour of begging before you condescend to part your legs. And while he's pounding away, hum your favourite song and sip a sherry. Better still, file your nails. Grin and bear it bravely, darling, even if you don't like it. You'll get used to it soon enough. Women have done it for hundreds of years. Why should you be any different?'

My ears turned hot and pink.

In school, I had been curious about sex in an academic, detached sort of way. I would worry about it, I always told myself, once I was happily married. It was a strange conditioning. The thought of actually having sex with a man never entered my head, despite my intense love for Paul, his ardent longing for me and the kiss he had impressed on my lips on my last night in Kathmandu. Stirred by some inept, half-formed comprehension, I had realised that I would have to sleep with a husband, whoever he may be, and experience his touch just the way I would experience childbirth or, maybe, a whitlow or a grand, dramatic sunset. But now these women made sex sound so dirty! In an instant, they took away the sweet fragrance of roses that had been strewn on my nuptial bed. Everything blurred, apart from the smell of whisky on Bobby's breath and the touch of his fingers on my bruised body.

Late at night Bobby would thrust his hands all over my breasts, kiss me with perfunctory nonchalance and then roll over and submerge me forcefully in his arms. In a tangle of bed sheets, my bra hurriedly unhooked, my sari hitched up and Bobby's pyjama strings unknotted, he'd enter me in a spate of lust whenever he felt he was in the mood, without any prior warning. My own, inept longings would remain unuttered. I'd hear his heaving and choking, and endure his frenzied chatter about how his next promotion would get us a bigger bungalow or a bigger car, even as he thrust away. For him, copulation was a game of power; of lust and winning.

I'd wait for him to do whatever he had to do quickly, letting my mind wander. I'd think of other times and other seasons and recall that golden, wonderful autumn in Nepal with all its delights and caprices. And then, once he would finish, the dark night would slowly drug me to sleep. I'd toss and turn and dream of a road twisting around the mountains. I'd dream of a crowded bus that would lead me back to a fabled city. And I'd wake up in a cold sweat knowing that my dream was now dead. And I'd set it on fire again and lay the embers in a heap on my pillow and weep into it silently, even as Bobby started snoring.

It was unlikely that my husband guessed anything about my past. He could never have confronted the fact that another man may have made off with my heart! He was, by nature, overbearing. But, hard as he tried, I wouldn't let him cancel out my earlier life. The past was all I had to hold on to – a whisper of approbation that brought back a secret smile, a confidence I thought I had lost forever. Yet, even as I resented Bobby's authority and refused to let Paul fade away from my thoughts, I had neither the courage nor the economic independence to walk out. I was, alas, too afraid to take a drastic decision.

My marriage was a fait accompli and there really was no escape. Who could have guessed, seeing me on my wedding day, that I had had the spunk to fall in love – that too with a blue-eyed American? And despite grudgingly accepting an arranged marriage negotiated by my family like thousands of girls before me, I still had the tenacity to cling to old, bittersweet recollections that lingered as a reminder of that brief holiday? I'd ask myself a hundred times if this was meant to be happiness – this lying buried under a man for a few fleeting moments, drowned by his lechery, his animal heavings, his spittle. Was sex something I needed to endure, unfeeling and blank, like a toothache or a foolish memory?

And when the first rays of light crept into the bedroom through the chintz curtains, I'd rise without making too much noise and rush to the bathroom to have a shower. I'd soap myself vigorously – rub my skin over and over with a loofah – to wash away the dirty stains of the night.

In the beginning, PomPom was just an irritating fly that I found hard to swat.

She insisted on partnering Bobby in the bridge tournaments at the club on the Saturday afternoons he was not playing golf. And she remained a permanent fixture at his parties, waiting on him like a slave. For every trifling attention Bobby paid her, she blushed and bridled, inviting lubricious speculation on the relationship from the city's veteran Hedda Hoppers. I glassily smiled and tried not to read too much into my husband's flirtations. But I had been warned that PomPom was the epitome of deception and infinitely thick-skinned.

Much as I tried to ignore her, I had to, alas, admit grudgingly that PomPom was attractive in a harlotish sort of way. She had about her a noxious air of exploding crackers and a perpetual, cheeky squint. She'd come to our home, often unannounced, wrapped in billowy georgette dupattas and clutching a bunch of expensive orchids as bribe. I couldn't stand the frippery in PomPom's clothes and manners. The scarves never quite offset her short and tight kameezes done in the latest style by French Tailors opposite New Market. Worn with smart churidaars, they accentuated her well-endowed derriere and camouflaged her rather frugal breasts, their protuberance small and not very attractive. Her appearance – so refulgent from a distance, so radiant and beaming – on closer scrutiny actually brooked irredeemable flaws. 'Good from far and far from good!' her enemies sniggered, poised on their high heels and buoyed by their spite.

According to them, her ears were oddly large and her mouth infinitely vulgar. Her badly pencilled eyebrows tried adopting a permanent semblance of seduction when she arched them to emphasise many half-lisped sentences, and her hooded lids drooped abnormally with the dust of electric blue eye shadow. The diamond pin flashing on her nose drew attention away from her huge forehead, where her hair fell in an infuriating fringe made famous by a Bombay film actress. In abrasive daylight she did seem a bit jaded, but at night, with some imagination and a few pegs of Scotch to prop up flagging fantasies, she could easily pass off as the local Queen of Sheba. Always fashionably breathless, PomPom tried every trick she could muster to pump out information on Bobby from me, flattering me with obvious skittishness. Such sycophancy was very annoying and I began to hate the way she took to addressing me as 'Didibhai'. 'Yes, Didibhai! *Ooof* course, Didibhai! *Nooo*, Didibhai! Three-bags-full, Didibhai!' she constantly bleated, fluttering her mascara-laden lashes. And as I breathed in deeply to check my temper, snapping at the stalks and doing the gladioli in a pretty porcelain vase, PomPom flittered around me like an errant insect.

When I initially started frequenting PomPom's beauty parlour, I hadn't realised that Bobby was in the thick of an off-and-on affair with her. Wives, alas, are the last to know! Apparently, it had been carrying on for years. What finally aroused my suspicion were the oddly timed phone calls. They would come just as Bobby got back from office and settled down to a cup of tea. Within minutes the phone would shriek and, like a jack-in-the-box, he would leap up and say cheerily, 'I'll get it!' and disappear into the bedroom with the handset. A week later, when the phone rang again, I picked up the receiver before Bobby could make a dash for the instrument.

'Hello?' I said carelessly, trying to hide my annoyance.

Click! The line went dead.

I simmered but let things pass. Next evening PomPom altered her ruse. Aware that Bobby was on tour, she called and, despite a bad attack of laryngitis, filled me in on all the slander she had overheard at the parlour.

'Oh, Didibhai,' she croaked like a bull frog. 'You won't believe me, but I've got to tell you what a horrible rumourmonger Cheenee Buttockbyle is!'

'Now what's Cheenee-di done?' I asked, trying to seem disinterested.

'She's snooping behind RajRani Sunanda Devi's back. Can you imagine, yaar? I can't even begin divulging the filthy lies she's spreading!'

'What did she say?'

'Disgusting things,' PomPom muttered and went straight into a vicious invective, describing a dinner party hosted by the Readymoneys to which I had not gone and Bobby had spent all his time kowtowing the RajRani. 'Believe it or not, Didibhai, all that her lovers are expected to do is keep her swimming in a sea of bed sheets. Next morning, of course, she rises from her four-poster and rewards them with expensive presents.'

'What rubbish!' I interjected, thoroughly miffed, having grown quite fond of the eccentric RajRani in these last few months.

A smile, not quite brought to birth, must have lingered on PomPom's lips as she imagined me turning pale with disgust. Unrelenting, she dropped her voice to a dramatic whisper. 'Her immaculate style hides all her not-so-immaculate conceptions,

Didibhai,' she giggled. 'My manicurist confirmed this to your Innie-Meanie-Cheenee at the parlour just the other day. I swear, yaar! The manicurist's sister works as an ayah in one of the lesser-known nursing homes in Lake Gardens, you see. They know *everything*!'

'PomPom, have you gone mad?' I snapped.

'I'm only repeating what Cheenee-di repeated to me, Didibhai. If you hadn't been so trusting, can you imagine what *we'd* have to face?'

'Oh come on! Who'd believe you're having an affair with Bobby?'

'I know, Didibhai! Thank God for that! But you must keep Cheenee Buttockbyle and that awful RajRani at an arm's length. I feel so protective about you, Didibhai – you're *sooooo* special!'

'I can take care of myself, thank you!'

I was as brusque as possible, and recognising my irritation, PomPom quickly changed her tune and asked in that ingratiating, horrible intonation that always managed to get my goat, 'Are you coming for your hair-wash tomorrow?'

'Yes, I think the appointment's for three in the afternoon.'

'See you then, Didibhai. Thanks a pile. See you tomorrow, yaar!'

Though her voice often faltered on the higher notes, PomPom, besides being a beautician, also prided herself as an amateur melody queen. Once Bobby had had his fourth whisky, his sycophants would encourage her to entertain them.

Much to my exasperation, Bobby's cronies started addressing me as 'Boudi' or 'Bhabi'. They reeked of Brut aftershave and wore shirts unbuttoned to their hairy navels. Shackled in heavy gold chains and diamond rings, I couldn't help noticing that the money they flaunted was so new that it bawled like a spoilt child for attention. Bobby needed his toadies much more than he needed a wife. They licked at the crumbs that fell off his lap so that they could get further orders for supplying packing boxes, gunny bags, paper containers and all kinds of other assorted goodies needed by the Company's marketing units. They sniffed around for opportunities to make profits despite the Big Boss's 'cut' that could be in cash or kind, depending on the actual billing amount.

Bobby's crowd was deferential though they claimed to be his friends. Falling on their knees to make the right noises, they lit his cigarettes, praised his tie, guffawed at his jokes and opened the car door so that he could slide in and roar away. And the minute he was gone, they cursed him from the bottom of their hearts for being such an unscrupulous rogue.

'Saala randichod! Bloody whore-fucker!'

PomPom was always ready to oblige them. Most of Bobby's parties would end with her ghazals as she'd cast her eyes down, clear her throat and begin lisping:

'Aashiyaaney ki baat kartey ho,
Dil jalaaney ki baat kartey ho...
Saari duniya ke ranj-o-gham de kar
Muskuraaney ki baat kartey ho...'

Of course her ghazal was meant to melt Bobby's studied indifference! After all, her heart belonged to him and she had no desire to see it break into a million pieces and lie scattered at his door! The pique, the subtle accusations ensconced in the lyrics were akin to Cupid's arrows meant to wound Bobby's pride. But much of the ghazal fell on her arrogant aashiq like water over a duck's back.

Bobby's faithful lackeys lolled around on the carpet, propped up on bolsters, and clapped fitfully or muttered 'wah-wah' or 'bahut-khub', sipping another round of whisky-soda and getting more and more sloshed. Encouraged, she continued into the next verse, unconcerned by the stifled yawns spreading over the mottled faces of the poor wives who sat in the shadows, dying to be spared. But Bobby's flunkies had strict instructions not to let PomPom down.

'Humko apni khabar nahin yaaron
Tum zamaaney ki baat kartey ho
Dil jalaaney ki baat kartey ho...'

RajRani Sunanda Devi of Natore finally put me on the alert.

I would like to think that she had taken to me immediately at the wedding reception itself. She later told me that she had been charmed by my honesty and my open smile. I was deeply flattered. Bobby knew which side his bread was buttered as far as the RajRani was concerned. Undaunted by the ripples she created when she walked into the party in a flourish of arrogance, wearing her solitaires and her patent Baluchari sari draped the Bengali way, without pleats, Sunanda Devi proceeded to confront us, chuck me under the chin and, to the absolute surprise of those who hovered on the dais, slip me a solid, old-fashioned gold mohur. Before I could recover, the princess turned to Bobby and cautioned, 'You better stop all your hokey-pokey at once, Bobby boy, if you know what's good for you! She's a jewel too precious to lose.'

'Of course, of course,' Bobby nodded, trying to cover up for his past proclivities.

'You blackguard!' barked Sunanda Devi, throwing back her head and laughing heartily. Then, turning to me, she announced, 'Come and have lunch with me this Saturday. We have a lot to talk about, my girl.'

'You must take her under your wings and shelter her, Hukum,

now that she's an integral part of your tea companies,' Bobby grinned.

Cheenee Buttockbyle, standing near the podium with a bunch of friends, snorted, '*Hokum* indeed! The RajRani looks like my part-time jhee who does the dishes!'

'Except that your maid would never be able to wear solitaires with such perfect élan,' Shireen Readymoney chuckled over her shoulder and walked away, draining her cocktail glass and buttoning up poor Cheenee Buttockbyle's mouth for good.

Bobby was all excited and nervous the day I was to lunch with Sunanda Devi, as if I were going for an important job interview. He was adamant that I be appropriately dressed and chose a pale blue Chanderi with discreet gold boti-work from a pile of saris that were part of my bridal trousseau. I watched, amused, as he rummaged through my cupboard and fished out a string of pearls with matching ear tops. The RajRani was an influential member of his Board of Directors, and, more importantly, a prized social asset. He didn't want me in any way to put a wrong foot forward and devalue such a priceless contact.

When I was finally chauffeured to the RajRani's 'palace', it turned out to be a bit of a joke, crumbling like Miss Havisham's wedding cake although it preserved enough Belgian chandeliers and louis quintz furniture covered in faded brocade to prop up its reputation. Pedestrians and tourists often wondered why this odd-looking structure squatted, legs apart, bang in the middle of matchbox apartments on Pretoria Street, as if ready to defecate with complete irreverence.

A brood of yapping Pomeranians ushered me in.

Certainly, RajRani Sunanda Devi had invested wisely to cultivate her whims. Educated at Roedean in Sussex, she still retained a touch of upper class English waspishness. And PomPom topped her list of pet hates.

'Don't you like asparagus?' she asked me at lunch, watching me struggle with the wilted stalks dipped in a bath of rather tart Hollandaise.

'It's absolutely perfect,' I lied, trying to cover up for my awkwardness.

'Good!' barked the RajRani. 'I'd rather stick to juicy asparagus than vinegary PomPoms!'

'She's quite ha-harmless,' I stammered, not at all convinced by my assertion.

'*Harmless?*' hissed Sunanda Devi, cutting me dead and brushing aside my attempt at diplomacy. 'My dear, don't be naïve! That slut will go to any length to feather her nest! She's even arrived at my doorstep at the crack of dawn last Independence Day and dragged me out of bed to hoist the flag at the club. Just because their chief guest let them down at the eleventh hour!'

I fell silent, quickly helping myself to some grilled bekti that Haider Ali, the bearer – replete in livery, turban and a faded red sash – came to show around.

'She knows how I hate these club doodahs, but do you think she ever listens?' Sunanda Devi's resentment quivered like a shaft of arrows as she continued with her attack. 'The bloody girl insisted that I sing *Jana Mana Gana...* on an empty stomach, can you imagine? Frankly, my dear, I don't give a farthing whether the "mana" comes before the "gana" or the "gana" comes after the "jana". What a hopeless muddle! Why can't we just do a *God Save The Whoever...* and be done with it?'

Then, clearing her throat, she fired her final salvo with all the hauteur of a seasoned thespian, 'Don't let her make you dance to her tune, Mohini! The whole world knows she has a terrible shine for Bobby. Men will be men. But don't let that bitch ruin your happiness.'

Sunanda Devi obviously knew what she was talking about. She was well acquainted with nuptials gone sour. Both her marriages had ended in acrimony and continued to remain steady grist for Calcutta's perennial cocktail mills. Her first husband, Dr Pannalal Lahiri, an eminent urologist, had died under mysterious circumstances and the reasons offered were as ambivalent as the RajRani's sense of style.

'Unusual, isn't it?' she cried, biting on a piece of garlic toast. 'Those weird Madagascan trifids in the garden just gobbled Panna up! Fi-fie-fo-fum! They had done it to two screeching parakeets not even a week ago – but to do it to Panna, just after we had returned from a Bharatanatyam recital! And he seemed so full of the danseuse with her huge eyes and enormous derriere. Panna was always soft on these dancing girls, the fool! Running around and sponsoring their shows, wining and dining them at the Three Hundred Club or the Golden Slipper and letting them take him for a ride. You know me, my girl, I wasn't one bit interested either in his tomfooleries or in the prima donnas doing all that Indian stuff that really bores me to death. Give me slim men in tight leotards any day!' she burst out laughing, recalling, perhaps, some stray encounter from times gone by. Then, patting her lips with the napkin she looked at me with a sardonic smile and continued, 'Well, Panna just vanished into thin air the following morning! Unbelievable! I had to have the wretched plants dug up from their roots and thrown into the Gonga, along with Panna's secret love letters and cigarette ash! It was all too surreal and sad my dear, but what to do? One of life's little ironies, I imagine...'

A good story, I realised, was worth all the lies it needed to make it credible. But I wasn't prepared for the onslaught of the next chapter that followed.

Sunanda Devi's second husband had proved tougher to slay. The princess had cared little for the illicit opulence of Rotten's Rajput forebears; what bothered her was his incipient kleptomania.

Rotten Mohan Singh would compulsively pilfer stuff from departmental stores and private homes, much to Sunanda Devi's chagrin. She tried amusing him in a million different ways but Rotten remained adamant. He'd neither be intimidated by her threats nor bite the bait laced with exotic holidays offered to diffuse his penchant for pinching anything that took his fancy. If it wasn't your poor bottom, it could well be a miniature Dresden shepherdess displayed on a delicate whatnot decorating a corner of your drawing room. Rotten was happily egalitarian and indiscriminate like many of his Communist friends. He didn't give a damn for class or creed. His eyes strayed from expensive items like a bit of art deco earrings in your personal jewellery box to a cheap wrist watch made in Japan cushioned in a shop's glass counter. Hiding his spoils in the servants' quarters, he would proceed to get dead drunk and then plead innocence till the RajRani discovered one of her most trusted watchmen double up as Rotten's conspirator. Montoo Mullick, the artful solicitor, had to be finally hired at an enormous fee to get rid of the thieves.

'Royalty all over the world is taking a beating, my girl,' Sunanda Devi's sigh was as elaborate as the lemon soufflé that lay untouched as she persisted, 'Look at the new user-friendly royal family in Britain! Prince Charles is trying his best to persuade the public to think of them as closer to the Larkins than the house of Atreus! He'd rather be father to Billy and Harry than Agamemnon and Menelaus! But I won't budge, my dear – never, never, *never*! My blood is too blue for a commoner like Rotten! And I don't care what people think about the divorce!'

'Thank you for such a delightful meal and all your advice,' I smiled, once my hostess had worn herself out with her stories. 'You've been so generous and sweet. And now you must come home and have a meal with us.'

'I will, if you promise to cook,' the RajRani replied, 'but remember, no PomPoms and chom-choms!'

'I will,' I assured her, grinning. Perhaps I had spoken too soon.

In the early days it was often some foolish request I had made or a minor disagreement that would end with Bobby hurling bitter accusations. Voices would rise and I would burst into tears and angry recriminations to ease my suspicions. I could never gauge Bobby's moods and slowly turned hysterical, even as his behaviour, treading the perilous path of nonchalance as the weeks went by, turned utterly reprehensible. My unhappiness surfaced from the fact that Bobby had no time for me and remained maddeningly superior. And I grew profoundly wretched and resentful.

That Tuesday, when he returned from office, tired and preoccupied, I stomped into the bedroom and announced, 'We have to go this Sunday to Amherst Street. Ma's invited us for lunch.'

'I can't,' Bobby replied, too tired to explain why. He flung his briefcase on a chair and stretched out on the bed.

'But it's Jamaai Shoshti!' I exclaimed, never having the astute foresight to marshal my arguments correctly. 'We can't let Ma and Baba down!'

Ma's invitation soon turned into a bone of contention. Like every traditional mother-in-law, she had wanted to host a lunch on Son-in-law's Day. But Bobby threw a fit.

'Why the hell can't you understand that I'm not in town that day?' he shouted, pulling at his tie. 'I've meetings lined up in Bombay for Saturday and Sunday.'

'I have meetings lined up!' I mimicked in rage, muddying the issue with imagined slights. 'Why can't you postpone them by a

week? Will your company fall apart if you don't go this weekend?'

'Look, I'm not willing to get into another argument with you,' said Bobby, trying to check his temper. 'Leave me alone. And tell someone to send me a cup of tea.'

'I wish you'd stop treating me like your secretary,' I shouted, with little authority over my thoughts. 'I'm not your bloody Perin Titlusvala or PomPom who's going to scrape and bow at your silly commands! Why do you take such pleasure in insulting my family?'

'Insulting your family?' Bobby asked, rising to my bait. 'I've said damn-all about them, Mohini. I just can't go. Period!'

'Because I'm a piece of boring furniture in your house?' I provoked.

'I've had enough!' Bobby shouted.

'I can't live in this house any longer! I can't, I can't...' I screamed back.

'This is just the beginning,' Bobby growled. 'Stick around!'

I tried to wrestle my next reproach into some shape but failing bitterly, cowered in front of Bobby like a dog that had been reprimanded. Bobby cursed, jumped up and rushed out, past my loud sobs. He drove off in all probability to the Saturday Club to hit the bar while I sank into a chair, whimpering in frustration.

Our marriage became a series of similar rows, mean and self-indulgent. This led to a perpetual state of tension – unspoken but palpable – blowing through the apartment. The next major war was over PomPom's stupidity, though I couldn't be entirely blamed for instigating the final explosion. PomPom had come to Bobby with the oddest request. Some of her friends, who were financing a film, wanted to shoot for an afternoon in a smart residence. What could be better than Bobby's home?

'It's an art film, Bobby,' she tittered at the club, not daring to look at me, 'and they're very good friends. Their budget is limited. Please, Bobby, we must help them out, yaar.'

'Who's the lucky star?' Bobby inquired, pacing up and down the greens and hitting an imaginary ball with an imaginary golf stick.

'Pretty Burman,' PomPom winked.

'Oh, the bombshell herself!' Bobby laughed, doffing his cap. 'Wife, what do you have to say to that?'

'Nothing,' I simmered with icy formality. 'It's your house!'

'Very well!' Bobby exploded. 'Next Friday then! I'm out of town!'

'Of course, of course,' PomPom simpered in that false and irritating trill, scurrying away before I could protest. 'See you later, alligator!'

The crew arrived on the appointed day, noisy and full of demands. The spot boys strutted around with great impunity. The director introduced himself as Sid Roy. His faded corduroys, patched near the knees, required immediate laundering. So did his manners. I took an instant dislike to him, hating the way he leered at me, alternately scratching his beard and groin. He reeked of sweat and alcohol. He screamed out instructions and took over the flat as if it were his own. I was at my wit's end, watching the crew push the furniture around, break a crystal vase and litter the floor with cigarette butts. Then, an hour later, Pretty Burman sailed in, the perfect icing to my already rising temper that had reached its inevitable point of fracturing.

Pretty Burman could easily pass off as high priestess of a special-needs brothel – a magical reincarnation of Vasantasena, harking back from times immemorial. Her detractors claimed she had tutored enough novices in her boudoir – sprawled on a chaise longue draped in purple brocade and legs enticingly spread – on how meaningful conversation could be held even after a lesson in rapid cunnilingus. Though her past record in Bengali commercial films was dubious, her fans could never deny that Pretty had a wonderful harlot's mouth, instinctive and sly, involuntarily opening and closing as if she were sucking in tongues. Most critics sniggered at how she had swayed and swung her way into every available scrotum till a few favoured roles came her way. Now, of course, having done a spate of art films, she was the coveted showpiece at every trendy party.

Her Chinese hairdresser of many years, Peony Wong, trailed her everywhere and secretly resented Pretty's hard-as-nails attitude. How unfair it was that she – her ever-faithful employee – who had initially wept with copious devotion, agitated by the actress's loud sobs on the screen, should be treated so impatiently! Later, she became distrustful, suspecting that the tears springing to Pretty's eyes at will had nothing to do with her heart, which was hopelessly barren and beat like a stone in her bosom, without an iota of consideration and kindness. Then, to her utter shock, Peony Wong discovered that Pretty had to use vials of glycerin to enact a melodramatic scene which, later, the audience lapped up in darkened movie halls, sniffling into their handkerchiefs.

The high-strung hairdresser was also eyewitness to Pretty's many peccadilloes.

The keyholes of quite a few dressing rooms at the Tollygunge studios were unusually large. Peony Wong took recourse to peeping through them when her mistress chucked her out on the pretext of wanting to rehearse her lines, undisturbed, with a promising director or a handsome co-star. The minute the door was bolted Peony Wong would see if the coast was clear and instantly drop to her knees. It always came as a bit of a jolt to watch Pretty furiously tugging at the flies of the visitors' trousers and pulling down the zippers, the better to ease with her gifted mouth their erect members. Peony Wong kept staring in amazement and wondering if fellatio, after all, was a secret cure for pernicious anaemia, because sometimes, when Pretty went on those dreadful diets, she did have – the poor girl – a terrible pallor about her. Yet her directors and heroes could not stop admiring her prodigious appetite and her detractors, her failed love affairs.

Peony Wong now looked at me as if I were a janitor on the sets and asked, 'Where's madam's room?'

'Madam' scanned the surroundings with a supercilious sweep. She waved out to the director and then bent to peer short-sightedly at the replica of an old bronze Nataraja from the Chola period dancing on a glass shelf.

'Use the guest room over there,' I brusquely pointed out and almost knocked down a light that had just been hoisted.

'Careful!' shouted one of the electricians, untangling a bunch of wires and cursing under his breath.

'Where's Madam's nimbu-pani?' demanded Peony Wong, grabbing me by the wrist.

I had had enough. I blew a fuse and was startled at the intensity of my fury. Walking up to the director, I shouted, 'How dare you people treat my home like a bazaar? How dare you make stupid demands? Please clear out immediately! I refuse to tolerate this any longer! Clear out at once!'

Pretty Burman instantly knew the situation had skidded out of control. It took all of her past lessons in diplomacy to calm me down. She scolded Peony Wong till the tiny hairdresser cried into her sleeves, letting loose a handful of the choicest expletives she knew in her native, high-pitched Mandarin. The actress then proceeded to give the rest of the crew a perfectly stage-managed dressing down before turning to me with profuse apologies and folding her hands in utter supplication. Finally, I had to thaw. The shooting commenced. But when Bobby returned from his tour, he could do little to bridle my bitter tirade.

Later – many years later – I came to know that the payment for the favour Bobby had granted had been Pretty Burman herself, warming his anonymous hotel bed for a night in Bombay. Though I seethed with rage, Bobby pretended to be oblivious to my feelings and frustratingly, I never had any real evidence of his affairs. Out of some freakish compulsion, I continued to drop in at PomPom's parlour, hoping to stumble upon a sure-shot red herring. But PomPom too gave nothing away.

Often she would pester me to visit The Good Samaritans, a charity shop suspiciously close to Bobby's office where she helped most Fridays, once she closed the parlour at noon and gave her workers a half-day off. Eager to show me a bunch of shadow-worked luncheon sets that had just arrived, she'd blather on and on about their sheer beauty and dexterous workmanship. They were painstakingly created by tribal girls in a faraway mission in Bihar, only to be subsequently soiled at some fashionable dining table by careless lipstick stains. Lifting my thick, dark hair, squeaking clean against her dirty conscience, PomPom would gloat in nervous elation, 'You've got to see them to believe them. In pastel shades and sheer organza. As pretty as soft clouds, Didibhai. Pure white on whites. *Sooooo* pristine that they'll make you drool, yaar!'

And I would listen, leaning back in my chair and staring at the ceiling. My life had changed beyond my wildest dreams. Why, I had even reached a compromise with Bobby to always include PomPom at our parties and private dinners.

It was such a bloody shame!

PomPom was waiting at the Bengal Club lounge when Bobby and I walked in. A few heads turned; a few smirks were smothered. But we, the proverbial ménage a trois, put up an oblivious front. Sinking into the huge Victorian sofas, Bobby ordered our drinks.

'So how was your day, girls?' he asked, waving his hand and calling for the bearer to come and take the order. 'Did you make it to the flicks?'

'Oh it was great fun,' PomPom giggled. 'Didibhai, wasn't that new Calcutta babe absolutely smaashing? She'd make Bobby such a fantastic maashooka!'

'I'm afraid you'll have to be more specific,' Bobby said, suppressing a yawn. 'I don't know enough Urdu to understand your constant barbs.'

'It's hardly a barb, Bobby-boy,' PomPom bleated, sufficiently peeved. 'I was saying it *sooo* romantically for you.'

'Oh, really? But she's out of bounds,' Bobby grinned, trying to compensate for the slight. 'The flower of the mountains is hooked and booked by a nawab already.'

'Good for her,' I glumly muttered, taking a sip of my vodka that the bearer had just served. 'How many Bengalis can boast of doing what she's done? Straight from Pinaki-da's sets and headlong into the glamorous world of Hindi films. Wow!'

'And what a figure!' Bobby drooled, indicating for another cube of ice in his whisky. 'Did you see her on the cover of *Star & Style* in a bikini? That was really brave!'

'*Star & Style* or *Femina?*' PomPom intervened, stirring her gin and lime and giving Bobby sidelong glances as she started to hum, '*It was an itsy-bitsy teenie-weenie yellow polka dot bikini that she wore for the first time she tum-tum-ti-tummed!*'

'Who cares?' Bobby interrupted, draining his glass. 'Any guy would give his left arm for her.'

'You bet,' said PomPom. 'And she's a hundred times more talented than that stup-pid Pretty Burman, yaar!'

'Oh Pretty's not stupid. She has several special assets, sweetheart,' Bobby pointed out with a wink. 'She's no ordinary fish in Tollygunge.'

Afterwards, sufficiently plastered, we made an awkward threesome and dined at the club's restaurant, too tired to go and watch Shefali's floor show at Prince's. Waving out to acquaintances, we scrutinised jaws that either dropped in surprise or tightened into smile-lines running deep with disappointment. PomPom dipped into the noodles with her chopsticks while I made some inconsequential, caustic remark to Bobby to camouflage my deep displeasure.

An air of pretence had permeated all our lives as a result of Bobby's dishonesty. PomPom and I – to save our fragile reputations – kept up the façade and worked slowly to winnow out old hurts. It did not cost much to pull a bit of wool over the eyes of veteran scandalmongers. And I was learning to do just that with uncharacteristic aplomb.

Everything about Bobby craved attention – from his highly polished shoes to his heavy cologne. I came to realise that with him there could never be any conversations, any exchange of ideas, leave alone kindness. There were only instructions I was supposed to follow. I didn't even have the option of returning to Amherst Street and hiding my face in the folds of my mother's sari. Slowly, as a sheath of sadness settled on me like fine dust, I succumbed to obedience and my robotic nullity.

Bobby always needed to control; to be hero-worshipped. His lackeys let him have his way as he went about cracking dirty jokes, making horrible sexist remarks and behaving like an overgrown school bully. With immense alarm I realised that he was becoming more and more malicious, self-centred and condescending as the days went by. Bragging about his personal equations with local ministers, non-Bengali bureaucrats and senior police officers, he'd actually drag me with him, in the initial months of our marriage, to what he called his 'routine sharaab and kebab sessions.' At these so-called binges at the club, his minions would surreptitiously pass his guests innocuous-looking briefcases – the kind a harried salesman usually picked up at Chaandni Market in Dharamtolla – which I soon realised were stashed with cash. Bobby would christen such bribes 'donations to the party funds' or, even better, 'speed money' to get work done on the fast lane.

I was the sacrificial lamb – Bobby Saab's brand new bride – that the invitees had ostensibly come to meet. I'd sit through the ritual, prettily dressed in a heavy Kanjeevaram sari and traditional gold ornaments, kajol darkening my eyes and exasperation darkening my mood, struck dumb and in awful trepidation while Bobby jabbered away. His manner seemed way too familiar than what one would normally expect of senior company executives dealing with strict official contacts. If their wives came along, I'd try and make some polite noises. But most of them couldn't carry forward a conversation beyond jewellery and saris and maidservant woes, or, of course, the latest scandals involving film stars. Of late, what had really caught their fancy was the recent re-run of Homi Wadia's mythological film, *Sampoorna Ramayana,* starring Mahipal as Rama, Anita Guha as Sita and Helen, of all actresses – for once without her skimpy outfits and outlandish ostrich feathers – as the seductress, Soorpanakha! The film, when initially released, had taken the nation by storm, with Helen swaying her hips and singing, '*Baar-baar bageeya mein koyel na boley...'* to a mortified Lakshmana in a garden abloom with English sunflowers and hybrid bougainvillea and a pair of scintillating skylarks – 'Hail to thee Blithe Spirits!' – hidden in the formal yew hedges. Every re-run thereafter had ensured that devotees flock to the darkened movie halls with the right touch of reverence. The bovine actress who played Sita was, of course, the apple of their eyes, the eternal sufferer they could identify with – the epitome of the ideal wife – so faithful, so virtuous, so pure like the pure ghee in which they fried their breakfast parathas, leaving their waistlines girdled with stubborn tyres. And while they eulogised Sita's virtues, their husbands got more and more drunk on free pegs of whisky accompanied by oily cheese balls, chicken lollipops and fish fingers. Then, when they were about to leave at last, one of Bobby's flunkies who had been waiting in the car, rushed up with the briefcase and a box of laddoos and quietly placed it in the visitor's virginal white Ambassador sullied with just the right touch of mud at the rear!

There'd be good-natured goodbyes exchanged at the portico amidst whispers of 'Kaam ho jaayega, saab,' or 'Don't worry, mate, the job's as good as done!' while Bobby grinned and shook hands and made quick appointments for the following week. And then, as the guests drove away, our affable Bobby Saab would loosen his tie, scowl and curse under his breath, 'That's fuckin' life, Mohini! All this is part of the fuckin' deal, god dammit!'

Initially, I had been confused, but the more adamant he became about his lifestyle, the more I began resisting his deceptions and affectations. He was used to ambivalence. Unfortunately, I didn't suck up to him like PomPom. Sometimes he'd remain impassive to my accusations and make me feel as if I were talking to a wall. At other times he'd use sly and clever ploys to tame me. He'd buy me a particularly expensive sari or a piece of jewellery, never forgetting to tell me how much it cost. Or he'd flay me with particularly harsh insults, mocking my family's social penury.

I was, alas, so easy to wound.

Over the months Bobby grew more and more intolerant and nothing that I ever did seemed to please him, not even the simplest domestic chores. My security in Bobby's home (he always said it was 'his home'; never 'our home') was always hedged with danger. As the months passed, I became inordinately tetchy, not quite knowing how to respond to his threats or even his rare fits of affection. He blazed with rude confidence, expecting me to be all docile and agreeable, clearly hoping I'd wag my tail in simpering placation. All Bobby wished for was that I abide by his decisions – from the food that would be prepared for *his* Sunday lunches, the saris I'd wear to *his* office parties, to the list of *his* favourite films I'd be obliged to see when *his* mood so deemed. He accused that he got no response from me, telling me that I only cared for the free perks he offered. I didn't rouse him enough; didn't have any gratitude for his generosity, always lost in some other world he could hardly penetrate. He said that I left him 'unstirred' – as though I were some bland curry, deprived of aromatic spices and left on the burner, unappetising and without a ladle that – bingo! – Bobby could use to shake up at his bidding.

Over and over he told me, in that pompous voice of his, that he had no time for slow coaches. He'd dress in a hurry, get into the car, blow the horn in furious bursts and shout, 'Hurry up, lazybones! I'm waiting!' He was the monarch of all he surveyed and his subjects had to keep pace with his whims and fancies.

If I returned late from New Market after my weekly household shopping, he'd demand, 'Where the blazes have you been? Don't you know I need the car?' If I visited Amherst Street on a weekday, he'd sulk, 'Your bloody parents always take top priority. I'm only a means of convenience, aren't I?' And if I ever fell ill, he'd bark, 'What awful timing, just when I need you by my side at tomorrow's cocktail party. Don't you know that the bosses arrive tonight from London?'

Bobby's initial louche glamour gradually faded. He had reduced himself to a reckless liar, constantly messing up his lines. His dishonesty required no consistency. And in the end I stopped fighting, stopped questioning, letting him do as he pleased.

It was all too much for me.

When he said, 'Let's have a frank discussion', it invariably meant, 'Let's get into a roaring argument.' And I construed as contempt his deliberate ignoring – the way he'd look through me as though I were a window pane, a piece of glass, whatever – it was all so insulting! Very often his ready answers – too pat for his own good – made it amply clear that he had been badly out of kilter. His wiles were no more than foolish repetitions of the same excuses, the same banalities. The very poverty of his vocabulary precipitated a more physical congruence. What he called my 'foolish imaginings' were as real as PomPom's squint!

With time, I began to pity his tricks. What could be bleaker? Grief, perhaps. But I was not ready for grief just yet. His lies and his cut-throat ambition, I thought darkly, would be his doom some day. Very few people had any inkling that I walked around, burdened with hurt, like a dog on a leash. The tides of my life with Bobby, along with the tides of his career, thrashed and spewed trying to occasionally sprinkle some sanity into our severed shores. No step we took together ever left any lasting imprint in the sands of our marriage. Yet the outside world kept applauding my patience, my upbringing and my wonderful compassion for the girls at Sarojini

Memorial Women's Union where I started working as a volunteer, goaded by RajRani Sunanda Devi who headed the charity.

Slowly, I realised that it was a rather short route from exasperation to indifference. But I took it willingly. Then, before our first wedding anniversary, I discovered I was pregnant.

Shireen Readymoney and Shobeeta Mitra immediately recommended a fashionable butcher, Bijoy Banerjee, whose stupid anaesthetist gave me an overdose and almost killed me on the delivery table. Dr Banerjee's chamber on Little Russell Street may have been the most fashionable address in town for pregnant women but my inept visits, while I was carrying Ruchi, left me apprehensive. The gynaecologist was a notorious braggart. He had bad teeth, no buttocks and a flashy watch he had picked up in New York. He'd talk big about his powerful connections and snigger at all kinds of unsavory details regarding a small coterie of women who happened to be his patients. The nefarious leer in his eyes always unsettled me. I'd sit before him with my legs pressed together, clumsy and trapped, as he'd carelessly write out a prescription for iron pills, conduct the most embarrassing 'internal check-ups' with his rubber-gloved hand every six weeks and advise me to read Dr Spock like some new-age Bhagvad Gita.

Nevertheless, I survived his butchery. And so did Ruchi.

When I finally returned home, I became determined that my daughter would do all the things I couldn't. I'd look at the vulnerable little mite, sleeping with her thumb pushed into her dribbling mouth, and hope she'd grow up in a less stifling atmosphere. I wouldn't allow anyone to inflict Ruchi with foolish rules and stupid threats. I wanted my baby to lead her life without preconditions. Ruchi would do all the things I had missed out doing. And do them with stupendous élan, free from blame.

New to motherhood and completely guilty of my inept tactics, I resorted to hushing the baby with spoonfuls of Woodward's Gripe Water. I'd watch Ruchi splay her legs about in her pen, thrilled at the plastic mobile with flying horses whirring over her face. And testing the temperature of the milk bottle on my wrist, I'd marvel at the perfection of those little fingers and toes, the beautiful eyes and pouting lips that could pucker into the most terrible tantrums or break into a glorious smile without prior warning.

I was thankful that I hadn't succumbed to hallucinations like my mother when Ruchi was born. In fact, during my first pregnancy, I was too young and too confused to have any clear idea about my responsibilities. Bobby was of little help. Hiding his disappointment at having fathered a girl child, he ensured that he was out of the city, on official tours, at least twenty days in a month while I struggled with the infant. In desperation I turned to Paddy Roy's wife, Queenie, to help me find an ayah, too intimidated to ask RajRani Sunanda Devi for help. After all, Paddy Roy was Bobby's 'best buddy' and an intimate office colleague. They'd known each other right through their Doon School and St Stephen's days and not a weekend went by without them meeting at the club for golf and beer.

I had become rather fond of Queenie in spite of knowing that she drank like a fish and could turn aggressive and truculent if she had had one too many. But something about her sharp tongue attracted me to her. She was basically lonely and without friends. And I couldn't care less if she went around her home every morning in a dirty kimono, hair scragged back in curlers, dead drunk and yelling at all those who dared to cross swords with her. When I finally called her and poured out my woes, without hesitation Queenie sent across Kanchiama, her Nepalese watchman's wife, who turned out to be a wonderful ayah. Then she started to regularly drop in to check how I was doing. For Cheenee Buttockbyle, our growing attachment spelt doom. Her moral high-handedness had always been grating and now the bee in her bonnet about poor Queenie's so-called depravity buzzed overtime. She had taken it upon herself to rescue me from the foetid miasma of my new-found friend's alcoholic excesses. And so she arrived one afternoon, unannounced, ostensibly to see the baby with an appropriate gift but really, to tick me off.

'Don't you know *anything* about Queenie's past?' she asked, spreading herself on a couch in the living room. 'Hasn't Bobby told you? I'm so surprised, my dear! Don't you know why Paddy treats her like a leper?'

'Cheenee-di, Queenie is a good friend,' I replied, trying to be firm. 'She's been more than kind, and that is all that matters.'

'Then go and join Mother Teresa instead of helping out at Sarojini Memorial!' A hint of accusation tinged Cheenee Buttockbyle's voice. She sipped her tea with nonchalance and I went about, exasperated, straightening some crooked paintings on the wall. 'You must be daft, getting taken in by all her sweet talk!'

'What has poor Queenie done?' I demanded at last, turning to face my guest.

'Darling,' pronounced Cheenee Buttockbyle, placing her cup down and rubbing her palms, 'she is, I'm afraid, N.Q.O.C.D.! Full-stop!'

'N.Q.O…? What did you say?' I frowned, puzzled.

'N.Q.O.C.D.! Not Quite Our Class Dear!' she smiled, all hoity-toity and superior.

But I refused to believe Cheenee-di who thought it was her birthright to criticise the world.

How could Paddy be a sadist?

He had been so charming, so utterly delightful, washed clean and smarmed down when Bobby had initially introduced him to me at our wedding that the subsequent stories about his degenerate brutality sounded too fantastic to be true. I had felt uncomfortable till Cheenee-di's sly insinuations were confirmed by PomPom. I'd bump into him at Shireen Readymoney's parties, but he always came alone or with Beethi – a pretty receptionist at a five star hotel, with a slightly horsey face, crooked teeth and salt-and-pepper bobbed hair – draped on his arms.

'Can't you see how cold and grey his eyes are, Didibhai?' PomPom exclaimed at the parlour, helping to shampoo my long hair a few days after Cheenee Buttockbyle's visit. 'He treats Queenie like shit and gets away with it, yaar!'

'Why does Queenie tolerate it?' I asked.

'Oh, that's a long story, Didibhai. Ask Bobby, will you?'

And PomPom switched on the hair dryer and broke into a fit of infuriating giggles.

Poor Queenie did have much to grieve about.

She had spent her childhood abroad, happy to have a father posted in Madrid as India's distinguished ambassador. Then suddenly, in a spate of mid-life calamity, 'Papa' fancied himself as a contemporary Don Juan and started to visit a dark-eyed señora with her head appropriately covered in a delicate mantilla over a high comb. The lady ran a delectable little casa de putas patronised by discerning clients in the Calle Montera that opened up to the main boulevard of Gran Via like the glorious, spreading legs of a seasoned hooker. All hell broke loose when 'Mumsie' finally found out and promptly fell ill.

Life changed harshly once they returned to Calcutta. 'Mumsie', poor dear, unable to take the shock and the city's seasoned wagging tongues, succumbed to gossip that spread like wild fire. Within a month after returning from Spain, a cerebral stroke felled her in the unlikeliest location. While limping across New Market with her faithful coolie close at her heels, she stopped to bargain for half a dozen Alfonso mangoes in the fruit and vegetable section, assaulted by the foetid air ripe with rotting banana peels. Before she could pull out her delicate lace-edged handkerchief embroidered by the girls at Women's Friendly and press it to her nose, a vicious wasp coasted right into her cleavage. Her head took a sudden turn and like a pigeon shot in mid-flight, she collapsed in the midst of all the hue and cry kicked up by the vendors. The tragedy hardly affected 'Papa'. Once he had shed his crocodile tears, within a month he shacked up with a local femme fatale who was, horror of horrors, twenty-three years his junior. That was discomfiting enough. But when he began sporting colourful Hawaiian shirts over red drainpipes at public 'do's, the daughter knew that she'd have to fend for herself.

Queenie didn't fit in anywhere. On a silly impulse, she decided to marry the first man she met. The guy proved to be an absolute scoundrel. For the lack of a Humberhawke as dowry he walked out at the eleventh hour, leaving her high and dry and with no other option but to flee to Art School in Chelsea. The echoes of the would-be groom's father thundering 'no carriage, no marriage' still clanged loud and clear through vintage Alipore lunch parties.

Queenie started to indiscriminately sleep around once she returned to Calcutta without completing the course. Her boyfriends were a series of slim-hipped and hard-drinking rogues, freshly accepted in plum jobs as tea tasters or management trainees in foreign owned banks and shipping firms. They slouched down the dimly lit corridors of Birkmyre Hostel or the various chummeries dotting

Burdwan Road, whistling *'It's been a hard day's night...'* and boasting about their latest conquest. Their Sundays were usually free. If they were not going to the races or playing tennis, they put Queenie to good use. Later, when the mantle of respectability started to burden their shoulders as they elbowed their way up the commercial hierarchy, they denied having known her altogether.

Gone were the days of casual bonhomie, beer-drinking sessions and after-work rehearsals for their amateur theatre group called Purple Curtain. Gone were the furiously adrenaline-ridden football matches, wild nights of racing cars down Red Road at impossible speeds or canoodling foot-loose and fancy-free nymphets in darkened movie halls. They'd smile at Queenie awkwardly, plaster her with booze and then melt into thin air with wealthier harvest they had learnt to profitably scythe at weekend bashes. The pressure of their jobs and their richie-rich girlfriends became more inspiring than the pressure of Queenie's weight straddling their torsos or their scruples.

Also, rather ironically, they discovered she had breast cancer.

Mastectomy became Queenie's only option to deal with a broken heart. She had not yet been equipped to confront the grotesque physical sensation of sharing her bosom with a malignant cluster of cells, proliferating like bubbles in a glass of champagne. The drugs she had to take had names like parody countesses in a pantomime: Bleomycin, Vinblastine, Adriamycin. And when she finally came home, permanently scarred, she grabbed Paddy Roy literally by the collar.

Bobby loved to tell the tale with malicious delight though he professed to be Paddy's soul mate. PomPom, if she happened to be around, willingly added the frills. Poor Queenie's life lay ripped apart for public mockery at many of our get-togethers as Bobby insisted that every Turk worth an erection had had a crack at her from Madrid to Calcutta.

'Paddy first set eyes on Queenie at a gala Merchant's Cup Night at Tolly when he was on the Entertainment Committee,' he revealed, letting his cronies guffaw again, though they had heard the story a hundred times before. 'Queenie was downing her sixth gin with enormous flourish at the bar and smoking a Sobrani. One more peg and she was pegged forever, right under her host!'

Apparently, without wasting time, Paddy had straightened the knot of his tie and sauntered up to Queenie with lazy grace. Placing his startling grey eyes into hers, he had said, 'Hello Beautiful, you look so tired that you ought to be in bed!'

'What a charming idea,' Queenie had exclaimed, jumping off the bar stool and grabbing the lapel of his blazer. 'Darling, your place or mine?'

'Does it matter?' Paddy had grinned, concentrating on her eyes and swaying gently to the band that had started to play *'All this and heaven too...'*

Queenie moved her hands from his lapel and let them encircle his neck. Amazed at Paddy's rock-hard ardour as he pressed himself against her, she pushed him to the dance floor with a laugh. His hands started to explore, up from her tight and well-rounded arse to her back, counting the bones in her spine, and then, in a flash, slipping around the ribcage to stray over her bosom. Unprepared for what he had touched, she saw the disgust in his eye flash for a split second. Then with a sardonic glint – a glint she would have to see many times later – he quickly covered up his initial shock.

'Darling, you are irresistible,' Paddy whispered. 'I can't stop myself now, I'm so sorry. I can't stop myself from not fucking you tonight!'

'I'm all yours, baby,' Queenie whispered back, grinding her hips against his and sliding her palm down his groin.

Tears suddenly filled her eyes. She moved her head to rest it on his neck, sucking and attacking him. Deliberately, nibbling past the slightly bitter aftertaste of his cologne, she confronted the fact that yet another man had discovered her inadequate body.

Queenie did not realise when she finally married Paddy that she would join the BWC (Battered Wives' Club) within a week.

Before making love, Paddy would insist on stripping Queenie, washing her down and sinking her in the old-fashioned bath that foamed with bubbles and rested on brass claws. His eyes never left staring at the rough scar where her breast had once swelled. The ritual gave him an instant high. Tearing off his clothes, he would initiate the drubbing, thrilled by the way she spewed and sobbed. Paddy used every ploy to keep her sunk. His beatings were relentless. Thankfully, in a while, everything blanked out against the blinding pain. Queenie vaguely heard Paddy, naked and domineering over her, with a massive erection, hissing profanities.

According to PomPom, Queenie's voice often spluttered and then rose like a litany late at night over the sound of the splashing water, unable to bear up with the hammerings or Paddy's cock that he forced down her throat. Her muffled shrieks were like a declaration of some strange, perverted kink as she sucked away. Somewhere, incongruously, she too enjoyed the torture that culminated in Paddy's huge orgasm and their landing back to earth with a thud.

Later, exhausted and toweling her down with profuse apologies, Paddy would look sufficiently shame-faced. Queenie bore the insults with stoic silence. Often, Paddy would leave home soon after. Queenie couldn't care less where he went. She'd stagger into the bedroom and pour herself a stiff whisky. She'd soothe the bruises with ice and pretend nothing had happened. Five hundred milligrams of Brufen smudged the sordid details. Her only solace in bed was the telly, and its final opiate, the weather bulletin, after the news at midnight.

Perhaps she'd disappear one day, Queenie had confessed, having finally spilt the beans to me on a sultry afternoon. She'd leave Paddy to his eighteen holes of golf, to a choice between soda and water in his Scotch, and the freedom to sleep with his girlfriend, Beethi Kanungo.

Initially, Queenie had found it odd to see Paddy's desk calendar marked with little red dots over five days every month. With persistence she found out that those were the days Beethi bled. Paddy loved sleeping with women during their period, pulling out his penis after the orgasm, all bloodied and victorious. He had tried cornering Queenie during her chums but she had kicked up a huge fuss. Beatings and blow jobs were all she was willing to tolerate. She firmly nipped any other aberration in the bud. So, on those red-letter days, Paddy would disappear and sleep with Beethi, allowing his sexual kinks to bloom in outdoor bowers.

Shocked by the stories Bobby never tired of telling, I pushed past all gossip and made it a point to spend time with Queenie at the Bengal Club library. Soon I discovered that my new companion was a voracious reader. And our taste in books was similar. The bond strengthened over the hot and humid days of summer as she slowly confessed about Paddy's tortures. Yet Queenie's many generosities made me realise how thoughtful and warm she could be, stripped of her mask. Her calm, aloof eyes gave nothing away in public. No inferences, no mood swings, no sudden hysterics brought on by sinister incubi. I had learnt by now that every Calcutta cupboard had a priceless heirloom and an equally precious skeleton, and women were made out to be sexual turnstiles through which all men had to pass. Escape for Queenie, inevitably, lay either in a tumbler of whisky or in the opulent world of literature. I let our common love for Rilke's poetry and the novels of the Bronte sisters, Somerset Maugham and Iris Murdoch override wagging tongues. Meanwhile, with some semblance of help, I also learnt to organise my life better and centre my attention on Ruchi. The months swiftly went by and within a year, in utter amazement, I was watching my daughter toddle and fall and get up and walk again.

Right from her childhood, Ruchi showed great determination to stand on her feet. Once she began going to a Montessori, I involved myself more and more with Sarojini Memorial Women's Union, encouraged by RajRani Sunanda Devi and a group of women the princess shuffled dexterously like a pack of cards at her bridge table. She even taught me how to play the game and make new acquaintances at the 'palace'.

'Mohini, my dear, I believe Cheenee's been at your throat again about poor Queenie,' she pronounced one afternoon, expertly rearranging two packs of cards. 'Pay no notice, my girl. I've got my spies working overtime. We'll kick her out at the next governing body meeting, the bloody bully!'

'Cheenee-di's a lot of sound and fury,' I said placidly. 'It's just her stupid temper. Actually, she's quite kindhearted.'

'Kindhearted? Utter bosh!' retorted the RajRani. 'I've asked Sylvia to come for tea this afternoon. I want her to take over from Cheenee. I'll fix Madame Buttockbyle in the next hour! She's getting too big for her boots! And her chin's shot up so high that I hope she ricks her bloody neck sooner than later! I'm sure Sylvia can help us get donations from England.'

'Is it necessary?' I asked, trying to placate Sunanda-di. 'We're going to do a big fund-raiser with Simi Garewal in any event. She was so wonderful in Conrad Rook's *Siddhartha*, remember? The British Council promotes culture, not charity.'

'Be quiet, silly girl!' flew back the rejoinder. 'I know how to tackle the Hammonds! Cheenee's been behaving awfully with the new wards rescued from Sonagachi. As for Indian money, the less said about it the better!'

'Darling, I believe some of the new girls have a past worse than Pretty Burman's,' giggled Shireen Readymoney, viewing her hand.

'It must be *sooo* dreadful to be poor,' proclaimed Reena Chakladar, a fashion designer who dabbled in kantha and had an appetite for stealing other couturiers' designs. 'Can't imagine twenty people sleeping in a single room the size of my bra. And yet they breed like bunnies!'

Reena Chakladar was famous for paying the poor village girls – who actually did all the intricate embroidery – a pittance. Shireen Readymoney had recently introduced her to Sunanda-di as her new bridge partner once Shobeeta Mitra decided to quit, and Reena lavished Shireen with half-a-dozen kantha saris in order to firmly stitch yet another loose hem on Calcutta's dubious social border. Reena was what Queenie described as the quintessential hoyden – a thoughtless little 'rich bitch', replete in her slacker gear that included a Hermes bag, Burberry trousers, a Dolce & Gabbana belt, Manolo Blahnik leopard-skin flats, a six-carat diamond ring, a Body Mass Index of less than twenty and a cosmetically propped up face covered in more makeup than a transvestite out on a geisha night. She couldn't even smile properly for fear of snapping the tucks.

'We've begun a school for orphans, Reena,' Shireen Readymoney explained. 'You should come and help at least twice a week. Perhaps some of our girls could even do your embroidery.'

'I'd love to,' responded Reena Chakladar evasively, toying with a wobbly conscience and pondering whether a one-time fat donation could be a better pay-off. 'But where's the time to mess around with charity?'

Sunanda-di was well aware of the blatant thievery that went on in the fashion world. Women in the kantha business came dime a dozen, circling around the Birbhum villages like hungry vultures. If only they were more generous, she thought, a stitch in time could actually save nine.

'Don't you people have a conscience?' she barked, trying to hide her anger and wipe away her opponent's belligerence with the Queen of Hearts.

'You keep the conscience, darling,' Reena Chakladar tittered, fondling her King of Diamonds before demolishing the set altogether. 'I'll keep the millions!'

Just as the last rubber was drawing to a close, Sylvia Hammond breezed in. Her skirt, in a pretty floral print cut on the bias, clung to her and made her look thinner than usual. And her enthusiasm was still staggering.

'Girls, girls, girls! I have a very exciting proposal!' she informed, breathless, before RajRani Sunanda-di could have her say. 'I want to start a Book Club. And I want all you babes to become members. Will you shell out your subscriptions now?' she laughed.

'What a good idea!' exclaimed Sunanda-di quickly calculating the benefits and digging into her handbag. 'We can henceforth educate our Ritas and Christinas without any bother!'

'You have to be chief patron, of course,' enticed Sylvia, slipping into a spare rattan chair. 'I insist, Sunanda. I'm just as stubborn as you, my dear! And I'm not taking "no" for an answer!'

Pleased at being handed charge without the bother of an initial committee meeting to ratify her credentials, the RajRani accepted without protest. Now she'd return the favour by offering Sylvia Cheenee Buttockbyle's post. The Book Club was a marvellous windfall – revenge had never tasted sweeter.

At the first Book Club meeting, I was made honorary secretary. Encouraged by me, Queenie enrolled within the week. Soon after, out of sheer boredom, Shireen Readymoney also became a member and dragged Reena Chakladar to one of the poetry readings. Reena, of course, would join anything or pull anything asunder if it helped promote her business. Sylvia presided over most committee meetings, conveniently held at the British Council veranda, though RajRani Sunanda Devi, determined to be the real star, insisted the book launches be hosted in her chandeliered hall room.

PomPom sent feelers to me and clearly indicated she longed to be part of the gang.

'It's *sooo* intellectual, yaar!' she gushed over the phone. 'Didibhai, can't I be accepted as a member too? Please, darling, you must get me in!'

'Can't right now,' I replied, knowing better. 'We're full up at the moment.'

PomPom fumed silently till Bobby, with Shireen Readymoney's collusion, forced me to jump the gun and agree to Jahnavi Somani's membership.

Jahnavi was the new public relations manager at his office and Bobby had the upper hand when he said to me, 'You know how bright she is, don't you? It was because of you that she got the job, remember? What's the harm in breaking a few rules?'

'But I've just said "no" to PomPom,' I protested.

'Oh, wake up and smell the coffee, honey,' Bobby laughed. 'PomPom doesn't know her elbow from her arse, leave alone Dostoevsky!'

A little more arm-twisting and the deed was finally done. PomPom, of course, never forgave Bobby. Or me, for that matter.

Initially, I was confused about Jahnavi Somani. Through PomPom's grapevine I had gathered that she belonged to an illustrious Muslim family, having thrown caution to the wind the moment she married Harish Somani, a Barabazaar Marwari with pots of money. She had also cleverly changed her original name, Jahanara Parveen, to a more acceptable Hindu appellation. But her woes, alas, could not be washed away by the Gonga.

Love had made Harish Somani blind. But when the razzle-dazzle of romance faded and he regained his sight, he also discovered that he was in the throes of a foolhardy situation. Jahnavi was more than he could handle. Had his folks found out about her religion, they would have instantly killed him and sunk his body in the local pond. He had faced the cyclone of 'ishk-wishk', as he liked to call it, with stubborn willpower and a battery of lies. Jahnavi's beauty had certainly helped. But, much as he tried, she refused to adjust to his lifestyle, his friends and relatives, stubbornly clinging to her half-baked, bakwaas ideas.

The compromises Harish demanded only managed to irritate Jahnavi. For example, she was used to rich Muslim fare but Harish insisted on traditional daal-bati-churma with dollops of freshly churned butter. He spurned her advances the days she visited her college friends and then tried to kiss him after returning home, having tucked into a rich Murgh Mussalam or a spicy kaleji curry done to perfection with calf's liver.

'Ooof! How could you? Are you a churail?' Harish would shout in disgust, pushing her away. '*Liver!* You actually ate Gai-mata's liver?

Hai Ram! Mother Cow will never forgive you!'

'Mother Cow tastes divine. But how would you know, jaan?' Jahnavi would counter in a fit of temper. 'You've grown up a complete goat, chewing grass!'

The differences in food habits were a minor impediment. The smaller problems could have been resolved had Harish shown some imagination in bed. But, regrettably, he'd simply get her to mount him whenever he felt horny, lifting his spine and pumping away as if she were a deflated car tyre. Later, once she had climbed down, without another word he'd fall off to sleep and begin snoring. Nothing frustrated Jahnavi more than dreary fornication. She tried several times to show him what to do a little more inventively. But he just wouldn't listen. Sex for him was simply lust. He wasn't interested, he said, in 'foreplay-shoreplay'. He wasn't even interested in erotic talk. Dry as the missi rotis he ate at lunch, his sex life bombed badly.

'Isn't it enough that I use Boroline?' he'd point out in the morning, lathering his face for a clean shave. 'Not like the others who make do with gobs of spit.'

'For goodness' sake, be less gross,' Jahnavi would yell. 'I only want you to make love to me properly. Why are you so fucking lazy? Why do I have to ride you like a bitch on heat all the time?'

'Because I work like the blazes to provide for your comforts and am dog tired at the end of the day,' Harish would bark back. 'Your nonsensical, unt-shuant demands drive me up a wall!'

Harish Somani simply lacked the savageness to make Jahanara Parveen, alias Jahnavi Somani, scream and render an orgasm she so richly deserved. And unable to live up to her expectations he ended up – the poor bloke – jitterbugging at the racecourse in khaki Safari suits and Ray-Ban Wayfarers when he was not sweating it out, overseeing his sugar mills in Hardoi.

Jahnavi was fed up of her tepid life. To break the monotony, she decided to get herself a new hairdo and a scintillating career much to her husband's exasperation. At PomPom's parlour she sniffed out that Bobby's company was on the lookout for a public relations manager. The job was right up her street. It demanded oodles of charm and little or no conscience. Having wilted under the boredom of herbivorous food and vegetarian sex, this assignment presented itself as a veritable Barmecide's feast straight out of the Arabian Nights. Without wasting time, she goaded PomPom to help. PomPom, in turn, arranged for her to meet me, and I, unwittingly, played right into Jahnavi's hands, melting at her well-prepared little sob story. Anyone who had studied English literature could find instant access to my heart. Jahnavi was lucky. As a shy undergraduate at Loreto College, my soft spot for Shakespeare had initially taken wings. Now, in no time, a few stray lines from *A Midsummer Night's Dream* parroted by Jahnavi worked their magic on me.

'My gentle Puck, come hither,' I repeated in a trance after her, watching PomPom's eyes turn into saucers. *'Thou remember'st since once I sat upon a promontory/ And heard a mermaid on a dolphin's back/ Uttering such dulcet and harmonious breath/ That the rude sea grew civil at her song/And certain stars shot madly from their spheres/ To hear the sea-maid's music…'*

Surprised at my insistence that he meet this brilliant girl I had discovered in PomPom's parlour, Bobby finally gave in and called for Jahnavi's bio data. Just a careless fall of her sari anchol in the midst of the interview, perfectly timed and more dramatic than any mermaid riding a hapless dolphin's back, did the trick. The strategy was brilliant. What God had gifted her in abundance, Bobby now glimpsed at leisure. And memories of the cleavage kept the Burra Saab happily overwhelmed. She landed the job within the week. I, of course, was unaware while PomPom fumed and fretted. She could not reconcile to the fact that she had been left high and dry, with ephemeral soapsuds all over her hands, while Jahnavi frothed up her life into one hell of a slather.

Like Bobby, the Book Club members too were enthralled by Jahnavi's charm. She became an instant hit with her strong voice and clear enunciation. But it was her criticism of George Eliot's *The Mill On The Floss* that ultimately won the day. As her nose pin flashed while her head turned from her sheaf of papers to the listeners, every member was struck equally by her good looks and her diatribe. Nobody knew that she had regurgitated an old essay from her college days, written by the best girl in her class. RajRani Sunanda Devi instantly recognised that she had found a new protégé and clapped the loudest once Jahnavi had finished.

But it was I who Jahnavi sought after for airing her troubles.

'Can you imagine, Mohini Boudi?' she exclaimed, as we sat at Flury's drinking tea one afternoon. 'Harish wants me to put sindur in the parting of my hair, cover my head and go fall at the feet of his taujees and taieejees in Barabazaar! What do I do?'

'It'll cost you nothing,' I suggested, having done the rounds myself in the company of Pansy and Petunia Pishimoni immediately after my wedding. Bobby had protested but the aunts were dying to show me off. They had taken me to pay my respects to some of the more conservative pish-shoshoors and pish-shaashuris who hadn't been able to make it to the wedding. Bobby had nothing in common with them, but they were relatives, after all. And blood, every Bengali babu worth his machismo and maachher-jhol knew, became thicker than water in the aftermath of marriages and funerals.

I hadn't protested against the initial visits. In fact, as I had placed the mandatory box of shondesh into a wrinkled hand, sweeping down to touch the feet of an old uncle or a widowed aunt, I had been instantly transported to my adolescent years. I could almost hear my mother insist that we girls pay obeisance to the family elders. Smiling shyly and draping my head with the loose end of my sari anchol, I had adhered to tradition, instantly charming the relatives. But soon the visits started to get tiring. Sometimes a nasty comment came wrapped in the scent of an innocuous paan. At other times they were preceded by a strong smell of cannabis.

'Oh,' a widowed jethi-ma had once exclaimed with disdain, her nose screwed up and eyeing my gold necklace through her bifocal glasses, 'that thing around your neck, dear, it's rather light – hardly any gold worth its name in there – is that all that your parents could afford?'

At other times, some of Bobby's poorer cousins with bloodshot eyes, unshaved chins and hastily stubbed out cigarettes said, 'I've just passed my B Com, Boudi. But I'm sitting idle at home, giving stray tuitions. Surely Bobby-da has lots of contacts that can get me a decent job. You need a source that's powerful. That's how the commercial world works, after all. You need a good contact to back you up!'

Yes, I could understand Jahnavi's apprehensions, though I encouraged her not to become inflexible.

But Harish's complaints kept multiplying. Having married in a tearing hurry, he now repented at leisure when Jahnavi started to come home late from office. What compounded his rage was her newly acquired friends, especially from the artistic community. They arrived in hordes over the weekends – scrawny and lantern-jawed, dressed in shabby kurta-pyjamas and Khadi Bhandaar jackets, shaan bags slung across their shoulders – to drink endless cups of tea and discuss their next exhibition that Jahnavi's company was going to sponsor.

Harish understood little about the finer nuances of modern art, save the garish calendars that hung in his grandmother's prayer room in their old home in Howrah. As a child, he had been quite in awe of the numerous gods and goddesses staring down from the walls. Lakshmi Mata floated on her lotus-seat draped in flashy pink and gold; Vaishno Devi rode her tiger across the Himalayan snow, robed in gaudy purple; Nandgopal crawled on all fours with a lump of butter smeared all over his mouth, reconciled to turning a deep shade of blue; Vishnuji actually became red, sprouting a water lily from his bare and sexy navel. That was the art he enjoyed. It was part of his life; part of his heartbeat; part of his psyche.

As a youngster, with his eyes tightly shut, he had sung '*Hey prabhu ananda-daata gyaan hum ko deejeeye, shigr saarey dur-gunon ko dur humsay keejeeye...*' at morning assembly in the company of a passel of other rowdy school boys. The headmaster of Bal Bharati Vidyalaya housed near Paarijaat Cinema in the vicinity of Salkia on Grand Trunk Road was a fierce Hindu fundamentalist. His allegiance to the right-winged Rashtriya Swayamsevak Sangh could never be challenged. And he had put the fear of Muslims and Mahadev into every student worth his Marwari lineage.

At home, as evening descended, Harish would loudly chant '*Om Jai Jagadish Harey*' with his cousins during the evening prayers, impatiently waiting for the prasaad sweets to be distributed. His aunts performed the arati and, still singing, circled a camphor flame under the noses of the children, having initially offered the fire to the gods. Why couldn't Jahnavi be like them? Why couldn't she convert? He could easily arrange for it at the Arya Samaj at a pittance. Arrey bhai, money always talks, and talks loquaciously – why couldn't the bitch get that all-pervasive fact into her silly head? Why couldn't she understand that after marriage girls were meant to bow to their husband's wishes instead of traipsing down office corridors? And all this nonsense about her job, her need for space and freedom – all this stupid business about art-shart, painting-wainting lay quite beyond the poor man's ken! Who cared two hoots about what you had suspended on your drawing room walls, as long as lots of rokda burned holes in your pocket!

Harish Somani by temperament could only sniff at profits. Refinement and aesthetics were as alien to him as the old woman on her haunches spinning fluffs of cotton on the moon. He was stiffly polite to Jahnavi's friends but hated them for addressing him as 'Horis-babu', or worse, 'Horse-babu'.

'Horis-babu! Horse-babu! What kind of chooteeas are they, wasting our time on precious Sundays? Can't even pronounce my name properly! Saala Bangaalis!' he growled.

'Don't you compare them to your Barabazaar types, with your crude language and your farts reeking of heeng!' Jahnavi lashed back. 'They are artists, not third-rate Marwari pimps stinking of asafoetida and posing as businessmen! They have the grace and culture to accept your uncouth ways!'

'Culture-vulture will not help,' Harish reminded her, trying to knock some financial sense into her head. 'Arrey, why do you have to beg them for hours to find out what their stupid scribbles will cost? What for? Just do the nakki aggressively and saltaao the deal! It's that simple! Everyone understands the sound of paisa. You married me for money – hai na?'

Jahnavi detested his arrogance just as much as she detested his paan-masala-chewing cousins and friends. She absolutely refused to bend to his ways and, instead, started in earnest to scout for external adventures.

Poor 'Horse-babu'!

With the beginnings of a pot-belly and a marriage gone sour, he gave up trying to gallop around the bedroom and soon metamorphosed into a lame, frustrated donkey.

To my utter amusement, I discovered that Sunanda-di had taken a fancy to Jahnavi's elaborate tehzeeb blended with large doses of rather contrary British manners. The protégé knew how to wear with maximum effect her aura of a latter-day Umrao Jan who could transform into a new-age Jane Austen heroine in the twinkling of an eye. She arrived at the Book Club meetings, a bundle of billowing silks and defenceless embroideries, or in dazzling jewels and vertiginous heels, depending on who was coming as chief guest. She liked to imagine she had bohemian leanings. And a few months later, after a failed attempt to unceremoniously topple Cheenee Buttockbyle from her post at Sarojini Memorial, Jahnavi's happiness knew no bounds when the RajRani roped her in to help organise a picnic one winter weekend to outshine Cheenee's annual lunch party.

The outing was scheduled to be held at Sunanda-di's famous farmhouse in Baruipur. The picnic soon became the talk-of-the-town. Trying desperately to be part of the gang, Jahnavi ran every errand demanded by the RajRani, all agog and eager to please, till Reena Chakladar could take such shameless sycophancy no more.

A private bus with all the frills a Japanese manufacturer could muster had been hired to ferry the ladies from the 'palace' to the picnic venue. They arrived with great slashes of lipstick and conceit, all set for the exciting expedition. Officiously, Jahnavi started to herd everyone in and, disgusted, Reena turned to me and hissed, 'You'd think she'd bleed champagne, the way she's going on and on!'

'She's worked very hard, poor thing,' I replied, slipping on my dark glasses. 'And isn't she looking chic in her white jeans and phulkaari jacket?'

'*Chic?*' Reena Chakladar retorted, settling into her seat. 'Just look at her! She may have the voice of an angel, as Sunanda keeps repeating, but her dress sense is worse than a baboon's! Just look at her doodh cans and her nail polish! My God, her bras would put any self-respecting hooker to shame, the way her choochees stick out like Mount Everest! She's such a bossy little so-and-so! Kick her over and she'll bounce right back like a slim Cinderella Weeble, licking Sunanda's arse!'

'Oh, don't be mean, Reena!' I laughed. 'She's just enjoying a little bit of attention.'

'Will you stop being the eternal martyr?' snapped Reena Chakladar, glaring at me and adjusting her scarf. 'Miss Holier-Than-Thou!'

The mood, however, considerably mellowed as the bus took off to loud cheering and the chorusing thereafter of popular numbers from Hollywood musicals all the way to the destination. '*Wouldn't it be loverly…*' and '*I'm gonna wash that man right outa my hair!*' were easily the chartbusters of the morning.

The girls arrived at the farmhouse, sighing and sputtering delighted little exclamations over the many full-blown roses nodding from slender stems to welcome them. What a pulchritudinous environment! What a flawless setting for such a splendid occasion! The greenery that stretched all around, after the fumes and flurry of Calcutta, was such a relief. A quick round of coconut water generously spiked with vodka chased Sylvia and me into the mood for a game of badminton. Even as I wrapped my sari anchol tighter and tucked it resolutely into my petticoat, the others cheered us on. Relaxing in elaborate deck chairs they soaked in the calm while Sunanda-di and Jahnavi walked around at a cracking pace, getting the buffet laid out near the swimming pool aided by a flock of servants.

The setting was impeccable, with marble and glass mosaic walks all over the garden, and a pretty shamiana that had been specially erected for the grand event. The lunch consisted of delicate fish croquettes flavoured with parsley, a robust meat loaf, garlic bread and a salad of crisp lettuce, yellow peppers and just-picked tomatoes still drowsy from the sun and drizzled with vinaigrette.

It was a perfect repast enhancing a perfect afternoon.

Post-lunch, gossip veered towards a discussion on arthouse cinema. Jahnavi lazily stretched her arms and waxed eloquent over Pinaki Sanyal's *The Lonely Wife's Letter*. Many of his movies were based on timeless classics and I wondered aloud why Sanyal had steered almost clear of contemporary stuff. My remark made a few eyebrows rise.

'Darling,' Queenie said at last, sipping another round of vodka and breaking the silence. 'Bengali men have always sat on the fence, the bloody chauvinists.'

'I entirely agree,' acceded Reena Chakladar. 'Look at Pinaki-da's films! Or, for that matter, any other Bong director who's been feted internationally. Where are the *men* in their movies? I mean the real macho guys? For Pinaki-da, Mrinalini's loneliness was only an artistic excuse. After all, don't forget he was madly in love with Monimala-di while making that film. She was his meek and ever-willing Eliza Dolittle. He even wanted to march her off to a dentist and straighten out her crooked, tobacco-stained teeth while his wife thundered and fumed and took an overdose of sleeping pills to fix him good and proper!'

'Oh, is that true?' Shireen Readymoney asked, intrigued, peeping from behind her huge shades. 'Who'd believe that the touch-me-not Pinaki Sanyal could actually get all het up and horny and have a volatile fling?'

'His films do extremely well in the festival circuits abroad,' pointed out Sylvia, 'fling or no fling.'

'Monimala is sort of erotic in her own uptight way, isn't she?' remarked Jahnavi. 'I think Sanyal was interested more in capturing Mrinalini's sensuality than her turmoil.'

'Oh, balls!' flared up Sylvia, uncrossing her legs. 'He was only portraying on celluloid what Tagore had written all those years ago.'

'But I want to know more about the affair!' protested Shireen, leaning forward and smirking. 'Did he manage to take the bitch to bed?'

'Stop being foul,' Sunanda-di chuckled, suppressing a yawn. 'Can't imagine Sanyal in any intimate action scene, rolling in the hay.'

'Pretty Burman's rubbished such gossip, of course,' slurred Queenie. 'According to her, he is too much of a gentleman to mess around with actresses.'

'Pretty is such a bloody hypocrite,' Reena Chakladar protested. 'I was supposed to do some costumes for Pinaki-da and she had tagged along, twittering like an early bird searching for a fat worm. However, none of her ploys to wangle a role worked. And in the end she was politely shown the door.'

'But how come she's the current arthouse rage?' asked Shireen. 'Has she moved on from her past and decided not to expose? Or is she...'

'Dahling, a leopard cannot change its spots,' Jahnavi interrupted with a sneer. 'Have you girls noticed that none of the Sanyal heroines dare to enjoy sex? Not one!'

'True! Very true!' exclaimed Sunanda-di, nodding gravely. 'Even that frustrated widow in his latest movie goes around with a tight grin instead of selling her wares! I have to concede she had nice tits but, alas, no spark! French film-makers would have treated her frustration with such aplomb my dear – a latter-day Lady Chatterley in Palamau's wilderness! Couldn't she masturbate or at least fake an orgasm to seduce her innocent lover?'

'I do it all the time to keep Peter guessing,' Sylvia confessed with a sudden laugh. 'It can be such a nuisance, but who cares? I don't want the cookie crumbling just yet.'

The girls turned to look at her, not quite believing what she had said. Had they heard right? Or was she speaking many of their minds?

Suddenly, like a spate of rain that comes without warning, the conversation swung rapidly from Sanyal's films to their personal sexual rondels. Teasing out astonishingly candid confessions – stuff they wouldn't dream of admitting to any man – they now found comfort in discussing what went on behind closed doors.

'In Madrid, I had once hired a lover who only shoved all kinds of horrible things into my privates, without actually wanting to sleep with me,' Queenie owned up, sloshed and oblivious of the faces around her arranged in various states of incredulity. 'I admit we'd met at a depression support group. But it wasn't worth the sex.'

Pin drop silence. Sylvia stretched out to squeeze Queenie's hand. Jahnavi found sudden tears pricking her eyes. Sunanda-di smiled nervously and I blushed.

Reena Chakladar, watching me go red, exclaimed, 'Mohini, my dear, don't look so dazed. There are more things in heaven and earth than are dreamt of in our mundane boudoirs!'

'Stop teasing her!' cried Sylvia, ready to defend me. 'Mohini is still such a bachcha!'

'Lucky girl,' shot back Reena, before confessing that she had recently slept with several Pakistani test cricketers. 'All they demand is a lusty suck of their thingamajigs,' she murmured, 'while they rave and rant in Urdu, reeking of garlic and spilling their spunk all over your mouth!'

'For goodness' sake,' demanded Jahnavi, unable to control her emotions. 'Why should we have to take it lying down?'

'How else would you like to take it, sweetheart?' asked Shireen Readymoney, curling back in her chair like a cat. 'The missionary position is such a saving grace!'

'I'd rather cradle my man's head on my shoulder and buoy up his body with my hip,' admitted Jahnavi. 'I'm sick and tired of being used like a deflated tyre! And you? What about you, Shireen?'

'No such luck for me, girls,' giggled Shireen, discomfited. 'My Pesi's gone off the boil. He's disgusting. He actually farts in bed!'

'I want to do it properly and lie below Paddy for a change,' said Queenie with a faraway look. 'I'm fed up of straddling him like a bloody jockey. My thighs get so badly bruised. But do you think he'll listen?'

'Women actually prefer it with circumcised men,' Sunanda-di revealed, experience writ large all over her face. 'There's something so basic about things hacked, isn't there?'

'Nonsense!' interjected Sylvia. 'Sex is a whole load of fun only because it's ridiculously clumsy.'

'Tell that to Paddy,' said Queenie, taking out a handkerchief from her bag and dabbing her eyes. 'I want to get sick each time he catches me by the hair and hammers me black and blue. What could be more revolting than being forced to slick back your fringe with your man's sticky semen?'

'Why do you tolerate it?' I asked at last, giving vent to my anger that had made my blood boil ever since Bobby had scoffed at Queenie's plight.

'Money, my sugar,' divulged Queenie, after a pause. 'As long as you've got money and position, everything falls into place.'

Totally outraged, I sat silently, unable to believe what I had just heard. Why were these girls pouring out such horrifying tales? What hideous compulsions had made them confess? Was it desperation or some perverted need to voice their hurt in a collective catharsis? How had such a private dam suddenly burst? I could have never imagined, watching them walk around the pretty flower beds edged with nodding phlox and carnations on such a perfectly beautiful afternoon, that they were beaten and abused. I could never have guessed, seeing them squeal and giggle and relax under broad-brimmed panamas festooned with ribbons, trendy slacks, expensive sweaters and paisley scarves, that they were shackled to the lure of money provided by a bunch of delinquents. Their shiny blow-dried hair, their impeccably done up faces, their Dior shades and their idle chatter about holidays in St Moritz and shopping sprees in London were so desperately deceptive. Watching them glide in and out of charity meetings and book club events in a cloud of Chanel 5, I had no means to sniff at the stink that pervaded their bedrooms.

Lost in these thoughts, I came flying back to reality with a sudden jolt. Wasn't I, inevitably, part of this gang? Wasn't I too succumbing to the creature comforts provided by Bobby and tolerating his affairs and his high-handedness? Henceforth, how would I ever descend into garrulous parties and face the crowd? Would I ever be able to hold a normal conversation with Queenie or Reena Chakladar or Jahnavi Somani or, for that matter, even Shireen Readymoney, without thinking about their private stories? I felt inadequate; disoriented. Had the dream I had nurtured in Kathmandu, painted with moonlight and infused with the fragrance of wild mountain gentian, softly faded away like an old, sepia-tinted photograph? Had Ma's hankering to find us good husbands as she assiduously poured a potful of milk on Shiva's phallus every Shibraatri and prayed for her daughters' welfare come to naught?

Oh God! Is this how all love ended?

That night, with Bobby still not back from the club, I watched over Ruchi sleeping fitfully and through the window glimpsed the moon, like some hibernating beast, uncurl from the palm fronds and slowly set forth to ride the sky. Could one really forget the past and move on, I wondered, watching the moon on its journey.

I was eternally obliged to Sunanda-di for getting me involved with the Sarojini Memorial Women's Union. In the beginning I had actually believed that I would be contributing fruitfully in making the lives of those less fortunate than I a little better. The assumption had been tinged with a sense of sanctimonious superiority. But now, sitting in Ruchi's bedroom, I felt defeated. I remembered some of the wards breaking down and weeping while telling me about their plight. Were their accounts any different from what I had just heard at the picnic? I wondered how long I could carry on wearing my mask like the others. Of course, unlike the wards at the Remand Home, I didn't have to refashion little rosebuds with the help of French-knots back into my life just yet. Compared to them, I lived in the lap of luxury.

Or was it a Fool's Paradise?

Two weeks after Ruchi's eleventh birthday, I realised I was pregnant again. I had gone to Kaalighat to pray for Baba's failing health and jostled by the crowd before the idol of the goddess, I was suddenly struck by the fact that I had missed my periods over the past two months.

How careless of me not to have thought about it earlier!

At that very moment, another surge of devotees pushed past me. The tiny saal leaf basket which held the offerings went flying out of my hands and the garland of scarlet joba blossoms fell unwittingly at Ma Kaali's feet. I stood rooted to the ground in a state of utter shock. Was this some kind of a premonition? Tears coursed down my face. I stared into Kaali's eyes, murmuring prayers and asking her, at last, to forgive me. Years ago, I had confronted her when she had come to my father's home in the guise of Durga, angry that she hadn't spared me from an arranged fate. Now, empty-handed, I bowed to her wishes.

In a moment of indiscretion, I had succumbed to Bobby when he had insisted on dragging me to Goa for one of his official conferences. Driving back home from the temple at dawn, I inhaled a strange odour – a combination of salt and mildew and dry fish and rambling roses that seemed to come from far, far away. It brought with it the smell of Bobby's armpits and the scent of my body unprepared for the surrender. The sea had been as hot as the blood in my veins. Now, with my eyes tightly shut and Calcutta's traffic speeding past aggressively, I listened once more to the sounds of the ocean rising and falling against the cliffs at Dona Paula. I saw the breakers rush to the shore and retreat again, wave after enormous wave. And then everything seemed to melt into Ma Kaali's omnipotent eyes.

I decided not to tell Bobby till I had taken the tests. A week later, after lunch, I couldn't hold back the news any longer. I thought Bobby would be upset or plain indifferent. But as soon as I blurted out that I was expecting again, he looked rather chuffed and kept staring at me with a foolish grin. For him, Ruchi had been an unintended accident. But now he longed for a son, he said, tapping his fingers on the table and demanding his pound of flesh. I laughed and told him to hope for the best.

I have to concede that Bobby had never physically abused me, and for that I was grateful. But it had been an unequal partnership from the start, a relationship that had left me bereft, watching him roar and thunder and take control. His temper and his unbridled concupiscence had driven me mad. But, out of a sense of self-preservation – because I had no other option – I had called for truce. There was no point in looking back. No point in crying over spilt milk. One has to carry on, regardless.

Now, for both of us, the time had come to settle scores.

'Get yourself the best. Just forget about the expenses,' Bobby muttered, before awkwardly patting my head and leaving for office. I didn't know whether to laugh or cry. Even in this magical linking of our lives once again, in this keen anticipation of a child who would fill our future days with hope and joy, money played its predictable role.

For Bobby, life began and ended with all the comforts that money could buy – a swanky car, a foreign music system, a bigger television. Mammon was the only god he worshipped. Expensive cameras lay languishing inside his cupboard because he found them too complicated to use. Paintings by some of the best-known contemporary artists gathered dust in the attic because there was no more wall space to put them up. But Bobby just had to buy anything and everything that caught his fancy. With money, he was sure he could make a bonfire of most things – his past, his enemies, his whims.

Even his wife.

Once the initial shock wore off I was like a bird, singing my heart out. I started looking forward to messy nappies soaked in Dettol and pretty bassinets lined in gingham and boxes of Lactogen, pushing the carpenters to work harder, the painters to finish their job faster, as I turned the spare bedroom into a nursery.

The girls at the Book Club seemed flabbergasted but I was past all caring. Fanning their curiosity with mysterious smiles, I decided not to take their prodding and poking to heart. Ma Kaali had ordained that I swell with new life. That, for me, was enough.

PomPom was dumb-struck when I ultimately told her I was going to have a baby. She looked as though she had emerged from a site that had just been bombed. Yet, with her predilection for platitudes she went about washing my hair and singing my praises till I instructed her to chop my locks really short.

'But what will Bobby say, yaar?' she asked in dismay.

'Who cares?' I laughed, savouring every minute of PomPom's shock and disbelief. 'I'm too happy to let anyone spoil my mood.'

She did as I bid and cocking a snook, I paid and left. The hairstyle was wonderful but the alarm writ large on PomPom's face throughout the morning, even better!

Sunanda-di played Mother Hen to the hilt and, rather insistently, started to call at all odd hours. If she wasn't asking me over for a meal, she would pose the oddest questions related to her past. I could never predict what she might come up with next. One afternoon, just as I was looking forward to a nap, the phone started ringing and I unmindfully picked up the receiver.

'Mohini, my girl,' Sunanda-di's imperious voice cut into my thoughts, 'you've seen my old albums, haven't you?'

'The ones in your study?' I asked, fumbling.

'Yes, yes. I'm talking specifically of the photographs taken at Panna's prayer meeting. For the life of me, I don't seem to recollect where I put them away. Do you remember what I was wearing?'

'Not really.'

'What's happening to you young people?' she retorted, piqued. 'You are just as bad as I am!'

'But why do you want to know?' I asked, taken aback.

'Because I don't want to wear the same Baluchari today! Have you forgotten that I'm going to the High Court for my settlement?

Rotten's sure to show up. And I don't want him to catch me repeating my sari for such an important occasion! No my girl, that'll never do! Never! Never! *Never!*'

Sunanda-di's calls were as erratic as her changing moods. She soon forgot her exasperation and called again, a few hours later, full of concern.

'I hope you are being a good girl,' she inquired, her voice laced with anxiety. 'Is there anything I can do? Is there anything special that you wish to eat, my girl? Pregnancies can be such a bother! Do you crave for some spicy Goan fish curry? Maybe a robust steak? Some tomato chutney? Don't be shy. Just let me know.'

'I'm fine, Sunanda-di. Thank you so much for your concern. I'll come on Saturday for the book launch.'

In the end I made an excuse and didn't go.

I didn't fancy confronting Reena Chakladar or Jahnavi Somani or Shireen Readymoney with their hundred probing questions. Queenie dropped in once or twice when she wasn't too plastered. But I was quite happy spending the afternoons reading and dreaming and trying to prepare Ruchi for the new arrival.

Ruchi took my pregnancy as a personal betrayal. Her temper swung from resentment to dark indifference. No amount of mollycoddling helped. In any event, she hated overt physical contact, and when I tried to take her in my arms and kiss her and talk to her about the baby, she burst into copious tears.

'I hate babies!' she cried, running out of the room. 'And look at you! You are so fat and ugly!'

For Ruchi's sake, I started taking a fresh interest in my appearance. When I went to pick her up from school, I wore a fresh Tangail sari, had my hair – now short and thinning – tamed with tortoise shell clips. I even tried a hint of make-up to cover the laugh lines around my mouth and eyes. But nothing pleased Ruchi.

Bobby left some money with me one afternoon, saying awkwardly that I should buy myself a piece of jewellery. I called Sylvia and she took me to Satramdas on Park Street and made me blow up a minor fortune on a gold bracelet encrusted with emeralds and diamonds. She even made me buy a pair of stiletto heels from Henry's at New Market. Then we breezed through Kundahaar off Lansdowne Road, tiring out the salesgirls before choosing three exquisite Dhaakai saris – absolute masterpieces – from the pile.

'This is your chance,' Sylvia proclaimed, sitting me down at last at a table for two at Skyroom and ordering an elaborate lunch preceded by prawn cocktails after our shopping spree. 'This is your only chance to get your own back at Bobby. Blow up his money, darling; don't feel guilty! He has enough rotting in the bank anyway!'

Slowly, tactfully I learnt to cope with Ruchi's fractious temper. It was best that I carry out my chores as normally as possible, suggested Sylvia, before the delivery. Whenever I felt inordinately happy, much to Ruchi's irritation, I couldn't help humming *'Ja re, ja re urey ja re paakhi...'* If only I too could fly away forever like the bird in the song!

'Stop it, Ma!' Ruchi yelled, edgy as usual. 'Why are you never quite on the note, always singing off-key?'

'I sing because I'm happy. I sing for my own pleasure.'

'Then go and sing where I can't hear you!' she retorted.

'Suit yourself,' I shot back and walked away, continuing to croon.

Ruchi had a marvellous voice. Her head mistress was very pleased when she played the lead at the annual school cantata, singing her way into the hearts of all the members in the audience. That summer, when she came to spend a weekend at Amherst Street with me, Ma taught her some of Tagore's lovely songs and she instantly fell in love with them. Ruchi was a perfectionist and could never treat her muse lightly. For her, I was the one making all the compromises.

My second pregnancy helped me push aside Bobby and his infuriating friends. I started to spend more time with Ma, inhaling again the scent of jasmine in her prayer room. It was the old scents that drew me back to my father's house – the scent of childhood; the scent of heartbreak.

A few years ago, Mini had ultimately decided to go away to teach in a school in Mussoorie, severing all links with Dibaakor-da. Soon after, in the aftermath of the Naxalite Movement, Dibaakor-da vanished. Bijoy-kaka did his best to find out where his son was hiding. He had even come to see me, requesting if Bobby could have a word with the police commissioner. I have to give it to Bobby for leaving no stone unturned. But, those days, almost every home complained of a son or a recalcitrant daughter being sucked into the quagmire of rebellion.

The Naxals were everywhere, disrupting traffic, setting buses and tramcars on fire, brutally killing those who resisted. The Calcutta University campus in and around College Street had become a hotbed of arson and activists. The urban intelligentsia met regularly at the Coffee House to discuss the pros and cons of avant-garde poetry. Some extolled the virtues of seditious pamphlets. Others romanticised the outcome of aggressive revolutions. Presidency College turned into the unofficial headquarters of the radicals though they genuflected at the feet of Kanu Sanyal and Jangal Santhal, their new-found heroes, who were plundering the remote tribal villages in and around Naxalbari in North Bengal. And Mao's little Red Book, secretly imported from China, was devoured by novices before they succumbed to a hopeless, impractical and violent ideology.

'Amaar naam tomaar naam shobaar naam Vietnam! Cheener Chairman Amaader Chairman! Mao Tse Tung Zindabad!'

There was slogan-shouting and protest marches everywhere. Red was the reigning colour of those brutal, agonising days. Dolly-kaakima went ballistic. Advertisements were placed in *Ananda Bazar Patrika* and *Jugantar,* begging Dibaakor-da to return. Days went by in fear and anxiety. Then, two months later, in the narrow lane behind our home, his body was found with brutal stabs and all his limbs broken.

He had choked to death on his own blood.

Dolly-kaakima had to be ultimately committed to an asylum in Ranchi to stop her from going around the house with a broom in her hand, her eyes transfixed, calling out to Dibaakor-da in piteous sobs. Her sister Molly came and took her away, not before making a huge fuss and blaming Ma for the tragedy. By then, Baba was a broken man. The old fire had gone and in its stead emerged a soggy hypochondriac, given to bouts of irritation and melancholia. To compound matters, Bijoy-kaka was found hanging from the jaam tree near Baba's chamber one morning, a week after Dolly-kaakima had been moved out, dangling on a piece of rope like a defeated marionette.

Baba immediately had his first massive stroke. Through all this harrowing grief, Mini refused to come home. Marriage was out of the question, not with all the rumours being spread by some relatives who had sniffed out the disgrace. And to keep further catastrophes at bay, Ma started spending most of her day in prayers with Shubha.

I never gave Bobby details of what was going on at Amherst Street, knowing that, if he found out, he'd forbid me from visiting my parents. I could take care of Ma, Baba and Shubha without dragging him into the mess. But I was always worried about Mini. What would she do, alone and so far away from home? Would she be capable of handling the little boys in her school? Who would take care of her when she grew old? Mini, with her nosebleeds every summer; Mini, with her head in the clouds and a penchant for sour mangoes that used to make Dolly-kaakima scream, 'Only pregnant women and prostitutes crave for pickle!'

Now, when I came to see Ma, she hardly spoke about the past. Reticent and nervous, she'd only talk to me in brief monosyllables and feed me a plateful of rice soaked in cumin-flavoured fish. I'd carry on, willy-nilly, filling her in on news about Ruchi and Bobby. She'd politely listen to my light-hearted banter – about my shopping sprees and new acquisitions – but I knew that her world had collapsed.

And Baba?

He simply lay in bed and grumbled about his health, toothless, sucking his jaw and staring at the walls.

'Ogo, shunchho?' he'd call out a hundred times a day, forgetting that Ma could no longer run errands at his beck and call. Consoling Baba was like consoling a shadow. Till it was time for him to be admitted to Neelratan Sarkar Hospital again and to let poor Ma stand alone in the queue with aching feet in the middle of the night.

'Why didn't you call?' I demanded next morning, rushing to the hospital.

'It was so late; I didn't want to bother you,' she replied. 'Your condition is delicate, Mohini. Bobby may not have liked it.'

I sighed impatiently and walked into the ward where Baba lay abandoned on a small cot, breathing with difficulty. In a while he opened his eyes and I watched him, bewildered, staring at my face.

'Are you happy?' he whispered in a slurred voice, trying to turn his head so that he could see me better. 'Or are you still angry with me?'

'No, not at all,' I said, pushing back a stray strand of hair from his forehead. 'The past is dead and gone. You get well soon and come back home.'

It was almost three weeks before he was released. Bobby did go and see him once, and an over-worked nurse tried to keep calm and handle his rapid-fire questions in the midst of the hospital neon signs and wheelchairs. But the second stroke that felled Baba had done its irreparable share of damage.

To the indignation of Shireen Readymoney and her coterie, I decided to make a sudden break with my social set, resigned from the Book Club at the first opportunity and changed my gynaecologist. Dr Tonmoy Chaudhuri – Tom to his jealous colleagues – had about him a gentle, avuncular quality. He was a distant cousin of Ma's and I trusted her decision this time when she suggested I see him at his chamber. It was the biggest disloyalty, as far as Shobeeta Mitra was concerned.

'Eta ki korli?' she admonished, when I bumped into her at B.C. Ojha's fish stall in New Market. 'You shouldn't have done this to Bijoy! He's been so good to all of us. Why, he was like a dream right through my hysterectomy!'

I smiled but said nothing. She proceeded to gingerly check the ear of a huge beckti and told the fishmonger, 'No, no, no! I want my fish really fresh, please, this won't do...' Then, looking me straight in the eye, asked, 'Bijoy's bedside manners are impeccable, aren't they?'

Before I could retaliate, she turned to Ojha-babu again. 'Yes, let me see that one,' she pointed out. 'No, no – that one at the back – I hope it's not a haddock being passed off as beckti!'

Hardly had the fish emerged from its murky ice bath that she declared to me, completely ignoring poor Ojha-babu, 'Never trust a fishmonger! Ha, ha, ha...' she laughed, before carrying on with her tirade, 'And then, when I wanted to go off those hormone-inducing pills, Bijoy said, "Shobeeta, you've got to put your sex life in order." I was so stunned... Yes, do skin it and remove the gills and the bones... I don't think...'

I had had enough.

'Shobeeta Boudi,' I interrupted, hitching my sari a wee bit to show off my high heels. 'I'm really happy with Tom Mesho. He pampers me and I feel really good.'

'That old ragbag – allowing you to wear heels at this time, if you please,' snapped Shobeeta, having insisted that the beckti fillets be cut into finer wedges. 'Paatla. Aaro paatla!' she instructed with some agitation, prior to facing me once more. 'Oh they're getting so careless nowadays! Everyone wants to turn into a capitalist overnight – make a fast buck without realising that the difference between capitalism and poverty is the difference between fine beckti fillets and hunks of tasteless carp... And why, for godsake, Mohini, are you wearing those dangerous slippers? If you topple in the middle of the market who'll save you? Are you wearing proper panties? Marks and Sparks I hope; not those gosh awful, shapeless things they make in India! Suppose the sari rides up your thighs? What will you do? Remember that stupid Jahnavi when she went for a toss at the Grand Hotel arcade? High heels, indeed! People will only laugh instead of helping you out. You know what these men are all about? Just dying for a free peepshow.' Finally, heaving a sigh, she ended her attack. 'Old dog Tom messed up with so many girls I know. Remember Queenie's plight after her abortion? Such a tragedy! Such an awful tragedy!'

'You can hardly blame Tom Mesho, can you?' I protested, turning to ask for a kilo of fresh tiger prawns, shelled and de-veined.

'Then who do you think needs the knuckle-rapping?' she demanded.

'Queenie herself, of course. All that drinking! It certainly wasn't Tom Mesho's fault,' I retaliated, carelessly pressing the belly of a succulent eelish that lay in a stack near me, all pale pink and silver.

Ojha-babu smiled brightly. 'Just arrived. Very fresh. Straight from Dhaaka, Memshaaheb,' he cajoled. 'Poddaar eelish! Daaroon! Should I pack some for Shaaheb's Sunday lunch?'

'No, no,' I exclaimed, 'Shaaheb can't tackle the bones.'

'Don't tell me you can't do him a smoked hilsa?' Shobeeta sneered, getting her own back at last. 'Nothing like a smoked hilsa that's properly done. I remember giving you my Barua Mog cook's recipe. He does it so well – over charcoal fire, with a half-inch coating of bran. Purnendu loves his smoked hilsa. So would Bobby, if you only tried.'

'We've gone off eelish, Shobeeta Boudi,' I smiled cheekily, and collecting my prawns, flounced away, clip-clopping on my high heels.

Something about Shobeeta and Purnendu Mitra had always put me off. She was inordinately officious and he had too many teeth crammed into his mouth permanently clapped over a dangling pipe. Purnendu was head of accounts and played golf with Bobby and Paddy thrice a week. And Shobeeta, ever the ubiquitous do-gooder, had done her best to browbeat me when I had initially stepped into Bobby's home as an inept bride. However, a few years later I noticed Bobby rapidly cooling towards them. Office politics had the knack of making and breaking friendships at the drop of an acerbic memo from the London head office. Though intrigued, I didn't bother to ask. They would still come to our parties and we would go to theirs, but something had inevitably soured.

Purnendu's rise up the corporate hierarchy, Bobby had told me, was phenomenal. His detractors claimed the credit should have gone to Shobeeta. Her father was a diehard Communist and his connections were put to good use. In the aftermath of the British shares being hurriedly diluted, Purnendu had swindled sufficient money before retiring prematurely. Bobby and his gang were peeved but found no evidence to nail him. Then, quite suddenly, Shobeeta forsook the bridge sessions at Sunanda-di's 'palace' and proceeded to join the Communist Party. Her heart must have broken at the thought of giving up the beautiful bungalow with acres of garden in Alipore. But the call of the 'red' was too tempting to resist.

On several New Year's Eve bashes, before she had started to spout quotes from Chairman Mao, I had seen her dancing at the Saturday Club, blowing into flimsy paper whistles edged with feathers and wearing a silly paper hat. She had joined the men in their loud hoots to make a skinny-looking Miss Lola wriggle her bottom faster, giggling and clapping and egging the poor girl on to fling aside her grass skirt a split second before the lights went out. It hadn't mattered to her then that Miss Lola was forced to publicly strip in order to feed several hungry mouths in her family living in a hovel off Chamroo Khansama Lane. Those days, Shobeeta was busy proffering her cheek to all and sundry so that they could kiss it and wish her well as they tipsily sang, *'Should auld acquaintance be forgot and never brought to mind...'* when the clock struck twelve. Then, almost overnight, she changed her colours. Out went her sleeveless cholis and in came the handspun full-sleeved khaadi blouses. Shobeeta was, indeed, a quick-change artiste of great dexterity and cunning.

'Oh, Shobeeta's suddenly become bum chums with the Bum

Front,' PomPom had sniggered at one of Bobby's parties. 'What an opportunist!'

'You mean the Left Front,' I'd corrected.

'No, no! The *Bum* Front. The way you Bengalis say it. But God knows where's the bum and where's the front, yaar! The coalition's such a muddle!'

However, before PomPom could catch her breath, Shobeeta had announced with great aplomb, sipping her nimbu-paani, (she'd even forsaken whisky in a hurry) that she was off to the Rajya Sabha in New Delhi the following month as a nominated member of the Communist Party. Poor PomPom, she didn't know where her jaws had dropped!

To celebrate Shobeeta's impressive appointment, Purnendu hosted a sitar recital at their new apartment. Ustad Alim-ud-din Khan had been hired at great expense to perform that night and the invitees were suitably excited. Khan Saheb's skill as a musician was well-known. So was his prowess in bed. Reena Chakladar, a die-hard fan, had tasted his genius on both counts and couldn't stop gushing over the experience. After one of our Book Club meetings, she had accompanied me to PomPom's parlour and insisted that prior to a recital Khan Saheb often stood stark naked before a full-length mirror. Surveying his body and flexing his muscles, in between sips of milk flavoured with delicate saffron from the valleys of Kashmir, he challenged a fabulous erection for at least an hour before getting down to tune his sitar.

'It's just like the ragas he plays,' Reena had exclaimed over a manicure. 'First the languid preamble in soft strokes; sheer jhaptaal in ten beats, sweetheart – Bageshree at its best! Then the well-defined exploration in a swift, mellifluous jod and the running of his fingers all over! You have to experience it to believe it! And suddenly, before you know what's up, it's time for the vilambit and the dhrut – oh, the incessant shower of his kisses, the nibbling, the playful biting! All that love talk in chaste Urdu – darling, he makes you feel like Mumtaz Mahal before turning you over and buggering you!'

The story could have been apocryphal or it could have well been true – having heard the girls pore their hearts out at Sunanda-di's picnic, I was willing to believe anything. PomPom kept giggling as Reena went on and on. But now I wondered if I'd become blasé. Was this really me? Was this really the Mohini who had gone to Kathmandu – Paul's Moh; Moh of the mountains – who had wanted to break all the rules like the fragile green bangles on her slender wrist? I looked at my face in the mirror and was shocked to see a middle-aged woman – tired and resigned and hard – staring back at me. Were the tears glistening in her eyes real? God! Where had Moh disappeared?

Having grown too big, and knowing that I was going to have twins, I was loath to go out unless it was absolutely necessary. But Bobby insisted that we show our faces at the recital as a social ploy. I dressed with difficulty, irritated, put kajol in my eyes and flowers in my hair and soon found myself standing at Shobeeta's door, accepting one of the fragrant juhi garlands she kept fishing out from a fancy reed basket to welcome her guests.

'Don't sit on the floor, my girl,' said Sunanda-di, drawing me away from the crowd and settling me on a chair next to her. 'You've been very, very naughty! Why haven't you come to see me?'

'My father's had a stroke, Sunanda-di,' I replied quietly. 'I'm trying to spend as much time as I can with him and my mother.'

'Oh, I'm sorry,' she whispered back. 'But, you must take care of yourself too. Is Bobby looking after you?'

'Don't worry about me,' I smiled, hoping that Khan Saheb would hurry up and make an appearance. But there was no such luck. Sunanda-di kept firing a volley of questions and I tried to give her non-committal answers, watching Bobby preen as usual at the bar with his cronies.

Getting restive, some of the guests started murmuring about the performer's famous transgressions recently washed up in the tabloids. The object of his latest desire, alleged the gossip rags, was Pretty Burman. Sunanda-di, as usual, reacted with her sharp tongue while Shobeeta's latest bosom buddy, the prissy and self-styled Tagore scholar, Bhobaani Sengupta, who sat a few chairs away from us, seemed visibly displeased by the banter. She kept re-adjusting her glasses, toying with the loose end of her Khaddar sari and expressing her disapproval by constantly clearing her throat.

'Are you feeling alright, Bhobaani?' Sunanda-di finally growled. 'Or is Bluebeard's ghost working overtime on you again?'

'I'm fine, Madam,' whimpered our starchy intellectual, startled, as if someone were about to brush a fly that had settled on her bottom. 'It's the air-conditioning, that's all. Always aggravates my throat.'

'Does it?' Sunanda-di was irascible. She opened her brocade batua, pulled out a small silver box and pinched out a stick of clove. Offering it to Bhobaani, she continued, 'Why, Bhobaani? Are you trying to draw someone's attention who couldn't care a tuppence for your Tagore mania?'

Bhobaani accepted the condiment and smiled weakly, too frightened to cross swords with her opponent.

Shobeeta had known Bhobaani though their sweaty school

and college days but lost touch with her when she became queen bee of the corporate world and Bhobaani decided to hoodwink her way into the haloed domain of Tagore highbrows, with a Doctorate from a bogus university in Orissa. They met again, years later, by happenstance. While waiting at the Delhi airport, they suddenly came face to face. Screaming like delighted school-girls, the long-lost chums fell into each other's arms and on the flight back home, renewed their camaraderie. To give her image a thorough overhaul, Shobeeta decided to use Tagore as a ploy and prove that, at heart, the poet was a die-hard Communist! There were enough funds lying around in sundry fellowships to help conduct the research. And sniffing out the money, Bhobaani Sengupta, the seasoned cur, immediately turned into Shobeeta's loyal partner in crime.

Always exuding a superior, touch-me-not aura, her salt-and-pepper mane carelessly plaited and fixed with an ugly rubber band, Bhobaani had the natural inclination to look like a sexless hermaphrodite. To the horror of Khan Saheb, who had a strong aversion for ugly women, she had accosted him recently after a concert and declared that she was his unalloyed fan as many of the ragas he played reminded her of Tagore's music. Khan Saheb had made a quick, perfunctory noise and fled down the corridor without looking back.

Bhobaani's marriage had been a disaster. But her enemies whispered that she now bedded fresh sophomores at the Georgia State University in Atlanta where she went to conduct workshops every autumn semester. Her sexual romps were an inherent part of academic service, giggled her rivals. According to their spies planted on the campus, Bhobaani, while fornicating with a bunch of horny teenagers hell-bent on losing their virginity, was also prone to declaiming Robindronath's erotic verses at the top of her voice. *'Wherever you turn you will see me/ My miserable voice and my sinister smile/ Will resound in all directions/ Because I have an insatiable hunger!*' she'd lustily recite from *Rahu's Love*, urging the rascals to pump away with all their might before jumping off, zipping up and shouting, 'Thank you Ma'am!' and allowing the next legitimate greenhorn his turn to take over!

'It's just too annoying,' Jahnavi hinted to her neighbour who happened to be the German Consul's prim and proper English wife. 'You never know what kind of haraamis dotted with freckles you're going to meet at firangee universities. Or at local parties, dotted with third-rate film stars.'

As Bhobaani pursed her lips and looked away, stumped by Jahnavi's blatant audacity, the woman from the Alliance Francaise – our current Marie Antoinette exuding cologne and culture – barked in short fits. 'I don't understand! Zis is Cal-kutta, after all. You find poets at every street corner, almost like ze prostitute. And a variety of 'omosexuals, posing *sooooo* macho, *sooooo* savage! So please explain yourself, ma cherie Genevieve.'

'There's nothing to explain, Claudette,' snapped Jahnavi. 'I mean exactly what I say. If you happen to be prowling through the corridors of a foreign university, you can certainly look forward to wanton adventures any time of the day or night. There are enough people here who can elaborate on their experience. But if you happen to be a diplomat at an undiplomatic party, you could end up with a really bad penny in your bed. And, by the way, I am not Genevieve. My name is Jahnavi!'

'What do you mean?' fumed Madame Consul General, hoisting her left eyebrow in nervous pique. Sylvia and Peter Hammond, who had braved finding seats on the carpet next to Claudette, looked away, trying to suppress their mirth. They seemed to be in on some secret I had no clue about.

'Well, for a start, it could be your awfully dull husband,' Jahnavi replied with alarming causticity, having witnessed the diplomat turn totally tactless at one of Pretty's mahjong do's.

'O, mon Dieu! Zis is too much! Zis is 'orribly, 'orribly fonny! L'amour est aevugle!'

'I beg your pardon!' Madame Consul General snorted, turning beetroot red.

'Zeese men! What to do with zeese men!' chuckled counterfeit Marie Antoinette as Jahnavi rose like driven snow to come and settle at my feet.

Shireen Readymoney, not too far away, had overheard the banter. She now declared to nobody in particular, 'After a while it's all the same. Tung…tung…tung! Ta…ta…thai! At a recital. Or in bed. Men are such bloody kutros!'

The room kept filling up with guests and gossip. But Khan Saheb remained locked in the guestroom. Amidst wild speculation, as the evening wore on, he finally made a grand appearance a good forty-five minutes late, smiling through his surma-laden eyes and apologising with profuse abundance. Then, most tenderly, he picked up his sitar. It seemed as if he were collecting a lover in his arms. The audience forgave him instantly.

'Wah-wah! Wah-wah!' they clapped, enthralled, and Khan Sahib began his recital.

Raga Jhinjhoti was the flavour of that late evening, though he started the recital with a semi-classical bandish in Bhairavi and sang along in a husky amoroso, eyes closed in some unfathomed ecstasy, sending the audience into raptures.

'Ras ke bharey torey nain…'

Shobeeta and her gang couldn't take their eyes off the maestro. He seemed to belong to another age; an age of ease and leisure, scented with the attar of roses. An era when fountains gurgled and sheer chikankaari angarkha-shirts, tied together with narrow bands, gave you a surreptitious peep at erogenous chests. An epoch where passionate kisses were planted at leisure against the soft cooing of white shirazi doves and the drizzle of scented fountains; and where the sound of silver anklets signalled the prelude to a night of erotic love-making on elaborate divans littered with zardosi-embroidered silk cushions and jasmine petals.

The devilishly good-looking ustad knew every trick of the trade to make girls defenseless with longing. I noticed that before breaking into a fresh round of adaabs after a particularly dexterous movement, he tucked a paan into his mouth and signalled to Reena Chakladar to come and press his feet.

Perhaps the rumours were true, after all!

From Shobeeta and Purnendu's musical soiree to my Shaad ceremony at Amherst Street – what a leap from one reality to another!

I had, somehow, managed to straddle both the worlds without complaining. But my parents and Bobby chose to inhabit their own individual, compartmentalised terrains. The few times Ma had come to visit me at Bobby's home, she was painfully awkward. The toys she brought along for Ruchi seemed so odd – the cheap little dolls she'd pick up from the Rather Mela, incongruous and moulded in a single sheath of ugly pink plastic – against the row of expensive English dolls in frilly skirts that shut their eyes most delicately when you put them to bed. Ruchi, however, loved her grandmother's gifts procured from the local fair held every monsoon near Amherst Street to venerate Lord Jagannath of Puri. When she showed them to Bobby with all the delight only children can muster over inconsequential presents, he grimaced broadly and walked away, leaving her to hide her disappointment and whisper,

'Never mind! Never mind! I love you, my Dollu Rani, you'll sleep in my bed! Daddy knows no better!'

I had told Ma not to bother with the Shaad but she wouldn't listen. A pregnant daughter and no Shaad? Impossible!

'If we could host the ceremony when you were carrying Ruchi, why shouldn't we have it this time as well?' she chided. 'How can I cheat my neighbours of their right to a lavish meal? What would relatives say?'

It didn't matter that the ceremony itself was so hopelessly antiquated and going to cost a packet.

Pregnant women in the distant past were fed their favourite dishes at lunch with exalted fanfare while a flock of married women, snickering and showing off the bright red vermilion in their hair, hovered around to keep her pleased. The ceremony was usually held in the seventh month of pregnancy. It hid ominous overtones. Nobody spelt them out but everyone knew why the would-be mother was thus pampered. It was her last chance to indulge herself, in case she died at childbirth. Now, of course, the occasion was just an excuse to make merry and show-off.

Poor Ma! Her predilection to keep up with the neighbours, her constant hankering for approval, her innate fear of going against the tide had always cost her dearly. An acquaintance would merely have to whisper, 'Didi, we've just heard such good news about our Mohini,' to get Ma all worked up and smiling back in that superior manner she was prone to adopt before less fortunate neighbours. 'Who told you?' she'd ask, in a voice tinged with the right amount of curiosity and umbrage, 'Beejee? Oh, Beejee and her big mouth!' and then, with a sigh, playing Barrister Bidhushekhor Dotto's wife to the hilt, she'd imperiously instruct Beejeepishi to sun the pickle jars. The best part of her story would be saved till the end. Tucking a paan into her mouth, she'd finally describe what a life of luxury I led in a perfect 'palace' in south Calcutta. And how happy was her wealthy son-in-law, now that Mohini was pregnant again.

'He's just gifted her an expensive bracelet, thrilled to bits about the news,' she'd crow. 'Emeralds and diamonds set in solid gold. God bless them! Such a happy couple! *Such* a lucky couple!'

Of course there'd be a befitting Shaad ceremony to announce the forthcoming babies! It would be a grand event worth Mohini's marital status. The whole neighbourhood would be invited to partake of the feast. And afterwards she'd go to Dakshineshwar and pay her personal tribute to Ma Kaali for bringing her youngest daughter such wonderful luck.

I turned down all overtures from Sunanda-di and Jahnavi who wanted to come along. Bobby laughed and said, 'Why don't you let them loose in your father's house? It could be such a revelation!'

'What nonsense!' I snapped back, knowing how self-conscious Ma would be, seeing the Book Club mob abrasively invade her home.

The world of 189/A Amherst Street was, undeniably, vulnerable – from the splash in the pond where the local boys swam to the fragrance of sandalwood coming off the gods or the cry of the Hindustani sil-kataauwallah punctuating the back alleys on quiet afternoons. It had about it a strange and stubborn innocence in spite of our complicated lives. Even the old trees in the compound, the sturdy jasmine creeper, the solitary jaam tree, the grove of mangoes and the cracking walls and staircase winding up to the roof looked defenceless compared to Bobby's brash domain at King Edward's Court done up in crystal and expensive marble and littered with Afghan rugs. That is where I had gone as a shy bride – where I had set up home; brought up my daughter; thickened my skin. My neighbours were Bobby's colleagues from the world of tea, a world so far removed from Amherst Street that I wondered now where I actually belonged.

It had taken me a while to wade through incessant conversations about 'first flushes' which had nothing to do with post-menopausal symptoms. And while Bobby spent his evenings playing tennis or slumping over the bar at the club with a drink, from our balcony I had learnt to spot the prostitutes at sunset, hidden under the clement shadow of St Paul's Cathedral, in the act of soliciting customers on the footpath. Bobby's world – whether business or private – depended heavily on hard-core hustling and whoring. The world of Amherst Street on the other hand – fragile and lonely – obstinately clung to its old-fashioned traditions, a little jaded and a little tired. A world that remained stubbornly conservative, hypocritical and quite oblivious to the dealings of commerce and changing times. I instinctively knew it was best to keep both these worlds far apart.

Despite my protests, Ma promised it would be a small affair and then called the entire neighbourhood. Cooks sweated over blackened cauldrons simmering the shukto, frying the fish and currying the crab. Baba couldn't watch me eat, but kept asking for a running commentary from his bed, propped against the pillows and sapped of all energy. I sat through the entire meal, letting small rivulets of perspiration run down my neck, irritated and without a smile, as some of Ma's friends blew into the conch-shell and burst into shrill ululations.

The elderly matriarchs put sindur in the parting of my hair, touching a pinch to my noa-bangle and the white conch shell bracelets Ma had slipped onto my wrists that morning. They chucked me under the chin and lovingly blessed me with a smattering of 'May you be the mother of many healthy sons,' or, even more approving, 'May you always remain married, my dear – shaanka, sindur okhkhoy thhaak Ma!'

Once the guests departed after lunch, Shubha slipped out of the prayer room where she had locked herself in.

'Come, Mohini!' she said excitedly, standing at the top of the stairs. Her hair lay in loose folds over her back, uncombed and dishevelled. 'You have to say "hello" to Krishno, darling. I've told him all about your baby. Come!'

'Oh, Bordi, why are you doing this to me?' I protested. 'I get so tired climbing up to the third floor.'

'Come, Mohini, come,' she kept insisting, oblivious to my condition, till I followed her unwillingly and entered the prayer room, panting with the weight I carried.

No one in the family was willing to accept that Shubha had lost her mind. Now she made me sit on a prayer mat, pouring forth a continual stream of shlokas inaudibly muttered with her eyes tightly shut. I couldn't help staring at the wondrous expression that settled on her face as she sat there, surrounded, perhaps, by some ethereal vision, some invisible substance of gorgeous yet sinister luminance that no one else could see. Thereafter, in a flash, she brought her face close to mine and whispered, 'My husband says you are a beautiful girl and you will have a beautiful baby! Look into his eyes, darling, just look! Can you hear him speak?'

'No Bordi, I can't,' I said, exasperated, watching her face crumble at my rudeness.

'Oh, my little one, you are still so impatient, so impatient,' she reprimanded, with a despondent shake of her head. 'I told you years ago about Krishno, didn't I? See, he is talking to you now. See, Mohini, see!'

Then she snatched the garland off the idol's neck and looped it around her own. 'He's my husband,' she said coyly. 'And he loves me very much. Does your husband love you too?'

What could I tell Shubha? It was plain as day that the depths of her torment had come to haunt her in a monstrous, mutant guise, leaving little scope for me to clarify to her that love was just as ephemeral as the scent of sandalwood perfuming her Krishno. Could I honestly reveal to her how different my world was now from hers? How full of bogus individuals who led double-lives, bursting with pretense and sham? Could I tell her about Queenie's plight or Reena Chakladar's dishonesty? About all those men who had let their wives down and women who had accepted such deception with frosty, vapid smiles? Could I disclose to her that behind every piece of my expensive jewellery lay some sort of compromise? Could I explain to her about the subterfuges Bobby regularly resorted to in order to save his skin? Could I let her know, without being ashamed, that my husband didn't love me, after all, like Krishno loved her and filled her with such unmitigated madness?

I left in a hurry, heaving myself up and clumsily negotiating the staircase, letting Shubha's laughter trail behind me. How long would she carry on like this? How long would Ma have to witness her bizarre obsession? What would happen to my poor Bordi when my parents died? It was so heartbreaking. So horribly cruel. And yet Shubha insisted that Krishno would protect her. Look after her forever.

Baba lay still in his bed when I eventually entered his room to say goodbye. There was a touching quality in the way he now accepted his embarrassing dependence on Ma. Much as he tried to speak, his words became more and more garbled. Looking up at me, confused and lost, at last he took my hand in his and held it for a long time. Then he did what he had never done before – he kissed my fingers softly. Ma stood, framing the door, with tears dimming her eyes.

It was the last time I met Baba.

My mother turned to stone after Baba's death. She had waited all her life to get to know him. But, ironically, the opportunity came only when he was dying. Bending over his frail body day after day to sponge and clean him and keep the bedsores at bay, she would look into his rheumy eyes silently pleading for clemency. The ignominy of two severe strokes, followed by cancer, had finally made him realise Ma's real strength.

The pain was so excruciating that the doctor recommended morphine every two hours. The gap lessened alarmingly as the weeks went by. Baba's stifled screams compelled Ma to acquit him of all his former misdeeds. The tentacle of the dreaded disease spread to his hips from his prostate gland. He couldn't take the insult of the little plastic pouch into which his urine, pale yellow and opaque, trickled through a catheter. Yet he took his own time to die. He'd ask Ma to cover him up when neighbours came to visit. He hardly spoke but let his tears do all the talking.

Only the dying, Ma said later, have eyes full of rain.

When I arrived after getting the news, there was just enough time to touch his feet in a last gesture of farewell and plant a kiss on his cold forehead. Some boys from the locality had been of great help and Ma allowed them now to take away Baba's body before a distant cousin put the torch to his funeral pyre. Prior to the bier being lifted, the priest intoned in his typical drone the ancient prayers, reiterating that the soul never dies. It is indestructible, immutable, eternal.

'Nahanyatey hanyamaaney sharirey...'

Yet I couldn't forget Baba's last, inglorious days – my Baba who'd go every evening nattily dressed for a drink to Calcutta Club and entertain his clients and friends at the Grand Hotel, while Ma went about the house washing down the veranda with Gongajol. Now everything was over. The neighbourhood boys and a few relatives left the gates chanting, 'Bolo Hori, Horibol!' and scattering khoi and loose change and a spray of pretty rose petals that blew away in the wind. It was so alarmingly, inevitably final that I started to cry.

Ma was made of sterner stuff. The assault of prayers and incense didn't move her one bit. She leaned listlessly on the door, oblivious to the pile of slippers at the threshold, letting the neighbours run in and out of the house and organise the funeral. I couldn't take this grief any longer. Fiddling in my handbag, I managed to find a wad of hundred-rupee notes and gave it to Ma.

'Keep it,' I whispered, wiping my eyes. 'You may need it.'

'You already do so much for us,' Ma said, taking the money but looking away.

Us? It was only going to be her now. Alone with Shubha.

It was all I could do to get away.

Two days later my water sac suddenly burst.

The rains were just retreating and Calcutta sweltered. A terrible crisis brought on by the Marxist unions led to a short supply of electricity, plunging moods and large areas into total darkness for hours. Generators worked overtime. Wherever I travelled, there seemed to be a constant hum, like invisible bees trying to pass on secret messages.

The sky was flushed a hot pink, chasing away the wan, exhausted, early morning moon. A gust of breeze blew into the bedroom. Bobby woke with a start and found that the air-conditioner had gone off again and I was crying. Without waiting to inform Ma, he rushed me to Woodlands Nursing Home, looking anxious and trying to mouth inept endearments.

The labour pangs intensified in the car. I had forgotten what it was like to be in this state. I clutched Bobby's hand, digging my nails so deep into his arm that he had to tell me I was actually hurting him. Somehow, I was glad. At last I had elicited a response! The pain jolted me from side to side like the sea's choppy waves, gasping and hissing, as they smacked the sand. Was I afraid of death? Would I be able to ebb and flow while waiting for the ordeal to be over?

Memories of the Goan sea and sun, all this while so vivid, now disappeared faster than the tan I had brought back home. Looking at the passing trees and some leaves that fell dead in a surprise gust of breeze, I wondered if this was going to be the final curtain call. Of course, I had known all along that I was going to have twins. But Death spoke to me now over the distant sound of the Arabian Sea – quietly – like a pale, blue moan.

Sunny and Vicky arrived in less than two hours, all bloodied and yelping, tumbling out of my womb within ten minutes of each other. The nurse told me later that one look at the twins and Bobby had grinned from ear to ear, as if he were entirely responsible for their birth. She had walked up to him holding two bundles in the crook of her arms and without warning, thrust their bewildered faces into his.

'Gentlemen, say hello to Daddy!' she had grinned.

The 'gentlemen' had squinted, set up a terrific wail, and their father had gone wild with joy.

To my utter surprise, Bobby went shopping for milk bottles, nappies and bed sheets. Later I discovered that PomPom was his ally. Much of what the twins wore came from The Good Samaritans. I was too exhausted to care. His enthusiasm was amusing because the babies, at whom it was directed, were too little to appreciate what he bought. If the stuffed teddy bears were too big for Vicky, little bunny rabbits arrived the next evening. Sunny wet himself on his father's lap with such regularity that Bobby was convinced I had taught him to do it out of spite.

After Ruchi's birth, I had gone to spend two peaceful months at Amherst Street. But now, sadly, that luxury was not possible. Ma came instead to see her grandsons and Ruchi promptly told her that she would flush them down the toilet bowl when no one was looking.

'But they are your brothers!' Ma protested.

'I hate them,' said Ruchi, all of eleven.

And I knew she wasn't lying.

Ruchi was true to her word.

Some unexpressed antipathy hidden deep in her heart instigated her into spurning Vicky and Sunny, holding them culpable for stealing me away from her – I, her mother, who had been her only true anchor, her only support despite the arguments and endless fights, before the twins arrived. Bobby, in any event, had never been included in her fragile little world, prone to dreams she wouldn't talk about and Tagore's songs that receded and surged in the gloom of her bedroom, as she sat alone by the window, white like a fragrant gardenia, singing her heart out.

Ruchi, at that time, was rebellious and often impolite. Her rudeness stemmed from her deep-seated insecurity, a response to the constant bickering that never seemed to leave her parents alone. Years later, she renewed her resentment against her brothers for being away at boarding school while she had to listen to raised voices and my subsequent sobs late into the night.

Over time, a part of Ruchi's heart became impenetrable – the way she would stop me with just a stare if I tried to take her in my arms and give her a hug; the way she would tick Bobby off and tell him how deplorable his friends were every time he tried to wheedle her into meeting them – especially PomPom, whom she came to detest.

What a fortress Ruchi had created to shut out her true feelings, with shadows lurking under her eyes and a smile that could freeze any adult with its supreme and silent mockery! I lived with an uneasy sense of guilt and was often left completely exasperated with her truculent moods and sudden fits of caprice. Why was Ruchi always so difficult, so outspoken, so dark? I remained constantly worried; a worry that made me often wonder where all this rebellion would lead to.

I did everything possible to include Ruchi in the trips with the twins to the zoo or when we joined Bobby, after his game of golf, for Sunday lunches at Tolly. But her offensive resistance invariably ended in huge arguments and ugly scenes. Ruchi coldly pointed out that animals needed to roam the wilds instead of staying locked behind cages for the gaping pleasure of spoilt brats and stupid adults – how would I like it if I were thrown behind bars with Vicky and Sunny in a public garden and Bobby's friends descended to ogle and poke and prod and laugh at us? PomPom was already doing that to our private lives at home, wasn't she? Did I also want the others to join the gang? She hated the zoo! But she hated Tolly even more, teeming with her father's fake sycophants hell-bent on sucking up to him. Why did I pretend to be blind? Why was I eternally trying to protect my self-created martyr's image? Did I have no self-respect? Was dancing to Bobby's discordant tunes my only ambition in life?

Much as I tried, nothing seemed to dilute Ruchi's ruthlessly forthright beliefs. And in the end, I let her be, lost within the little cocoon of her idealism. The twins were just as unsure about her as I was. At every opportunity Ruchi would smack Vicky's head if he happened to get in her way. She would tick off Sunny if he flew paper airplanes into her room and threaten the twins with dire consequences if they dared to ride the staircase banister and come sliding down, yelling off their heads. Ruchi found comfort only in music. And the songs Ma had taught her over that one weekend at Amherst Street – songs that had set the little girl free from her father's gilded cage – sometimes melted her heart, allowing a surge of tenderness to take over.

Most strangely, by the power of some remote, umbilical binding – a link that neither her brothers nor I could comprehend – she would suddenly soften, smiling brightly and coming forward to help me blow the balloons for the twins' birthday parties, hang up the streamers and fetch the cake from Nahoum's in New Market. Sometimes, if she was feeling generous, she even organised the games, letting Vicky and Sunny's friends run around – pell-mell, sweaty and flushed – all over the lawn in front of King Edward's Court, looking for clues camouflaged by the kamini bushes. She would volunteer to take care of the music too, stopping it at random as the rowdy gang sat cross-legged on the grass and noisily passed the cushion around. The high point would be, of course, the bursting of the khoi bag filled with parched rice, a fistful of coins and tiny little plastic toys that would come tumbling out of the suspended container shaped like Donald Duck or Mickey Mouse. The children would scramble on their knees to grab the goodies. And then, finally, with the candles being blown out and the cake cut over the boisterous shouting and singing of '*Happy Birthday To You!*' Bobby would appear with his expensive cameras and start clicking photographs, ruining Ruchi's mood and chasing back the black clouds. Ruchi's ambivalence left Sunny and Vicky thoroughly intimidated.

Before leaving for boarding school in Darjeeling tucked away in the mountains, the twins would trail me all over the house, wearing paper masks, gaudy plastic goggles or pigeon feathers in their caps, pretending to be Red Indians. Nothing pleased them more than going out with me to the Nehru Children's Museum or driving down the Strand, without Ruchi-didi, singing the latest songs they had learnt at nursery school. It was usually *'How much is that doggie in the window?'* or *'I'm H-A-P-P-Y; I am L-O-V-E-D...',* replete with all the actions taught to the class by their music teacher. They loved chucking coins into the river and making a wish, or simply watching the country boats sail across the waves.

'Ma, when I grow up I want to be a fisherman,' Sunny said one winter afternoon, his face flushed with excitement, watching a fisherman cast his net into the river. 'I'll take you with me on a boat to many exciting countries and we'll leave Daddy and Ruchi-didi behind.'

'Why can't we take them with us? That would be really nice,' I declared, tousling his hair and trying to be inclusive. 'And what about you, Vicky? What would you like to become when you grow up?'

'I'll become an engine driver,' Vicky said, puffing out his cheeks and making little chugging sounds like a train as he went round and round me in elated circles. 'And I'll marry you, Ma! I promise!'

I threw back my head and laughed till I could feel the tears smarting my eyes.

'And Daddy? What will we do with Daddy?' I asked.

'We'll make him go to office and earn a living... and play golf... and... and... and... sulk like Ruchi-didi!' said Sunny, grinning with delight.

A week after their visit to the Strand, as Bobby happened to be out of town on one of his official tours, I decided to take the twins to Amherst Street. Ruchi refused to come along. Initially, she made an excuse about too much homework and then, as I continued to persuade her, she walked off in a huff. There was little I could do to make Ruchi change her mind. I finally left with the boys, unable to understand – in my anxiety to maintain peace in our home – that Ruchi was actually terribly heartbroken. Not even the bait of Shubha's songs could tempt her.

Ruchi had been the apple of her maashi's and grandmother's eyes till the twins arrived and Ma transferred all her loyalty and attention on the boys. This hurt Ruchi deeply. Everything about Amherst Street, softly crumbling, seemed to nowadays revolve around Sunny and Vicky's visits. Even Shubha had been forgotten, lost in her fits of mad rapture.

The twins were terrified of Shubha – of her unkempt appearance, her fits of laughter that invariably ended in bigger fits of copious weeping, and her constant babble in the prayer room. The more she tried to charm them with her songs, and cuddle them and feed them with proshaad, the louder they screamed in fright and ran helter-skelter. Ironically, unlike her brothers, Ruchi had struck up an unguarded friendship with her aunt on the very first day they had met. The pujo area, smothered in the fragrance of sandalwood and dopaati flowers, had held a perplexing enchantment, both claustrophobic and fascinating, for the little girl. The gods with painted faces seemed frozen in time. They stared back at Ruchi from their miniature brass thrones dressed in faded satin and tinsel and covered in a soft, sad film of dust. Shubha diligently lit the joss sticks and included her niece in her constant flirtations with Krishno, teaching her how to weave a garland, sharing secrets and singing for her – singing all those lovely bhojons that Meerabai dedicated to Giridhar-Gopal. As Shubha's voice filled the room, every verse stretched to endless hours of longing – poignant, unattainable and yet so real.

Ruchi could not reconcile to the fact that she had stopped being worthy of Dimma's regard. Just because she was a girl? Just because she spoke her mind? Just because she could not get along with her brothers who were thoroughly spoilt by Bobby? Had Dimma forgotten those wonderful songs she had taught her? Songs that spoke of the many moods of nature? Of the vagaries of love?

'Shokhi, bhaabona kaahaarey boley? Shokhi, jaatona kaahaarey boley? Tomra je bolo dibosho-rojoni bhaalobaasha-bhaalobaasha… Shokhi, bhaalobaasha kaarey koye?'

My friend, what are feelings after all? What's pain? The love you go on and on about night and day – well, what's this elusive thing called love anyway?

Had Dimma really forgotten all the affection and praises she had showered on her granddaughter before Sunny and Vicky had intruded?

I couldn't deny that Ma pampered Sunny and Vicky to distraction. She waited for them eagerly, calling me at least a dozen times to find out what they'd like for lunch.

'Ma, please don't fuss. Just do us a khichuri and fry some fish,' I often snapped. But Ma would have none of my brusqueness or my suggested menu.

'Certainly not! Can't do a slapdash affair for my grandsons! Should I make a nice jhol of magur? It's not very bony, you know.'

'Vicky hates magur, Ma.'

'Then doi maachh? And some fresh mango tok and payesh?'

'Do as you please,' I smiled, unable to contain my mother's excitement.

Traffic was a nuisance and it took almost an hour to get to Amherst Street. Ma waited at the porch – dressed in white – shorn of all adornment but for a single gold bangle encircling her wrist with a solitary safety-pin dangling from it. Time had mellowed her face and cast its mantle over her frail shoulders, tired, like sunlight dozing on the red floors of her home in winter.

After Baba's death, the twins had become my mother's biggest obsession. She spoilt them with their favourite sweets and indulged every childish demand they made.

'Dadubhai,' she called out excitedly, watching them tumble out of the car, 'look what I've got for you?'

'What? What?' the twins chorused, racing up to her.

'Guess?' Ma enticed, adjusting her spectacles. 'Just guess, Dadubhai!'

'Can't, Dimma,' Vicky lisped, having recently lost two of his milk teeth. 'Coconut naadus?'

'Wrong!' Ma chuckled. 'I've got you kites!'

'You mean kites we can actually fly?' asked Sunny in utter delight and disbelief.

'Yes, my precious! Kites you can actually fly!' said Ma, gathering her grandsons to her ample bosom and kissing their foreheads.

'Oh, wow, Dimma, you rock!' the boys shouted, thrilled. And before I could stop them, they raced up the staircase, dipping their heads out of habit in front of the gods in the prayer room, before scampering, unafraid, to the rooftop.

By this time, Shubha had gone away from home. Ma had taken her on a pilgrimage to the Himalayas and on their way back from Bodrinaath, they had stopped to spend a few days at Akaash Baba's ashram in Rishikesh. Shubha decided to remain there.

Ma now chased after the twins, limping up the stairs but

determined to not succumb. She had deliberately chosen to forget how much she had protested when I used to fly kites with Dibaakorda just because I was a girl.

Time is such a great leveller. Such a cunning, heartless healer!

The years rolled by. The house at 189/A Amherst Street lost all its former glory. The pond was overrun with water hyacinth. The boundary wall gaped with holes through which the neighbourhood boys would slip in on quiet afternoons to steal mangoes. The thakurdalaan developed cracks and needed urgent repair. The chandeliers were either sold or stolen and the numerous books in Barrister Bidhushekhor Dotto's chamber finally donated to the High Court library. I decided to take the ormolu clock and place it next to an old satsuma vase in the drawing room at King Edward's Court. It was the lone reminder of my childhood days, of the schizophrenic years of growing up in the two disparate worlds of north Calcutta and Loreto Convent. Both worlds now inevitably lost. Like my father.

And then a final blow felled Ma forever, forcing her to go to the hills and live with Mini in her school quarters. Every hope in life seemed over for her – the hearth she had tried to save and the daughters she had tried to protect. Krishno Thakur did not spare her from his cruel, cosmic net. The notes of his magic flute had just been a careless interlude. Now there was only silence. Old relatives, who came to see her off, wisely nodded their heads, wiped their tears and whispered that no one could escape their karma. Not even inadequate, foolish Shubha, my Bordi.

Shubha had turned into a recluse at Akaash Baba's ashram, seduced again by the Blue God. Night after night a gang of sadhus had forced her to swallow a lethal potion made of equal parts of honey and poisonous dhatura leaves. They had promised that the concoction would end all her miseries. Miraculously, within a few weeks, she had begun to notice that Krishno had started to arrive at her doorstep at dusk and coax her to drink further from his divine chalice. The more she thirsted, the more he would pour his magic brew into her goblet so that at all odd hours of the day and night she'd sit in a trance at the community keertons, singing away in a mad frenzy.

'Horey Krishno horey Krishno, Krishno-Krishno, horey-horey! Horey Raamo horey Raamo, Raamo-Raamo, horey-horey!'

Shubha became addicted to the draughts. Even the widows in the hermitage couldn't wean her away. From the crack of dawn till late into the night she'd remain intoxicated, tottering through her daily chores with a permanent, idiotic smile. She'd fall at the feet of the idol a hundred times a day, weaving him fresh garlands despite pricking her trembling fingers with the sharp tip of the needle. She'd light lamps and beg him to hold her tight. And she'd curl into a tight, foetal ball, hands tucked between her knees, and fall asleep at the idol's feet, murmuring his name constantly in her dreams.

Ultimately, one dawn, led by Akaash Baba, the sadhus lured Shubha to a secluded waterfall in the mountains edged with wild ferns. They lied to her, saying Krishno was waiting there to carry her away to Brindabon.

'Krishno has come for *me?*' she had asked, ecstatic. 'Has he come at last to take me home?'

'Yes,' a young sadhu had fibbed, barely able to hide his sneer. 'He has come to be with you forever.'

'Gobindo! Gobindo!' Shubha had cried in great joy and burst into song.

She had blindly followed the mendicant, her mind wandering hither and thither, flying across an inebriated sky like a flock of untamed swallows. The other hoodlums, barely covered in scanty loincloth, lurked at the cascade. They advanced to dunk her under the frothing chute, almost choking her to death. Akaash Baba laughed and waved a peacock feather to seduce her, before ganging up with the crowd. Then they tore away her sari and bathed her in the pool of their lust, wrenching her limbs, bruising her neck – thrusting, thrusting, thrusting.

Shubha had writhed in agony and called out to Krishno again and again for help. But no help came. And an hour later, devastated and bleeding profusely, she jumped into the turbulent Gonga, sinking without a trace. Her decomposed body was found downstream a fortnight later, confined between boulders and a spray of water weeds, bloated and rotting beyond recognition. Only a fresh marigold garland, thrown into the waves by careless pilgrims, lay trapped around her neck.

Soon after the tragedy, Bobby arranged to have Ma sent to Mini. The house at Amherst Street was put up for sale. Rapacious Marwari realtors began visiting his office and quoting their price. The twins eventually left for boarding school and, later, Ruchi for Santiniketan. But distance and time did little to bridge old resentments. Ruchi, like her Shubha Maashi when she was alive, always remained unpredictable and remote.

Bobby couldn't help sniggering when I decided to make sure that, like Ruchi, the boys too developed some interests outside their limited academic world before they went off to boarding school in Darjeeling. The twins were around nine when Vicky, the quieter of the two, expressed a desire to learn the piano. An upright pianoforte was immediately bought and a tutor, old Mr Braganza – Sylvia's uncle – promptly hired. Sunny wanted to paint and I had him enroll in art classes at the Birla Academy on Southern Avenue over weekends during summer vacations. At every given opportunity I dragged them to concerts and exhibitions at the Academy of Fine Arts, which also happened to be one of my favourite haunts.

With ice cream smeared all over their lips, the twins followed me around through the vast galleries. Then, on one occasion, we bumped into Montoo Mullick, the solicitor.

'Mohini!' Montoo Mullick exclaimed, spotting us at the main exhibition hall. 'How wonderful to see you! You look like the splitting image of Goddess Paarboti descended from Mount Koilaash with her sons! Oh my goodness, look at them! How tall they've become!'

'I'm taller than Vicky,' Sunny said promptly.

'Are you?' Montoo Mullick chuckled. 'Come, let me see.'

'No,' Vicky grumbled. 'Because I know I'm taller.'

'Now, now,' I scolded. 'This is no place to fight.'

'Do you know that the paintings are done by Prokaash Moni, one of my dearest friends?' Montoo Mullick tried to impress the twins. 'Do you like them?'

'No,' they chorused.

'Why not?' asked Montoo Mullick, surprised.

'Because they're just like you. Ghastly!'

Thoroughly embarrassed, I smacked their heads as Montoo Mullick threw up his hands and burst out laughing.

Montoo-mama, as far as the twins could remember, had been in and out of our home, dropping by in the evenings without notice to drink Bobby's precious single malts and fill him in on all the legal gossip running rife through commercial grapevines. Bobby was enthralled. The more complicated the yarns about the rise and fall of the share market or the fluctuating fortunes of chairmen and managing directors, the more sinister the tales about individual ruthlessness and deceit, the more Bobby warmed up to the shrewd lawyer. He didn't mind how much Montoo drank – though, normally, he would have been extremely choosy about whom he obliged with his precious Glen Drammonds and Glen Morangies – as long as vital information could be extracted and, later, put to good use.

Montoo Mullick's past was dubious but he exuded a vast reservoir of charm. Bobby could always depend on him to think up devious strategies that would feather his nest and keep Pesi Readymoney and his tribe miles away. I found Montoo overbearing but the twins were entertained by his silly jokes and stories from Indian mythology.

'So what if I wasn't born at Amherst Street,' Montoo often told them, sitting them on his knees. 'I'm your uncle, your mama. I've known your mother for years, even before she married your daddy. Your Dimma treated me like her son. Did you know that?'

'But you can't be Ma's brother if you didn't come out of Dimma's tummy. Why, you didn't even pop out of her ear like Karna!' Vicky protested. 'You're telling lies again, Montoo-mama.'

Montoo Mullick smacked his bottom playfully, letting him jump off and run away.

'Montoo-mama, do you always tell lies?' Sunny asked, staring at him through his huge, dark eyes.

'Why do you want to know?' countered Montoo Mullick, grinning.

'Because you promised to get me a Tintin comic and you didn't.'

As a little boy growing up in his grandfather's home on College Row, a wiry Bihari servant, Bhola, used to massage young Montoo with mustard oil before his daily bath. The kneading usually ended in naughty asides and fiddles. Later, drugged by the humid heat of summer afternoons, Bhola would lie with his victim on a narrow bed and gently pull at his pajama strings, slipping his hand, past his navel, to feel his naked ardour awakening from slumber. With every delightful spasm a demon would be slain. Bhola knew his erotic mythology better than any master trouper. Over the years, story-telling became an addiction. The strokes got heavier as Draupadi was disrobed or Lokkhon was impaled or Orjun was seduced or Honumaan was forced to leap across the skies.

These fantasies never left the crafty lawyer even in later years.

However, once he became a well-known rogue floating through the corridors of Calcutta High Court in his distinguished robes, Montoo Mullick was loath to discuss his past. He hated any references to his youth spent in north Calcutta – to the pomp and pageantry of Phaata Keshto's annual Kaali Pujo or to the avid kite-flying sessions that overtook the rooftops, with Bhola as his faithful accomplice, during the festival of Bishshokorma. He never spoke of remaining glued to his grandfather's Murphy radio, listening to Shondha Mukherjee sing '*O bok-bokum-bokum paaira*...' during Onurodher Ashor. He even tried to forget how he would gorge on the famous babu-shondeshes from Shontosh Mishtanno Bhandaar during Bijoya Doshomi. It was a past Montoo did not wish to remember. Neither did he wish to recall why, as the orphaned grandchild of one of the city's most famous goldsmiths, he had been ultimately disowned.

Only I knew. And this fact made Montoo very insecure.

I had seen him as an awkward teenager at his grandfather's shop, helping behind the counter where I'd often accompany Dolly-kaakima and Ma on hand-pulled rickshaws to buy gold earrings or pretty filigreed lockets. On our way home, after we had stopped to pray at the Siddheshwari temple in Thonthonia, Dolly-kaakima would whisper how the boy's wayward mother had run away with the neighbourhood Romeo. What shame she had heaped upon her poor father – the much revered patriarch whose employees were famous for their workmanship all over the country! Within a year, her love-story had ended like all ill-fated love stories – replete with a baby in her arms and an abusive and alcoholic husband who had kicked her out. She returned home and then, in the style of a true Thomas Hardy heroine, conveniently died, leaving the poor grandfather with no other choice but to bring up her abandoned infant.

Montoo Mullick's transformation from a shy and insecure adolescent to the humungous and insufferable lawyer had certainly been astonishing. Despite the many rumours floating around, I was too embarrassed to discuss what I knew about Montoo's antecedents with anyone. Not even Sylvia.

Having moved into a smart little apartment in Jodhpur Park, Montoo Mullick soon became famous for hosting wild parties where orgies were the reigning flavour. He had enough clout to override the displeasure of his neighbours who were sick and tired of the loud music and strange-looking men fleeting in and out of the neighbourhood after sundown with lipstick smeared all over their mouths, elaborate eye make-up and odd wigs. Over the years Montoo's indiscretions turned compulsive as he took to picking up whatever was available at all odd hours. If the boys from the discos had fled, he was happy to drag back a rickshaw-puller or a coolie who looked reasonably clean and reminded him of Bhola.

I met him again, many years later on a winter afternoon, while lunching with Sylvia at the Bengal Club. Imperious Montoo walked into the dining hall with a golden-haired young man and, spotting me, stopped dead in his tracks. He waved out self-consciously and before I could call him over, quickly proceeded to a quiet table at the farthest corner.

Sylvia laughed, watching Montoo flee. 'We've got to tell Montoo to stop interfering with little boys' arseholes,' she whispered.

'Do you know him?' I asked, amused.

'Who doesn't? He's the most celebrated blackguard in town, fixing deals and wheels within wheels! He's the best lawyer any crooked shadow could chase!'

'And his guest?'

'Oh come on, Mohini! Everybody knows that young purser,' Sylvia barked. 'He's the freshest pick this season with Calcutta's gay crowd.'

Montoo's date was certainly Adonis reinvented.

Bruce MacIvor, according to Sylvia, was a true-blue Dundonian. His impressive reputation had been privy to more men in skirts than he cared to remember – men, who from the waist up were replicas of Sean Connery and from the waist down, Mary Queen of Scots without her knickers. Sylvia had met him a few months ago at a consulate party where he had made a play for every Anglo-Indian boy worth his Scottish surname and willing to dance to his bagpiper. Till he sniffed out Montoo Mullick's loaded wallet.

Sinking her fork into the rather tender loin of roast lamb swimming in piquant gravy and mint sauce, Sylvia – ever the animated raconteur – continued to regale me with colourful stories while sniggering at my naiveté. Unmindfully, I heard her out, revealing nothing and wondering all the while what had compelled Montoo to change so drastically.

Montoo Mullick had gathered about him a slightly abstracted air, one that is often observed in flawlessly ugly people. He enjoyed being ambiguous. With time, his clique increased. So did his list of clients. And Bobby was more than happy to hire him, when they eventually met, as soon as he had a glimpse into Montoo's clever but supremely devious mind. Ruchi hated him with a vengeance and unlike the twins, refused to call him Montoo-mama or accept his gifts.

Even at that age, she could sniff out bad fish.

Ruchi's sharp mind and sharper tongue could clip a thorny hedge with singular ease. Bobby, chary of her short temper, was incapable of realising that she had most probably inherited it from him! But she had also inherited my innate artistry and, perhaps, some residue of compassion that often made her feel enormously guilty for constantly being on a short fuse.

Ruchi's friends at Jadavpur University, where she was reading Comparative Literature as an undergraduate, initially found her enthusiasm for Robindroshongeet galling. What an odd fish! They'd rather be at The Pink Elephant, the currently in-vogue discotheque at the Grand, but much as they tried, Ruchi refused to accompany them. The boys would have willingly spirited her away to the dance floor had she deigned to scatter even a few crumbs their way. But, alas, Ruchi remained all awash with a glittering, unassailable 'Rabindrik' aura and, browbeaten, most of the devotees ended up feeling hopelessly intimidated by what they perceived – quite wrongly, of course – to be her innate Tagorean snobbery.

Finally, realising she had a god-gifted voice, their exasperation slowly turned into unwavering enthusiasm. Something about her articulation arrested their attention. With every passing week, her fans multiplied and soon Ruchi made Tagore the 'in' lyricist on the campus. She sang his songs with such simplicity and yet with such deep feeling that, at the end of a rendition, her admirers found a little lump choking their throats. Some of them started cajoling her to perform at the Annual Music Festival hosted by the Students' Union. Ruchi yielded and was happily embarrassed when the *Bengal Gazette* gave her a glowing review. But she said nothing about it at home.

I chanced upon the newspaper a week later and was thrilled and hurt by equal measures. Rushing into Ruchi's room, I accused, 'Oh, darling, why didn't you tell me?'

'I wish you'd knock before barging in, Ma,' Ruchi snapped, irritated, looking up from the book she was reading.

'I'm so pleased,' I said, ignoring her asperity. 'We must tell Daddy once he returns from golf.'

'Don't you dare tell him anything! Don't you dare show him anything!' Ruchi flared up, shooting out of her chair. 'Ma, I'm warning you! *Don't you dare!*'

'Why? What's wrong?' I asked, nettled at what I considered Ruchi's constant criticism of my efforts to make peace between her and Bobby.

'Nothing that *you'd* care to know,' Ruchi yelled. 'I'm not a hypocrite like you!'

In a fit of anger I plastered a slap across Ruchi's cheek.

'Don't you start taking me for granted too,' I shouted. 'I've had just about enough from all of you!'

'Then why have you kept quiet?' Ruchi accused, unrelenting. 'Why, Ma, why? Why is your life one big compromise; one big act of martyrdom?'

'Stop it!' I commanded, looking away. 'You've never bothered to find out what I go through in this house!'

'So you think you'll make me bother now by slapping me? You won't!' Ruchi spat out, letting her temper get the better of her as she grabbed me by the shoulder. 'You won't, simply because you don't know the difference between honesty and lies. Your life is one big fraud, Ma! And Daddy hates my music. You know that, don't you? Then why do you want to humiliate me? Only because you've been humiliated by him all your bloody life?'

Horrified, I ran out of Ruchi's room.

Next morning, at breakfast, there was a chilling silence.

'Jam?' I asked Ruchi brightly, trying to thaw the gloom and looking across the table draped in crisp, blue-checked gingham. 'It's gooseberry, darling. Your favourite.'

'No thanks,' Ruchi said in a touch-me-not voice, concentrating on her mug of coffee.

'But you must have something to eat, Ruchi! Another toast?' I coaxed, trying to catch her eye. 'You spend the whole day at college without eating a thing – that's why you are so thin!'

'Ma, don't nag. Please!' Ruchi snapped, unmoved, putting her mug down.

'I'm not nagging, Ruchi. I'm only concerned,' I said. 'You know you have a very long day today. You'll rush off to your singing classes after college and not eat a morsel. Or you'll go to the canteen and stuff yourself with all that spicy rubbish, and then grumble about a tummy ache.'

'Oh, Ma, why do you always exaggerate?'

I sighed and began buttering a toast. Bobby rustled the pages of the *Economic Times* that hid his eyes, impatient to get to office before the morning rush.

'Daddy, am I coming with you?' asked Ruchi.

'If you stopped squabbling with your mother and hurried the hell up,' Bobby growled, bringing the paper down to look at her over the rim of his glasses.

Punctuality, Ruchi knew, was one of her father's lesser-known virtues. She pushed back her chair and rose without preamble, hurrying out of the dining room.

'Don't forget to take your sandwiches – they're on the kitchen counter,' I called out.

Bobby glared at me and whispered with some ferocity, 'It's your entire fault!' and without waiting for me to protest, commanded, 'Now hurry up if you want a ride with us to your Charity girls!'

I rose quickly, wondering whether most marriages were plain tedium like ours. Did most of them simmer endlessly like unappetising soup – boring and atavistic – with bits of wilted cabbage floating over the scum? The deception of small, cherishing attentions that Bobby would shower on me in public was nothing but nonsense meant for the benefit of others. And maybe life was a hopeless muddle, after all.

Preoccupied, Bobby drove down Southern Avenue, trying to keep his temper under control. Traffic poured out of every lane in schizophrenic floods, threatening to descend into chaos. Ruchi sat beside him in silence. I was the lone rider in the back seat, lost in my thoughts. I sighed and tried to blank out my mind. Ruchi pretended to concentrate on some hurriedly scribbled notes in a dog-eared exercise book. The car jolted over numerous potholes against Bobby's muffled inventory of curses.

I watched the gulmohar trees along the lakes that had burst into full bloom. Plunged out of winter, with hardly a spring to talk about, Calcutta was waking to a sultry summer that would soon get too oppressive to bear. Pedestrians were already wilting under its weight, trying to scramble onto buses or yelling at taxis that refused to stop. Some urchins ran howling down the pavement, chasing a kite. A mother stood near a milk booth – frazzled and ill-tempered – smacking the head of her little son in his smart school uniform, in an attempt to force him to eat a banana she had already peeled and simultaneously asking him questions from a book she held open under her nose.

The pavement had turned into a scarlet carpet littered with gulmohar petals. Gazing through the gnarled trunks towards the measureless expanse of the tarn beyond, where a few stray punts were still being rowed, I realised that even in such stifling weather, the Dhakuria Lakes were beautiful. Slowly, Ruchi turned to look at the sky and caught a glimpse of the last flock of Siberian cranes flying in a low arc in the distance. In sudden delight she cried out, 'Look, Ma, look!'

I turned to where Ruchi drew my attention and, laughing, stretched out my hand to gently clasp her shoulder. She nuzzled my hand with her cheek, smiling. Then, very softly, she began humming, *'Megher koley-koley jaye re choley boker paati...'*

Borne on the lap of clouds again, fly a flock of cranes...

Bobby glared at her and blew the horn louder in a clumsy attempt to drown her voice. The traffic was becoming more and more aggressive and Ruchi's humming was getting on his nerves. To add fuel to fire, I joined in.

'So when's my nightingale cutting a disc and taking the country by storm?' he asked Ruchi lightly, disguising his sarcasm.

'Soon, very soon,' Ruchi retorted with an air of solicitous condescension. 'But sadly, I don't think you'll be around to see it happen, Daddy! Your nightingale would have flown the nest by then.'

'Why? Are you fed up of University already?'

She rewarded his question with a cold stare.

'Not at all!' she pronounced at last, taking pleasure at seeing his smile slowly fade. 'But I like my music classes better. Do you mind?'

Bobby decided not to pursue the conversation further. In his attempt to provoke her, he had only earned her scorn. He was barely aware of how demanding the Comparative Literature course was at JU. But Ruchi didn't mind, knowing that she'd be able to escape, come evening, and rush to Dokhkhini in time for the special Robindroshongeet classes. Somehow, Tagore's vast repertoire of music made her less tense. She'd often spend hours reading the verses over and over, hushing her agitation with their innate compassion and wisdom. Sometimes, if she was in a good mood, she'd even sing some of the songs for me. For one so young, Ruchi had a startling perspicacity to understand the poet's feelings and pour them out with intense emotion.

'Aamaarey tumi oshesh korechho, emoni lila tobo, phuraaye pheley abaar bhoreychho jibono nobo-nobo...'

You have made me endless, such is your pleasure... You have emptied me again and again and filled me once more with new life in equal measure!

Suchitra-di, her teacher, was already planning to talk to Bobby and see if he'd allow her to continue further.

Paying her father no attention, Ruchi went back to reading, forcing him to drive in silence. The mood of reconciliation suddenly changed to one of stifling claustrophobia. Bobby steered past jay walkers, jamming his brakes and gritting his teeth. Moments later he swerved into Gol Park, drawing the vehicle sharply over to the curb so that Ruchi could get off.

Ruchi slammed the door behind her without a proper goodbye and rushed across the road. Dodging the auto rickshaws that darted forth with no regard for rules, she swiftly negotiated her way to the queue at the 9B bus stop. Bobby reversed and veered off towards Gariahat, catching a brief glimpse of Ruchi through the rear mirror as she stood in a crooked line with the other passengers, back to her notes.

'Why the fuck can't she get the chauffeur to drop her instead of taking those ramshackle buses? Pushing and shoving her way for a foothold in that sweaty crowd – bloody hell!' he yelled at me, as if it was my fault. 'Why the fuck can't she be like the twins? They fit in so neatly with my crowd. Ruchi is such a stubborn idiot! All because of you! Why did she have to refuse that plum scholarship to study at East Anglia? What's so great about Jadavpur with its peeling, graffiti-infested walls, pseudo-intellectual faculty and volatile unions? Hah! And those Robindroshongeet classes! Such middle-class nonsense! She'll finish up in the gutter with some penniless musician! Why can't she go for piano lessons to Shireen Readymoney? That would easily kill two birds with one stone – keep the boss's wife happy and knock some musical sense into her stubborn skull!' As he continued his harangue, a mini bus missed ramming into Bobby's car by a hair's breadth. The driver craned his neck from the window to get a better view and abused, *'Ayee saala boka-choda, chokh nei, na ki?'*

You stupid fucker! Are you blind?

Thankfully, before Bobby could retaliate, the lights turned green. The cars behind him started to honk in an insistent chorus, trying to get past before the sparring degenerated into fisticuffs. Their impatience forced him to turn at the nearby intersection and escape into a narrow lane.

Bobby got off at his office and the company driver then proceeded to take me to Sarojini Memorial Women's Union. The Home was housed in a confusion of small tailoring shops and tumble-down buildings in one of Calcutta's less fashionable areas off Park Street. The car squeezed past a constricted road, overflowing with trams, fuming taxis and hand-pulled rickshaws, made narrower by some men working around faulty cables. Then, inevitably, it came to a halt. Within minutes, the traffic jam turned into an endless snarl. Vehicles started piling up and then doing exactly as they pleased. Thank God, Bobby was not driving.

A fat and helpless policeman created more confusion by struggling to bring the situation under control. But no one took his whistle-blowing and hand-flaying seriously. The rickshaw-pullers smirked and trundled along. A boy insisted on spinning a top in the middle of all the commotion, tripping over a pack of street dogs that milled around, undecided whether they should sniff around for a juicy bone or a bitch on heat. A cat sat on a broken wall and carefully licked its paw. Dodging past two speeding cyclists, a group of hermaphrodites danced and clapped, swaying their hips and cursing. A fruit seller refused to move his basket from the kerb, almost coming to blows with a furious Sardarji riding a motorbike. And, to add to the disorder, a pair of women in burkhas, engaged in animated conversation, merrily stepped off the broken pavement and almost got crushed under a shrieking ambulance.

In the midst of this supreme chaos, I sat in the car trying to tame my thoughts, as perplexing as the traffic outside.

Unlike me, who constantly tried to fit into the jigsaw puzzle of Bobby's life, Ruchi always had a mind of her own, even as a baby. She'd bawl through the nights, forcing Bobby to move into the guest room. Later – years later – I often wondered whether the seed of discord between them had sprung from such initial willfulness. I remembered what the nuns at Loreto often said, 'The mills of God grind slowly but they grind exceedingly small.'

But then, we had been too young and too carefree to heed their warnings.

Startled out of my contemplation, I looked out and faced the confusion. Would this continue to be my fate? This harsh sunlight and the hurly-burly of getting past each day, trying to keep father and daughter apart; trying to knit some semblance of balance into my home; simply trying to cope?

Every morning I would prod myself to wake up at six and run to New Market to buy fresh fish, fruits, vegetables and sometimes, if I was feeling generous, a bunch of early winter chrysanthemums. Then, rushing back for a quick shower, I'd take a lift with Bobby and Ruchi and proceed to the Home for destitute girls where I now helped manage the kitchen. Was my life really like any other, humdrum and lackadaisical? Or was it a hopeless disaster?

The car finally managed to find its way to Sarojini Memorial Women's Union and pulled up outside the gate. I alighted, still lost in my thoughts, remembering how poles apart Ruchi had been from the other children even at kindergarten. Some stray memory put a bounce back into my walk. I went past the sleepy gate-keeper towards the office where Sujata-di, the superintendent, in a plain cotton sari and wreathed in pious smiles, waited for me.

'Ah, there you are,' she said, letting me slip into an empty chair. 'We were just discussing the paucity of finances. You know how desperately we need to get the hostel roof repaired, my dear. Any ideas?'

The humungous Cheenee Buttockbyle, sub-committee member of the administration wing, leaned forward. Beads of perspiration had already collected around her forehead, fringed by her Nefertiti-like severely dyed hair. Glaring at us, she launched into a bitter criticism, combative and ruthless, aiming her darts at many of the other committee members.

'Darlings, I'm just about fed up with everybody,' she ranted. 'I've told the high and mighty RajRani Sunanda Devi a thousand times that we need to be more professional, but sadly, she is missing again this morning. Why should she remain our chairman when she isn't woman enough to get up on time and move her fat you-know-what to appear for important meetings? Haven't I been asking you girls to put together a foolproof plan instead of collecting money in dribs and drabs? We don't have two coins to rub, but all that you girls seem to do is tuck into your shingaras, drink your coffee, make promises and then buzz off!'

Shireen Readymoney could not take this tirade any longer.

'That's most unfair!' she protested. 'None of us are sitting pretty on our butts, Mrs Buttockbyle – and that includes the RajRani! In fact, I've dashed off several letters to *your* husband's office asking for donations, but there's been no response.'

'Don't you know that at the moment the steel industry is in a bloody mess?' countered Cheenee, aggressive as ever. 'I'd like to know what *your* husband's office is doing to help us out!'

'Oh, they had sent us a generous cheque not even six months ago,' Sujata-di intervened. 'But much of the funds, I'm afraid, have been used up by the weaving department.'

'And what are the inmates weaving, pray?' snorted Cheenee Buttockbyle. 'Another series of nightmares we won't be able to sell till doomsday?'

I looked at the quarrelling women, sighed and reached for my cup of coffee. Taking a tentative sip, I tried to forget, at least for a while, my own dreary life.

'Mohini, my girl,' said Sujata-di, jolting me out of my reverie. 'Do you think you could approach Bobby to bail us out? Perhaps he could put us on to some of his clients?'

'I could certainly try,' I fumbled. 'But I don't know how far I'll succeed.'

'Why don't we pay him an official visit?' suggested Cheenee Buttockbyle. 'He won't throw us out, will he?'

I knew what a task that would be – getting anybody to throw Cheenee-di out, once she had made up her mind to barge into someone's office.

I smiled sweetly and suggested, 'You make the appointment, Cheenee-di. I'll come along.'

Just at that moment, as if in sympathy to protect me from the tyrant, the lights went out. The ancient ceiling fan dissented and stopped whirring. The ladies groaned in unison. Cheenee Buttockbyle immediately lumbered out of her chair.

'Bloody load-shedding again,' she hissed, whipping out a Japanese hand fan from her bag. 'What's happening to Bengal, my dears? Everything is going to the dogs! All this Communist business but not an ounce of jyoti in our lives!'

Fluttering Mount Fujiyama all over her sweaty face, she sailed out in a huff.

'If only she'd load-shed her bossy ways,' vituperated Shireen Readymoney, gathering her file and preparing to leave as well, 'we could fund-raise in peace!'

I caught Shireen's eye and smiled. She winked back.

'Do run along and see what's happening in the kitchen, Mohini,' said Sujata-di. 'The girls should have finished cooking by now.'

I nodded. It was a short walk to the canteen where the midday meal was about to be served.

Waiting for their standard thaali lunch, men from nearby offices in tight trousers, terelyne shirts and wilted ties noisily discussed local politics and *Sholay*, the latest blockbuster from Bombay. Two Anglo-Indian matrons from the neighbourhood, black as the Ace of Spades but with faces ridiculously powdered and lips painted to the hilt, staggered in on six-inch heels, tiffin-carriers in tow. In a sing-song gurgle, one of them placed the order for 'dol and rice and fish curry in mustard sauce, juldi-juldi!' with great authority before alighting on a nearby chair to smooth down her semi-transparent, laddered stockings that hid fat varicose veins. In the far corner, a group of adventurous society butterflies wrapped in crisp organdie saris and sleeveless blouses, 'slummed' it out, good-naturedly cursing the parshey fish bones and digging into the rice with their fingers. The eatery was certainly a big hit, in spite of Cheenee Buttockbyle's constant objections.

I stepped into the smoky kitchen and watched the wards perspiring profusely as they worked while a transistor emitted Lata Mangeshkar rendering, *'Yun hasraton ke daag mohabbat mein dho leeye/ Khud dil se dil ki baat kahi aur ro leeye...'*

What irony! Do women really have the power to wash away the relentless lashings of pain with make-belief love and tears, even as they try and comfort their grieving hearts? Here I was, cooking my own goose at home while offering my culinary services for social welfare!

The fumes of smoke and the sting of freshly ground onion were so strong that my eyes began to smart. The girls went about their task with vacant faces. Some peeled a mound of boiled potatoes. Others pored over huge cauldrons, stirring the mixed vegetable dalna. Yet others stuffed cream cheese into potol-gourd they had delicately hollowed. In silence, I gave thanks to Ma Kaali for small mercies. Watching the girls slog away and the rest of the world swelter, how could I ignore the comfort of an air-conditioner humming me to sleep every night? How could I disregard the huge Contessa gliding down Chowringhee, while I looked through the tinted glass and saw the office secretaries jam-packed in overcrowded trams, reeking of Charlie perfume and perspiration? At least I had been spared the torture of stray dabs of talcum caking in my armpits, trying to balance my life on rickety footboards of overcrowded public transport!

That summer Ruchi's graduation results were declared. Her friends and admirers were jubilant. Not only had she got a first class but she also stood second in her batch. They pestered me to throw a party to celebrate. For a while, everybody basked in her newfound glory. But soon the future began looming large.

Much as Bobby persuaded her to continue with academics, Ruchi became more and more determined to train as a singer. Applications were sent to music schools all over India, before she was finally accepted at the Sangeet Bhavana in Santiniketan. Trapped between my daughter's passion and my husband's practical outlook, I often got into protracted arguments with both. But in the end, Ruchi had her way. And before I could gather my wits about me, she pecked me on the cheek and dashed off to Bolpur by the morning train.

Guy Tourdes had arrived on a year's sabbatical to Kala Bhavana, the art school, housed next to Ruchi's department. A foreigner let loose in the red laterite desert of Birbhum was nothing unique or new. During Tagore's lifetime, many seekers from abroad had come there, including eccentric professors from China, philosophers from France and nudist artists from the remote town of Nagykaniza in Hungary. But here was Guy, handsome and carefully hushed, who had become, without his knowing, an intimate part of the secret lives of girls in the post-graduate hostel.

In one of her light-hearted letters to me, Ruchi claimed that

Krishnokoli and Golaapkoli, the Maity cousins – 'with mighty big boobs and mighty little grey matter' – were especially smitten by his studied languor and dashboard abs.

'Ki daroon dekhtey!' they drooled, watching him ride past on a battered old bicycle, smiling at them shyly. 'Ki handsome!'

Ruchi's acerbic humour spilled out in her letter: 'Doe-eyed Rotna Shorkaar, with a single frangipani nestling in her wild hair, often casts him her best "come-hither" looks from across the wooden table while sipping tea with Shutopa Dhor, her best friend, at Kalo's teashop. Lolita Lobongolota, straight out of a sculpted panel from Khajuraho, whose plunging neckline ensconces perfect melon breasts in the confines of a batik blouse, passes him subtle hints that she is more than willing to become his slave. But Guy is not interested. After all, he's in love with me!'

Ruchi met Guy one spring afternoon when he had stopped to watch the students of Sangeet Bhavana rehearse for a performance of one of the poet's operas for Dol, the Festival of Colour, ushering in spring. He gazed at them sing and dance in the open-air theatre, scratching his scant, auburn beard with an air of indifferent amusement. Then, suddenly, his eyes had locked with Ruchi's.

As she told me later, 'Ma, I think love *can* happen at first sight, after all. See what's happened to me?'

Her voice had faltered as she began one of Chitrangada's beautiful solo numbers. An errant breeze kept blowing a disobedient strand of hair across her face. She had barely noticed the Flame of the Forest nearby set its branches on fire as the hour grew heady with the cry of the kokeel.

Guy watched intensely, fascinated as much with Ruchi's voice as with her exceptionally beautiful eyes. She had bent her head over the harmonium, determined to continue with the verse, feeling all the while that her heart would lurch into her mouth if she did not distract its intense hammering. Turning away, she had tried to lose herself in the beauty of the song: '*Ketechhey akela birohero bela akaasho-kushumo-choyoney...*'

My days of separation slipped by, as I beheld the crimson sky...

Within a few weeks Ruchi had not only sunk herself into the depths of Guy's deep green eyes, but also hung her future by his ponytail. They became an inseparable pair on campus. Holding hands, they'd walk past the playgrounds in a trance, turning beyond the avenue of saal trees to find a quiet corner to chat and get to know each other. Ruchi's friends mercilessly teased her about her new obsession. Unaware of their jealousy, she'd laugh and hum her favourite love songs, hugging her pillow.

When she was home for the summer holidays, I chanced upon her diary one afternoon and inspite of my guilt, read some pages.

Oh Paul! Paul! *Paul!* My beloved god of the mountains! My daughter was also in love with a white man and I fervently hoped that her romance would not be doomed like mine!

In later years, once the children had grown up, I often wondered why I hadn't mentioned Kathmandu to Bobby – even as a joke – or, for that matter, why I had never asked Paul, in the first flush of our romance, to give me a photograph as a souvenir. There was nothing palpable now that kept alive those memories. No tangible tokens or mementoes or snapshots to burn holes into my conscience. And so, as Mrs Bobby Sen, I had held my pain around my fingers like a swarm of stinging bees and kept up my public charade without fear. After Ruchi was born, I had even learnt to stay out of Bobby's hair. With a sense of perverted victory I had realised that the Pretty Burmans and PomPoms of the world could never push Bobby into anything beyond casual, meaningless affairs. He would never have the nerve to divorce me and jeopardise his freedom or his career and social status.

The fragile security of matrimony and its small mercies now made me laugh. How banal, how obtuse was the assumption that a piece of paper signed before a marriage registrar or fragrant garlands exchanged in public could turn night into dazzling day!

Now, Ruchi's feelings for Guy struck me like a fresh, sharp shower of rain. My daughter, my little baby girl, was in love! And her love was honest and full of hope, so simple and right! It exuded a fragrance that seemed so pitifully heady. I shut my eyes against the erupting past and saw Ruchi's love laden with dreams I hadn't dared to dream.

Ruchi had written in her diary:

That year the monsoon came late.

After the gruelling summer holidays, when I returned to my classes, I realised we were in love. There was no getting away. For Guy, this was not just another casual affair, another fling. I had felled him with my random, deliciously bittersweet moods. In panic, some of Guy's more ardent devotees began declaiming how vividly they fantasised about him, willing him to hold them in his tightly muscled arms. Guy remained quite oblivious to the stir. For him, it was only me. His Ruchi. His beautiful Rrrru-cheee-rrraaa. And allez-vous-en, the others disappeared into the shadows, grating their teeth!

Guy didn't want to spend a moment away from me. He waited for my music lessons to end in the late afternoons so that he could take me out to an early supper, past Uttoraayon, the sprawling estate where Robindronath used to live – past the poet's shimmering prayer hall in delicate stained glass – to the little shacks near the post-office.

When he had initially expressed his feelings, eating mundane bhaat and daal and crisp slivers of aalu bhaaja, Guy's voice had strangled in a spate of emotion. His eyes had filled with sudden tears and I had sat back and marvelled at his intensity.

'We have a lot of catching up to do,' he had whispered. 'You and I, my love. Can you imagine, we've lived through so many lives, travelled across so many universes, so many centuries, always loving each other? And we didn't know? We didn't know till now?'

I nodded, unable to express my innermost feelings. In my stomach, suddenly, there was a violent constriction, a pain I couldn't quite explain. It socked me with such severity that I turned my face away, unable to look at him. How ridiculous it was – how utterly sad – that while his eyes only sought mine, I was forced to gaze at a prosaic glass of water, and then sip it slowly to pacify my turmoil!

How was I to tell Guy that all I had witnessed till I met him were lies and deceit? How was I to tell him that my parents were so unhappy that they hardly talked to each other? That their life together was a ludicrous compromise, ridiculed behind their backs by those who proclaimed to be their dearest friends?

Across the road lay a trash-can spilling its guts. It reminded me of my parents' marriage.

'Don't!' I cried at last, slowly letting the tears fall. 'Don't say things that hurt, Guy! I know what I feel for you. Yet, foolishly, I hide them in my heart. Because I have seen nothing but fights and suffering at home.'

He reached out for my hand and said softly, 'But you have to see the world through my eyes now. I am only a hollow bamboo; you have to sing your songs through me.'

I raised his fingers and brushed them with my lips,

wondering whether I had not conjured him up out of thin air, after all; out of that fatal imagination I had possessed and boasted about to my brothers. Guy smiled gently, a smile that was wet and fresh like the watercolour he had just completed, swaying with feathery kaash flowers in autumn. And watching his eyes softly crinkle – all emerald and liquid – I knew that God had, despite everything, spared me from a broken heart.

In that dappled, cowdust hour, between late afternoon and dusk, as he walked me back to the hostel, Guy sought out my hand and kept it firmly in his grip, before drawing it closer to his heart.

Then, one afternoon, when the monsoon clouds at last darkened the sky, pregnant with rain, we ran across an open field, laughing, oblivious of the slender chor-kaanta thistles that had cunningly lodged a spray of sharp husks in the edge of my sari. We let the first torrential shower pour over us in probing runnels as I flung myself into Guy's arms, unmindfully shaking my wet hair. Raindrops trickled down my lashes and soaked my face. Looking into his eyes, I burst into song: 'Ami roopey tomaaye bholaabo na, bhaalobaashaye bholaabo...'

I will not bait you with my beauty but win you over with my love...

After months of thirsting, Guy, swift finagler of my heart, finally pressed his lips against mine – pressed them tight – unmindful of the falling rain, letting my firm bosom crush against his chest as our tongues met at last in flames of sweet fire. And Guy drank the heat – deep and long – and sealed out all doubts.

For me, kissing Guy was like coming home at last.'

The next thing they did was run away together, creating a minor scandal. But, ironically, I was happy – very happy – for my daughter.

Book Three

TOMORROW

When I get older losing my hair
Many years from now
Will you still be sending me a Valentine
Birthday greetings, bottle of wine?
If I'd been out till quarter to three
Would you lock the door?
Will you still need me, will you still feed me
When I'm sixty-four?

—THE BEATLES

Vicky and Sunny, away at boarding school, were left largely untouched. They had met Guy but once, when he had come home for a cup of tea. Bobby had immediately dismissed him as one of Ruchi's 'puppies'. I had been suspicious. But knowing Ruchi's temper, I had held back from probing.

Then it became too late. Too late to make amends. Bobby raved and ranted and accused me for what he called Ruchi's 'perfidy'. He vowed he'd never allow her to enter his home again. She had blackened his face; demeaned his social standing; dragged his name through mud. Come hell or high water, nothing would make him relent. I remained silent and unobtrusively, once Bobby's fury subsided, tried to establish some contact with Ruchi with the help of Sylvia's diplomatic links. Ruchi did write back but remained adamant.

After weeks of anticipation, a brief note had arrived from Paris to tell me that she was well. But no amount of coaxing would make her appease her father. Or, for that matter, get formally married to Guy. Ruchi, from then on, remained persona non grata as far as Bobby was concerned.

With my daughter gone, I felt more and more cornered. Not in my wildest imaginings could I have known, watching baby Ruchi hungrily suckle away, that in the pace of just two decades she'd have the guts to bolt with the man she loved. My own mother had relied on her dreams and her pujos to escape from the dreary reality of her life. Shubha had fled to a world of intoxicated make-belief, diminished into utter lack of self-confidence by the men who had rejected her. Mini had retaliated by walking the razor's edge, and I had glimpsed a brief sliver of hope in those faraway, snow-clad mountains. But it was left to Ruchi to face up to the cold and bullying winds of tradition; to defy and choose her own path. And vindicate my beliefs.

In the early years of my marriage, as a dismal sadness settled over me, I would often silently accuse Paul of being a complete coward. Why had he deserted me? Why had he not turned up, despite my entreaties, and taken me away from Amherst Street? Why did he never bother to get in touch? Why had he been so heartless?

Why? Why? Why?

Not for a moment had I considered – venting my spleen and trying to hush Ruchi to sleep – that he could have simply left Kathmandu or, worse, met with a fatal accident. For me, Paul was invincible – how could he die? How could he betray me? Vanish into thin air without a clue? How could he just disappear from my life altogether?

I was not looking for the tried and tested comfort of clarifications. And every time I called Sylvia to voice my anger, I was left, alas, in a state of utter confusion. Ultimately I allowed the dream to expire of its own accord. After countless bouts of weeping in the bathroom and months of depression, I learnt to confront the world – a little brittle, a little bitter but certainly sadder and wiser than I had ever been. As the years went by, my husband's slaughterhouse became my castle. And then, miraculously, Ruchi justified much of my suffering by defying Bobby and escaping to France.

As a young girl, I had unwittingly learnt from my mother how to bear the cross of what Bobby's corporate crowd came to admire and call 'Mrs Sen's superb selflessness'. Selflessness? My foot! It was simply a defense mechanism that saved me from searing pain.

Consequently, I have spent half my life trying to work out

what I had done to deserve such a fate – so loud and outsized that it has worn me out. I would have been comfortable had the gods directly suspended their swords over my head, without telling me the many inescapable lies about Death. Death, after all, is so real, so comforting and puts everything into perspective. But my mother insisted on feeding me with constant subterfuge about Life, in the age-old tradition of mothers forever trying to fit us up with weapons they have fashioned out of their pain. An old hand at reinventing her personal experiences, Ma tried dressing me like a counterfeit goddess – a fake Durga, clutching a fake shield and sword, garlanded with fake flowers and garbed in fake glitter. She was more than up to the task of deceit. Only I didn't know that over the years, along with dispensing drinks and hors d'oeuvres and small talk, I'd have to cast off all that my story needed to stand for.

After Baba's death, when I used to visit Ma in the afternoons to escape from the claustrophobia of King Edward's Court, she would aim her little lectures at me with quiet determination. Ma would usually be sitting on her bed in a chemise with a hint of lace. Her sari, neatly folded, would be lying on the clotheshorse. She would insist on combing my hair and tying it into a neat chignon as she kept admonishing me to accept my good fortune with a little more gratitude. After all, Bobby was the family's thakur-jamaai, the ideal son-in-law. So what if my marriage had begun floundering? I was being unreasonable, as always, when I should have made it my business to pour over Bobby's life like steady, abstemious rain! Women couldn't afford to take notice of temporary thunders! Our job was to keep everything stitched into place!

'At least he leaves you alone. At least he loves his children,' she would insist, jittery about any unseemly revelations. 'So why are you always cribbing? He has only raised his voice, hasn't he? So many women have to put up with beatings and torture, you foolish girl!

That hasn't happened, has it? No? So Shib Thakur has, at least, spared you?'

'But I feel so neglected, Ma,' I'd protest. 'He has no time for me. We can't even talk without getting into an argument.'

'Your Baba is dead and gone now. But we too were like any married couple, ill-tempered and a little frayed around the edges, condemned to routine – so what?' Ma would shout. 'That's the lot of any woman coming from our background. Bobby provides you with enough money to run the house, gives you the car to come and visit me all the way to Amherst Street, takes you along on his official tours abroad. Why can't you see the brighter side? Why do you always look upon life as a ruin? Why can't you stem your tears and reconcile to the fact that what you have is much more than what you deserve?'

Then, voices would be raised, as Ma would drag back the Kathmandu trip, with her usual jeremiads and contemptuous accusations, ripping apart old wounds I had tried my best to heal.

Poor Ma! But for her sharp tongue aimed at the servants and her daughters, she had always been frugal. Ever since I could remember, she used to constantly tell us not to waste food, not to argue, not to flaunt wealth. And her homilies about life began and ended with, 'Silence is golden!' If silence was good enough for Draupadi and Sita, it had to damn well be good enough for her girls! Had she been able, she would have attached our mouths with permanent zips so that we could never provoke her with embarrassing questions. My betrothal, she always insisted, had come like a generous cloudburst, attached with prestige and a perfect rainbow. Why was I being so stupid, wanting to throw it all away? Had I so easily forgotten how cursed my life would have been – how terribly impoverished – had Bobby's pishimas not arrived to salvage the situation?

I would sigh and look at Ma, exhausted, trying my best to

understand her suffering. My mother's reprimands were conditioned by centuries of subservience, reiterating the hopelessness of middle-class Bengali morale that created paragons of womanhood inflicted with prejudiced responsibilities. Wives were forever moulded into wax-dolls that had to be acceptable to men. They were expected to emerge from the cast, molten and ready to receive their pre-arranged tasks. There was no scope for flexibility or deconstruction; no way for tried and tested roles to evolve.

Watching my mother shed tears, I had wondered why women were always expected to be a little stoic, a little jaded, softly sighing away their lives in soot-ridden kitchens or at cocktail parties – depending on their fate – with no identity they could dare to call their own? Perhaps I was fortunate. In spite of my indiscretion, my love for a white man so alien to our culture, my face hadn't been permanently blackened before I was turned out in full public view. Instead, prior to my departure, I had been carefully dressed in rich Varanasi silk and adorned with expensive jewellery and intricate embellishments on my forehead. A lavish ceremony and feast, against the background score of a plaintive shehnaai, had helped prepare my bier. And in death I had looked so beautiful that afterwards the guests had exclaimed how in a long, long time they hadn't quite seen such a beautiful bride leave her father's home.

Du'gga! Du'gga!

Bobby's growing impatience and selfishness after Ruchi had gone away was beginning to get more and more on my nerves. The sharp little barbs about Ruchi and Robindroshongeet and Guy's 'villainy', aimed at me like poisoned arrows, never gave me the chance to let him know that Ruchi had written, saying how happy she was with her lover. I dared not bring up the letters and subject myself to a fresh round of derision and abuse. Despite my mounting frustration, I remained lulled by habitual indecision.

I had just returned from Sarojini Memorial when Bobby came back from office to carelessly announce that we'd have to go to an official 'do' within the hour. It had been urgently fixed, he said, to meet a new client. I protested. I had made plans to visit Sylvia who was not keeping too well. Bobby lost his temper. And only after a huge argument did I let the tears dry and start to wrap around my enviously thin waist a handpicked Sambhalpuri sari.

Satisfied at having won his way, Bobby dived into the shower. Cautiously, I layered my eyes with kajol and ran a lipstick over my mouth, wiping the residue with a sheet of tissue. Bobby emerged from the bath, naked, rubbing dry his hair with a towel. His tight little buttock came into view, reflected in the looking glass. I paid him no attention and continued circling a small dot between my eyebrows. He walked up to the dressing table, carelessly picked up the comb and ran it through his hair. It didn't matter that he left behind stray strands on its narrow teeth. Turning briskly, he fumbled through the chest of drawers in pursuit of clean underwear. After an impatient fiddle that put his manhood into place, he slipped on a Ralph Lauren shirt, pulled up his chinos and hurriedly knotted his parachute-silk tie. Ramdeen, the bearer, had already polished his shoes. Slipping into them quickly after putting on a pair of grey socks, he grabbed his blazer and shouted, 'Come on, wife, we're bloody late!'

Then he ran down the stairs, whistling *'She'll be coming round the mountains when she comes'* and twirling the car keys on his forefinger.

'Coming! Coming!' I shouted, beleaguered, quickly spraying my throat with a drizzle of Madame Rochas. The anchol of my sari fell away and I cursed the tailor for cutting the neckline of my blouse so low. It was all PomPom's fault, wheedling me into trying out new designs! God, there was no time to change!

Tightening the screw of my earring and wishing I could do the same to my marriage, I took a final look at the mirror. With a quick adjustment of the pleats and a nod at Ma Kaali's picture on the nearby chest of drawers, I rushed down the stairs, click-clacking in my heels, slipped into the car and drove off with Bobby to the Readymoneys.

Official cocktail parties followed a dreary routine. Inevitably, there was an assortment of senior directors and vice-presidents, women with taut breasts from the publicity department, underhand journalists and a sprinkling of the boss's favourite juniors who mingled with guests outside the pale of the incestuous tea trade comprising a handful of jaded film stars, second-rate musicians and dancers, and third-rate artists. They were there strictly as decoration to make a splash on the illustrated pages of newspaper supplements.

Bobby and I walked in to see Sudhangshu Bhattacharjee, the inveterate business correspondent of *Bengal Gazette*, holding court with Pesi Readymoney and Chairman Chugh. He kept running his hands through his shock of unruly hair and surreptitiously scratching his behind. The man was an unalloyed scoundrel. With generous help from his principal correspondent, Rafeek Sen, he had managed to fish out some really nasty stories about a juicy bedroom scandal splayed across ruffled sheets in one of the tea gardens near Siliguri. And now, as he repeated some of the gory details to Pesi and the Chairman, their crumbling faces behind their frosty smiles delighted him. The imminent bribe would certainly be worth two in the tea bush. The local Jezebel currently warming Sudhangshu's bed would, no doubt, be thrilled. A pedigreed bitch known for her enormous sexual appetite, she had recently ensnared Sudhangshu as much with her skill at putting together a Burmese Khow Suey for lunch as through a display of unbridled lust immediately thereafter. She ascribed her seductive powers to the exotic maalish-sessions she enjoyed for three hours every morning, being pumelled and kneaded by an Amazon in order to retain her beauty. Sex and massages, I have to concede, helped her look like a Greek heroine's ageless bust gathering dust in the Louvre!

Jezebel's cunning and Rafeek Sen's carnal preferences had come in surprisingly handy to dig out scandals that Sudhangshu could later use for arm-twisting and blackmail.

The lackey was black as pitch. And the colour of his skin invariably ignited his concupiscence when he went on assignments to the hills and happened to catch adolescent Nepali boys defecating in the dark. His boss soon discovered the flunky's predilection for well-rounded bottoms that he liked to bugger. And on their next round of beer, it was 'bottoms up' for both. Sudhangshu Bhattacharjee was willing to let Rafeek Sen frolic, writing his travelogues and opprobrious little art and book reviews in exchange for juicy news his lovers could sniff out – true or false, it didn't really matter – as long as they could be put to good use later for extortion.

Sudhangshu Bhattacharjee now stood leaning on one foot next to Pesi, ever willing to place the other right into a fresh round of chinwag. His florid jowl wobbled as he regaled his audience with old yarns about Ramdoolal Dey's forays into the business of buying sunken ships and fresh tales about the recent slander that threatened to scupper a new project. None of the rumours were overt but Chairman Chugh bit into his jaws.

Damn Ronnie Lamba! He'd have to sack him forthwith, before things got out of hand!

Chairman Chugh's thoughts were interrupted by visions of Bhattacharjee's vulgar headlines and subsequent inquiries. The directors at the head office in London had already gone into a sulk following the financial results that had been announced at the AGM last week. At the moment, Chairman Chugh was in the doghouse and his British bosses none too pleased at the company's frugal profits. He certainly didn't want further trouble. I discovered soon enough that Bobby had been asked to sniff out what it would cost to expedite a decent burial for that annoying Siliguri tittle-tattle. Feelers had been sent but the haggling hadn't stopped. Sudhangshu Bhattacharjee had not yet bitten the bait.

I nursed a vodka, aware of all the clever little ploys going on around, right beneath my nose. Bobby was back to being his charming self, his eyes a-crinkle and a smile playing on his lips, making some light-hearted, easy reply when Sudhangshu Butt – as the rogue was christened in absentia – finally strode up to him and asked what was the most devoted couple in Calcutta doing with their private lives. I looked away, seething. But Bobby kept a tight grip on my elbow. He was unaccustomed to feeling defensive. He stared steadily into Butt's curiously obsidian eyes to stop him from probing further. Bobby's team at office was all set to finish him off and make the spiteful troublemaker eat his words. Yet Damocles kept laughing and dangling his proverbial sword.

Bobby often muttered that Butt needed his butt kicked real hard!

Once Sudhangshu had sailed away, Bobby took a quick sip from his whisky while craning his neck over the bundle of heads milling around. In a bid to let off steam and silently search for an ex-lover's attention, he allowed an eyelid to minimally fall that I was able to note with some discomfiture. Thus, fuelling my constant suspicions, another casual rendezvous was fixed.

The party was abuzz with small talk like the sting of polite bees. The air-conditioners hummed. A consortium of lashes, stiff in their intent not to bat, eyed a set of energetic management trainees with quiffed hair and razor-sharp sideburns revolving lazily on barstools, charmingly bored. Virulently painted lips blew them intermittent kisses. Paying scant heed to the passes, the boys preened and flexed their muscles, carrying forward an animated conversation on locker room shenanigans involving genitalia measurements post a rigorous game of rugby. According to them, sexual ambivalence was quite an appropriate asset because you were never sure which way your manager vacillated. One of the studs had discovered why weekends promised pretty interesting trimmings when he was asked to come in to work one Sunday afternoon and ended up in the bossman's chamber with his trousers down, sitting on bossman's hallowed chair and getting not only a thrilling blow job but also an equally thrilling hike in his pay packet. The mist of expensive perfumes and aftershaves masked the stench of double lives. It was a perfect circus enacted at least three working days a week to feed the city's business interests and its bubbling sexual underbelly frothing behind the corporate, self-gratifying spirit of carpe diem that threw together birds with exotic plumage and beasts sporting voracious appetites.

Bobby was still distracted when Paddy Roy, who had overheard some of Sudhangshu Butt's canards, turned to ask, 'Did Ronnie really ply the garden manager's wife with eight pegs of whisky to get her knickers off?'

'Oh, that was hopeless,' said Bobby with a short laugh. 'An hour's fornication wasn't worth the airfare to the Dooars!'

'Don't rule out an arrest for that bugger if Butt finds out,' pointed out Den Dhingra of corporate accounts. 'Ronnie's as mundane and tasteless as an angel's arse. But he's also just helped himself to a huge bribe.'

'Have you read Bossman's handwritten memo today?' said Goli (Gulbahar) Singh, a junior tea taster. 'Boy, it was chilling!'

'Why are you prone to odd fits of bum-licking?' asked Bobby smoothly. 'Don't you have anything better to do?'

'Ronnie's bedroom skirmishes will soon become open warfare,' laughed Dhingra. 'Take it from me, he'll end up popping penis enlargement pills once he gets the sack!'

I detested such talk and passed a caustic remark. Momentarily, Bobby looked at me as if I were capable of arousing interest after all. But with some exotic bird alighting on the scene just then and cheeping into his ears before dragging him away, I found myself deserted and alone once more.

Possibly because of the vodka I started to feel unsettled – even wary. Was it fatigue or plain stretched nerves? Involuntarily, I massaged my eyes with the tip of my thumb and ring finger before spotting Shireen Readymoney across the room. She was talking to a chic Punjabi entrepreneur belonging to a latter-day 'Cult Of The Clitoris' whose Sapphic flowerings had managed to entice a pushy Bengali heroine into bed. I had come to know through PomPom's grapevine that the heroine had finally discovered what no hero had helped her locate – the elusive G-spot that gave her a new lease of life and an ecstatic sense of liberation. And, overnight, her lover had turned into an avant-garde film producer, wanting to back projects with an all-female crew. Next to Miss Dyke stood the stiff and prissy English wife of the new German Consul General. She was bedecked in beads and a clumsily worn salwar-kameez from Delhi's latest ethnic cornucopia, Fabindia. What a fool she had made of herself at Shobeeta's sitar recital! Looming large beside her was that opportunist bitch, Tina Suri. Draped in a Bomkai silk sari, she was busy sucking up to the little crowd, a tantalising strip of voluptuous boredom. Her hair lay open like her numerous affairs as she took tentative sips from a glass of wine she held with great affectation. She had recently milked dry a poor, innocent painter from Gujarat with a penchant for garba and dhoklas, before abandoning him after his cerebral stroke for more lucrative pastures. Sylvia had sussed her out long ago, well aware of her insatiable sexual appetite and her proclivity for arse-licking. There she was, bustling around Shireen, pretending to be a connoisseur of watercolours, along with the ever-opinionated Shobeeta Mitra and that pushy impresario – now what was *her* name? Meenu something-or-the-other, with her snake-like eyes and famous for having caused quite a flutter after being rudely slapped up and kicked out from an arts organisation supported by powerful Sindhi industrialists. The scandal had taken Calcutta by storm not even a month ago. But the unscrupulous hussy was back in circulation, indiscriminately bedding a sundry collection of slimy film producers and batting for free votes to run a defunct NGO that was, ironically, famous for fighting for the cause of sex workers! Did I really want to plough my way through the chattering crowd to go and meet them? The routine was so tiresome and Bobby was still drinking.

Gosh! When would we ever leave?

The cocktail rituals, with its hypocrisies of 'Hello, darling, you look *sooooo* gorgeous! New jhumkas?' or 'Give me the lowdown on the last Book Club meeting, sweetheart – every teeny-weeny, dirty detail!' or 'Why didn't you show up at so-and-so's party? It was such a hit!' interspersed with flying kisses hid hours of loneliness as the night thickened and we returned home at last, with Bobby a little high and a little abusive about his colleagues. I tried to wedge my feelings in between his unhappy tirade. He set about switching off the lights and shouting at me for not leaving him alone. Pulling at his tie and messing up his hair, he told me in a slur that he was 'too bloody tired' to face my badgering. Then he bundled himself off, leaving me discarded in the corridor. And I stopped thinking about the past and the future, about the tears still stinging my eyes. I crept into the bedroom, undressed and flung my sari on an easy chair, compelled by my need to find my own space, rather like an animal marking its territory. And relying on a newly formed habit, I dragged my feet to the flask on the bedside table, poured out some water and popped back a Valium, in a futile attempt to drown Bobby's snores and my own, unspoken sorrow.

How relentless are the brambles of memory! There's a photograph on my dressing table captured on the Darjeeling mall. I remember stopping a tourist to click the picture. There we are, frozen in time, a happy ménage – Bobby in his standard flannels and blazer, I in a silk sari and a Kashmiri shawl, the twins in their school uniforms and Ruchi with a ridiculous scarf wrapped around her head and huge ear-hoops. I can see my arm protectively resting on her shoulder. But Bobby rules the frame, combative and handsome, smiling self-consciously.

Looking at the photograph, who would believe that my marriage was a sham?

In our society, divorce is a dirty word. It immediately labels a woman 'cheap', 'loose' and 'available'. Overnight, men who had professed undying platonic camaraderie turn into leering wolves. It usually transpires when they happen to catch you at your vulnerable worst. An apparently innocent invitation to dinner or to the races or to the movies transmutes into a game of surreptitious passes. In the beginning, nothing is overt. But the way they start looking at you, the way they throw their arms around your shoulders, the way they make innocuous overtures compels you to become the unwilling connoisseur of other male eyes. You turn into easy prey even as your women friends titter when you are not around, either in empty sympathy or in whispers loaded with furtive insinuations. 'Poor thing! She must be so lonely!' some opine, playing their next rubber at a weekend bridge session. 'Lonely? You must be joking!' exclaim her rivals. 'She's taken the bugger to the cleaners, my love. She's loaded like she never was when they were together! That's why all that male attention! It's all about the money, honey!'

No parent wants the return of a prodigal daughter. And to save fathers from collapsing due to instant heart attacks and mothers from shooting up their blood pressures, married girls are supposed to look the other way and carry on with their lives, never mind if their husbands stray and heap upon them daily insults and grief. Girls from good homes learn to suffer and make the best of bad marriages. They learn to hire their little toy-boys or get serviced by good-looking chauffeurs on lonely afternoons in neglected garages or on the back seat of the car on a secluded stretch of the highway when no one is looking. But, dahlings, they *never* ever ask for a divorce!

Today, I can look at the intrusive sunlight flare through the curtains and watch the destruction without flinching. I wanted to make my life beautiful. But it didn't quite fold out according to plan. And I did nothing. Nothing at all to thwart the sadness. Till one quiet afternoon I decided I had had enough. I knew Ruchi would never come back. But today I can confess it was because of her that I finally decided to break my silence.

Just before Ruchi disappeared, I was overcome by a strange foreboding that things were not all right. Sensing imminent trouble, I had gone to visit her in Santiniketan. But she seemed more than happy to see me. One evening, after returning from her music class, she told me about a new song she was learning.

'It's beautiful, Ma,' she said, coming to sit by my side. 'It's in Raag Jaunpuri. One of Otul Proshaad's best. Shubha-maashi used to love it, remember?'

Like Ruchi, Shubha too had toiled over her music. But nobody had given poor Bordi's musical skills any credit. Ruchi now began humming the song softly, humming back old memories and hurts. I had known that song well, having heard Bordi hum it time and again when she was in the prayer room, lighting the evening lamps at her beloved Krishno's feet.

'Ma,' Ruchi exclaimed, shaking me out of my reverie, 'are you listening?'

Then, without waiting for a reply, she let her voice soar into the dusk.

'Stop!' I screamed, unable to control my rage. 'I hate it! I hate this song! I *hate* the lyrics!'

Ruchi paused mid-verse, stunned at my outburst. Speechless with shock, she stomped out of the room. I didn't stop her. I didn't have the strength to explain what I was feeling.

'Tobo choronotoley shoda raakhio morey...'

Keep me forever at Thy feet...

What was the purpose of such worthless sentiment? Why did devotion have to degenerate into such crushing defeat? Who was this omnipotent Lord with feet of clay? Who was He who couldn't stop Shubha's mind from wandering like leaves blowing in the wind, without direction or purpose? Why couldn't He give Mini an iota of relief and redemption? He that demanded unconditional love – where was His support, His fabled strength? Why didn't He come forward to protect us when we were suffering?

Men, men, men! I was sick of men! Sick and tired of their

egos! Oh, the insecurity of manhood! The sheer brutality of their dominance! Even in the prayer room at Amherst Street there had been no respite. The male gods ruled the roost, from Shib Thakur's overt phallus to Krishno Thakur's cunning flute!

'Dinobondhu, korunashindhu, shaanti sudha diyo chitto chokorey...'

Oh Friend of the Poor! Oh Ocean of Bliss! Soak my thirsty spirit with Your nectar of peace...

But which god had the potency to flood the desert that was my heart? In that wild mirage, shimmering with false hope, who would show me some clemency? Which of them would descend from Paradise and stretch out his hand to protect me? To offer me shelter? To give me the right to speak out my mind? To protest against injustice? To grant me some assurance that things would look up in the future? Would I find that enchanted shore where grief expanded into great waves of merciful emptiness? What cooperation had my father extended to Ma? What unalloyed masculine capabilities had he shown so that she could find peace and tolerance in her husband's home?

I felt so horribly trapped. So inadequate and abandoned. What could I do? What could I tell my daughter so that she would feel less rejected? Could I honestly tell her that through all these years, in my father's home and in Bobby's jail, I had been but an unpaid, dolled-up serf? An absolute coward cringing under male muscle and power? A worthless commodity that could be bought and sold in the marketplace by the whims of pitiless warlords and their masculine authority? Yet, out of utter shame and grief, I chose silence as my weapon and didn't say a word. For what is silence but the pricking voice of one's conscience, the uncertain heartbeat, the withered crackle of dead promises? What *is* silence but imagination's wild hooves and wind-tossed, harrowing memories?

I didn't call Ruchi back; didn't try to placate her or explain what was tearing me apart. The knives stabbing into my flesh were invisible. Ruchi wouldn't be able to see the lacerations. My silence would be my greatest strength. And in the end I knew I'd walk away, uncrushed like a fragile mountain flower.

Perhaps, some day, my daughter would understand and finally forgive me when she read the book I now decided to write.

Soon my manuscript became an obsession – a lover to whom I could return every day and pour out my heart. The hours, unhurried, clung to me as I settled my thoughts on a piece of paper. I had to tell my story. To whom? Perhaps to Ruchi. Or maybe to the twins. Or to the girls they would marry. Perhaps to all the other Mohinis out there who were waiting for a nameless friend to come and hold their hands. I didn't care. I just had to write.

When the house was quiet, I'd sit at my desk and scribble through the better part of the afternoon, letting my pen scratch away. With furious speed I unburdened my mind, writing on and on, unmindful of the cup of coffee I had brewed for myself and then left neglected to turn cold. With each chapter, I wondered what my acquaintances would say. Would Sujata-di ridicule me for exposing my emotions so blatantly? Would the wards at the Sarojini Memorial Women's Union kitchen scoff at me when they heard about the book? Would Ruchi understand my silences, my pain at last? Would Sunny and Vicky be horrified and disown me at the first opportunity? Would Bobby throw me out? This book would be my last baby that I was not ashamed to mother. It would be mine and mine alone, without the stink of righteous legitimacy.

After a lifetime, almost, I wondered where could I find my personal nest. Where was my real home? It was certainly not in the shadows of Late Barrister Bidhushekhor Dotto's dilapidated mansion or in the lockup of Mr Bobby Sen's plush apartment. Perhaps, I'd have to seek it deep within the recesses of my heart, freed from all bondage. I'd have to build it with all my inner reserve so that my existence would no longer depend on the diktats of men and social mores. It would be filled with the scent of my womanhood. Perhaps my home was, after all, my own body that I hadn't yet recognised – unique and impermanent, succumbing to the changing seasons – to the boisterous flowerings in springtime and to the softly falling leaves in autumn – but the only habitation I'd ever know. Nobody could take that away from me. I wouldn't have to measure eternity by the hour as just another cycle that birthed new buds, new leaves and new lives out of what had faded. My need to belong, to be loved and understood, would speak for itself. It would sing its own songs that did not require anybody's approval.

Through writing the book I was absolving my past. I knew at last that no matter how many prisoners men captured or how many times they struck women down, they'd still lose everything to enter the darkness of sleep each night. To enter the womb that gave birth to their sons and bite the dust from which they came and to which they would have to inevitably return.

Perhaps, I was on a journey to try and understand what forced men like my father and Bobby to behave at home in a manner so contrary to their public image. I tried to demystify the paradoxes of a woman's cloistered life in a traditional family and comprehend what compelled men to act like boors. Faces, like Dibaakor-da's paper kites, floated in and out of my mind's sky. And I could hear once more the bells toll in the prayer room. Hear the Chinese pheriwallah entice Dolly-kaakima in his sing-song voice and spread out his pagoda-encrusted pillowcases on the veranda table, or watch the Kashmiri shawl seller display exquisite pashmina stoles for Ma on quiet winter afternoons. With my eyes tightly shut I could see the incense smoking in the prayer room again. The lamps flickering. And the homing doves fill up a long-neglected sky at dusk.

The house where I was born had been full of furtive whispers, peeling off the walls and curling around my childhood like a mongrel's tail. Today, Amherst Street has a different name. Old wine in a new bottle. Even the house is gone; Baba and Shubha are dead. And poor Ma is probably cowering under Mini's verbal blows in the hills. Yet, the return of inconsequential details kept me amused and agitated, as I tried to take apart the world in which women, irrespective of their social status, were forced to conform. I wondered now where had we sisters gone wrong. By having loved? By having been defeatists and hidden the fear of loving in our hearts? By not nudging awake long-lost springtimes? By being unable to handle the repercussions of decisions we never took? By not speaking up against injustice? And again I remembered Kathmandu and its delicious burden that has lain in my heart for so many years, caught between sunlight and the nimble autumn rain, pulling me into a secret valley abloom with wild, unfettered flowers. Old breezes sifted and sighed through my body. And I wrote on and on.

Even as I poured forth my feelings on paper, letting a great fire in my heart finally lie in a heap of embers, Bobby's life suddenly turned topsy-turvy. At one of the board meetings he was asked to supersede his boss. Of course he was over the moon! Now, without any compunction, he'd get all that he had fought for, tooth and nail.

He'd show them the stuff warriors were made of! He'd now be the next chairman at last!

'Of course, he will,' Pesi Readymoney had seethed in visible rage after the board meeting, 'precisely because he's so vulgar!'

At the official party that evening to mark Bobby's imminent promotion, Shireen, with a canapé poised between thumb and forefinger, glided across to congratulate me. The peck flew past my ear and the canapé disappeared into her mouth. Between crunching the crisp slice of toast topped with liver pâté, as if she were masticating poor Bobby's brains, Shireen, the uncrowned arbitress of etiquette, simpered, 'Darling, what good news! So when's it going to be all pukka-pukka and official?'

'I've no idea,' I replied, embarrassed.

Shireen hissed like a viper. Turning to Paddy Roy she whispered, 'At the risk of ruffling apro dikra's feathers, sweetheart, I must admit that Bobby-boy cuts an almost dignified figure against my poor Pesi. Just look at him! He really does have the bluster of a perfect vulgarian, doesn't he?'

But Bobby was let down in less than a week with nothing to show but egg on his face. Pesi wasted no time sending a battery of faxes in connivance with some junior officers to the head office in London, proving without doubt Bobby's underhand deals – his hobnobbing with corrupt bureaucrats and powerful police officials, his illegal flutters in the Stock Exchange and his weakness for accepting bribes and jumping the gun. Decisions changed overnight. At an emergency meeting, the final verdict surprised all the directors. Bobby could only blink and go blank for a few seconds. Had he heard right?

Pesi J. Readymoney had pipped him to the post.

I heard the news from Paddy while on duty for the entire day at the Sarojini Memorial Women's Union office because Cheenee-di had been rushed to the hospital in a coma. That was bad enough. And now this!

I tried calling Bobby several times but Perin Titlusvala took the calls and said he was stuck in an important meeting where she dared not disturb him. I let Sujata-di know what had happened without getting into too many details and took a cab home quite unprepared for what I was going to confront.

The servants were in their quarters, off for the afternoon. Sunny and Vicky were home for their vacation but had gone to the movies with their gang. I slipped into the apartment quietly, only to hear PomPom groaning in the guest room. I tip-toed to the door and did what I should never have done. Today, the details are insufficient and blurred. But as I peeped through the keyhole that day, I wish I had left the house just as soon as I had entered.

Bobby had had neither the time nor the energy to strip.

'Hurry up!' he hissed, fumbling with his fly and the lid of a Charmis Cold Cream bottle he had plucked off the dressing table. 'I've got to rush into a crucial meeting in the next twenty minutes and Mohini may be back any second!'

'Don't, Bobby, don't!' PomPom pleaded, tugging at the strings of her salwar. 'Don't always leave me in a lurch, yaar! Don't make it sound so dirty! Be nice to me, Bobby! Darling, kiss me, please kiss me!'

Bobby only grunted and pushed her down on all fours, savagely entering her from behind – an animal mating a bitch. He saw her vertebrae sticking out through a haze of fine golden down and became frenetic. Thrusting harder, he growled, 'You third-rate randi! You whore! Do you really think I love you? Do you really think I'm going to break up my marriage for you? No chance, baby! No chance!'

His hips grated against her buttocks, hurting out such

godforsaken ecstasy that she shouted, 'Harder, you bastard, harder! I don't give a shit about your marriage. She's such a bloody saint, your wife – is this how you do it to her too? Is this how you ride her when I'm not around? Does she like it this way? Does she?'

To shut her up Bobby came in a series of urgent spasms, drawing his hand over her mouth and squeezing out the last drop of semen before collapsing like a house of cards. She bit into his palm, struggling against his grip, and whispered profanities in a stifled voice. It was all over in a few, furious minutes and, panting, he pushed her away in cold revulsion.

'Fuck off! Fuck off, you filthy slut!' he hissed, cleaning up with her soft chiffon dupatta. Then brushing back his hair and pulling up his zipper he left, banging the door behind him, unmindful of her whimpers as she lay, defeated, curled up on the floor.

Bobby was in such a hurry, perspiring profusely, that he hadn't noticed me, trembling and fixed to the thick curtains hanging across the divider that separated the living area from the balcony. He hurried to the main door and was out in a trice. I thought I was going to faint. I felt like throwing up.

I wrenched myself away and ran down the stairs. The echo of my footsteps seemed deafening. I was mortified that neighbours would pour out of their apartments any minute now and catch me before I could flee. They'd discover my shame. Laugh into my face. Clap their hands and scream, 'You stupid idiot! Didn't you know? Didn't you know what was going on? Didn't you have the common sense to quit before it was so late? What a fool you are, Mohini! What a bloody fool!'

Hot tears poured down my face as I thought of the twins and the fresh lies I'd have to invent in order to break free. What was I to do now? How was I to face the world? Through choking, stifling sobs I looked back on those times when I had contended with the sly smirks plastered on several faces at the club and tried to ignore the insinuations. But now… O dear God! What was I to do now? Now that I had actually *seen* the filth?

I somehow managed to walk to the Victoria Memorial and sink into a bench, my heart beating wildly. I was quite unaware that two hours had passed while I sat there trying to untangle my thoughts. There I was, Mrs Bobby Sen – indefatigable, immaculately turned out but, alas, irredeemably insulted and kicked in the gut. The pain was unbearable. What relevance did those years of weighing lies and defeats in dainty teaspoons hold? How would I bear such mortification? Who could help me out?

Divorce! The idea hit me straight in the chest like a well-aimed bullet. I'd have to swallow my pride and ask for help. Perhaps I should seek Montoo Mullick's assistance. I could even go and confess to Sunanda-di. All I knew was that, somehow, I would have to protect myself. Yet I continued to sit, confused, watching the sun sink in a heap of useless embers. After all these years, would I finally be able to burn the bridges I should have long before?

Bobby came home very late that night, drunk and irascible, cursing Pesi Readymoney. He immediately locked himself in the guest room where he had copulated with PomPom. I was unable to confront him, accuse him, shout him down. In the deathly silence of night my blood froze and by the time I woke up with a splitting headache, Bobby had left for the golf course.

Then, before I had decided my next course of action, the telephone shrieked.

'Mohini, do sit down. I've some awful news. You've got to be brave,' Paddy's voice came in a crackle of confusion. I was walking through a nightmare as he told me Bobby was gone – felled once and for all on his beloved golf course just as he was tee-ing off from the ninth hole. I could see him laugh and say something suitably rude before collapsing. Only Bobby had the audacity to do this to me.

As always, Mr Bobby Sen had called the shots. He had booted me below the belt by dropping dead without prior notice. I was left totally ill-equipped to feel any sort of grief. It was a thunderous shock for he belonged so much to life. To a life I had detested. To a life brimming with lies and trickery and betrayal. To a life the world applauded for awfully wrong reasons but didn't have the courage to challenge. And now Bobby's laughter rang through it all, mocking and egging me on. 'What will you do now? Face the wolves alone, Miss Self-righteous Twit! Face them alone and let them tear into you!'

A part of my life came to an abrupt halt. I rushed into the bedroom in a fit of frenzy and didn't dare to pause till I had reached the bed and sat down with a thud. Then, breathless, I grasped at my heart in an inadequate attempt to make it stop beating in such furious spurts. I felt horribly betrayed. Surely Bobby should have warned me well in advance! Given me some indication, however cryptic; some inconspicuous signal so that I was not left so utterly unprepared!

The phones started shrieking persistently. Soon, a motley crowd swept into the living room, clutching bunches of white tuberoses or carrying ominous-looking wreaths. The alarming eloquence of death had levelled all walls of resentment. There was a mad rush to be the first to offer a string of insincere condolences and then just as hastily scurry away. There I was, gripping the polished head of my nuptial bed and wondering where I could escape to, freed from the debris that had suddenly fallen all around me, and there they were, waiting to sooth me with their sly licks of sympathy even as Bobby was laughing his head off somewhere!

All I had wanted was a peaceful summer holiday in Kalimpong

where Mini was now working as headmistress of a new school. Sunny and Vicky wouldn't have minded had I slipped away to be with her for a week or two. Ma, thank God, would be spared the immediate shock, though I was already trying to phrase in my mind a telegram to her that would explain the truth adequately, without upsetting her too much.

Just when I was on the brink of taking a grip on my life, Bobby had spoilt it all and was having the last snigger. Damn Bobby! He had no right doing this to me!

Much as I hated the thought, I knew I'd have to face the visitors in a while, once I had changed into a crisp Tangail sari that looked sufficiently white and woebegone. Something non-committal, perhaps with a black, fish-scale border and just a few discreet florets in brown or purple scattered over its bleached expanse. Anything beyond the predictable, especially in shades of red, would bring on instant heart attacks! The burden of widowhood was too fresh, too raw just yet. But at the back of my mind I knew I would have to get used to its mundane obligations.

I'd have to find the strength, somehow, to tell the visitors what had happened and how much I appreciated their concern. I'd have to, however vestigially, give in to the preconceived demands of my new role, at best an infuriating bother and at worst a bloody nuisance. My exasperation would seethe within me, undiscovered. I'd have to sit through the torture of facing the mourners, smiling vapidly and blinking back my tears, letting the little herd get the better of me with their empty sympathy and clacking tongues. And just as I would think up ways of demolishing the crowd, Babulal, the Oriya bearer, in his smart white uniform and red cummerbund, would interrupt the act by bringing in the tea and very discreetly show the steaming cups around, and I'd foolishly sip its scalding comfort and come hurtling back to earth.

I saw thin strips of sunlight fall across the floor, as another round of visitors trooped in. Sunny stood bathed in a pool of gold and Vicky floundered in the shadows. Poor boys! What a way to begin their holidays! And they wouldn't ever know the truth! Thank heavens, Ruchi was not around. Sunny had tried locating her all morning but, as a professional vocalist, she was on a tour somewhere in Germany.

I rose with great difficulty and walked into the study, wondering how Ruchi would react now that her father was actually dead. She had despised the daily bickerings and the nightly arguments that would invariably leave my nose red with the friction of sodden tissues. The furnace in our home, so assiduously stoked by Bobby, had kept Ruchi in a perpetual state of apprehension. Then, one night, when she had silently watched me move out of the master bedroom and slip into the spare guestroom, whimpering in quiet defeat, she had gone up to Bobby, still loitering in the corridor, and hissed quietly, 'I wish you were dead!'

Now that her father had so conveniently obliged, would it prick Ruchi's conscience?

I went to the writing table and blindly pulled at one of the drawers where my manuscript lay in an untidy pile. For a moment, looking at those pages filled with the past, I wondered at my naiveté. I also doubted what had made me remember and record with such unflinching force the toll of all those years that had transformed me into an absolute coward.

Filled with remorse, I tried reining in my emotions. Tried pushing away all thought so that the throbbing ache in my temples would subside. Impulsively, I tugged at a neatly handwritten sheet of paper. A photograph fell into my lap instead. I stared at the picture through a fresh spate of tears, letting the sharp stabs of pain take their own sweet time to wound me. Ruchi smiled back, her dark eyes gleaming. My Ruchi was always there by my side, even if she had gone away.

Above the hum of the air-conditioner I could hear Calcutta's corporate world susurrating, waiting for Bobby's body to arrive from the hospital. I knew the twins were standing at the corridor to receive the mourners. At twenty, they were strapping young men and extremely good-looking. But the blow of having lost their father was shamelessly visible.

Still in my hideout, I could spy on the charade. I noticed Pesi and Shireen enter, almost on cue, with well-rehearsed expressions of shock. Vicky shook Pesi's hand and Sunny suffered Shireen's peck. They talked awkwardly and in hushed undertones. And when they had nothing more to say, Pesi and Shireen left.

Then came Queenie, envying my luck, I am sure. She kept patting her bobbed hair she had recently dyed a shocking blond.

'Have you had breakfast, darlings?' she asked. 'Even in sorrow we have to be fortified.'

Vicky frowned, remembering that he had got the news just as he was about to attack his fluffy cheese omelette.

'Ma will be with us in a while,' he said. 'Why don't you go in?'

'Bugger Bobby,' muttered Queenie under her breath.

A series of loud sobs came from the distance. It had to be that vamp, PomPom, creating a scene. Ruchi would have told her to shut up at once. If I had had the strength, I'd have kicked her out without any qualms. The twins were more forgiving. They let her snivel for a while before escorting her in. I boiled with sheer frustration and could feel my blood pressure shooting up. How dare she walk into my house after that sordid afternoon with Bobby! What bloody cheek! The shameless slut! The ignominious memory of their filthy coupling hung like a shroud over my heart. Yet there she was, sniffling and pushing her way into our living room, stealing the limelight.

As I tried to get a grip on my nerves, Purnendu Mitra's aromatic tobacco preceded his entry. He had outdone his show of grief in an off-white khadi panjaabi and a crisp black khadi designer dhuti that could be easily slipped on and zipped up without the bother of tying it the traditional way. A slatternly, middle-aged Bengali seamstress in collaboration with a homosexual tailor had pushed hard to make these dhutis trendy. Soon, the city's Brown Sahibs decided to go 'all Bengali' with a vengeance during condolence meetings and Durga Pujo soirees. Chewing on his pipe, Purnendu now clutched at his dhuti's fanfold and thumped Sunny on his shoulder.

'What a tragedy,' he muttered. 'What an unnecessary tragedy! I was with your father at the Bengal Club two nights ago. Never thought he'd die this morning...'

Shobeeta, of course, began chattering without preamble, pushing Purnendu aside.

'What happened, my boys? What *happened*? Oh, I can't get over this! I am still in a state of shock! I can't even begin to imagine what Mohini is going through. Was it a heart attack or cerebral thrombosis? Poor girl! She doesn't deserve this. *Bhogobaaner ki shaasti!* Did he drop dead at the seventh hole? Can you imagine, I had just put the frying pan on the fire and was about to fry some chicken. Mrs Venugopal had given me an old family recipe. Chettinad Murgi. Absolutely delicious. Have you tried it, Vicky? It's just superb. I'll make some for you as soon as the mourning period is over and send it through the driver. That reminds me. Do you know your grandfather's gotro? The priest will need it, shona muni, when he's performing the last rites.'

Sunny and Vicky knew that talking to Shobeeta was like opening a series of Babushka dolls. The more excited she became, the more she developed a concentric series of personae, each of which fitted perfectly inside the other, waiting to burst out of their shells.

She wrung her hands helplessly and continued, 'And then, just as I was about to mix the gravy with the coconut milk, the phone rang. Can you imagine? I thought it was Mrs Venugopal and asked Panchhi to answer the call. You know Panchhi, the maid, don't you? She insists on calling you "babalogs" even now. Stupid idiot, she's just gone and got pregnant again. For the sixth time, if you please! I told her she must get her husband to agree to a vasectomy, never mind if he has to come all the way from Barabanki. But do you think these men will listen? All of them – uneducated rascals! And then, she comes and begins bawling at the top of her voice and I keep asking her, "What's happened, Panchhi? What's *happened?*" And she tells me between sobs, "The Babalogs' daddy-ji is dead! Babalogs' Mummy-ji has terrible ill luck! Hai bhogobaan! Hai bhogobaan! What will she do now?" And I get such a jolt that I forget all about the Chettinad chicken and almost fall into the fire!'

Jahnavi Somani arrived just then to divide attention. Pushing her designer shades over her crown, she squeezed out a tear or two and simpered, 'Oh babies, what do I say to comfort you? Poor, poor Bobby-da! We were supposed to plan the biggest PR campaign next week for our latest packaged teas. And now, this?' Shobeeta nodded and would have broken into another interminable round of meanderings had Purnendu not intervened.

'Jahnavi, my dear, I need to discuss a little bit of work with you?' he said. 'A new client needs help. I recommend you see him soon.'

'I'd love to,' Jahnavi smiled, forgetting her show of grief and brightening up at the smell of moonlighting and money. 'Can we meet tomorrow?'

'Boys, boys, boys,' boomed Montoo Mullick, striding towards the twins with his arms outstretched. 'This is the most awful news I've had in years. I'm so completely shattered. Oh my god, my heart goes out to you, my loves. My heart goes out to poor, poor Mohini.'

Quickly swooping down on Vicky, Montoo Mullick worked his paws like lightning across his victim's buttocks.

'What happened?' he asked in suppressed delight.

'A massive heart attack,' informed Sunny, watching his brother turn red.

'Where? At home?'

'No Montoo-mama,' said Sunny. 'As he was about to tee-off.'

'At the golf-course? Oh my god! And then?'

'And then? Nothing! He died on his way to Woodlands.'

'Terrible! Terrible!' Montoo Mullick repeated like a parrot.

'You better go in,' commanded Vicky, blushing and letting his gaze fleetingly pass across Montoo's eyes frozen for a split second in an audacious wink.

I retreated hurriedly into the bedroom, blind with mortification. But a soft knock on the door shook me out of my stupor.

'Sylvia?' I whispered.

'Yes, it's me, Mohini. May I come in?'

She hurried across to hug me. For a moment we stood locked in each other's arms, letting the tears flow.

Sylvia held me by the shoulders, smiled and said, 'Get ready to face the world, you dumb cluck! The wolves are waiting!'

'I will, in a moment,' I murmured. 'How did you know?'

'Vicky called. So did Paddy. From the nursing home,' said Sylvia.

'Oh,' I sighed, turning away and slumping into a rocking chair.

Sylvia was on her annual visit from London to see her mother. Her brothers, Ian and Jimmy, had left Ripon Street years ago. Ian had found a job as a welder in Canada and Jimmy had made the sea his home. Their mother had to be packed off to the old people's asylum run by the Sisters of the Poor on Lower Circular Road because she did not want to live abroad. Initially, I had tried visiting Auntie Nellie once a month. But within a year her memory had started to crumble.

'Why have you come? Is it Christmas? Are the boys back home?' she'd demand. 'Why haven't they put up the tree yet? Where are the buntings? The candles I got from New Market? Oh dear, oh dear, who'll bake the cakes now? Has Charlotte Guzman supplied the wine? I had ordered *jamun* wine, darling. Not *raisin*! And has the khana-coolie come with the sausage curry? Have shepherds washed their socks by night? Or are they still watching their flocks? Ha, ha, ha… what a joke! Mohini, you shouldn't come so often, my girl, your mother gets so bloody takraari over the phone men! And now Sylvia hasn't turned up from school. She'll be my death, that girl!'

I had found it hard to confront poor Auntie Nellie going to pieces. Afterwards, once the twins arrived, my visits became infrequent. Sylvia understood. Sylvia knew everything. She held my hand now, letting me weep. Then she walked to the cabinet wedged between the windows and brought out two glasses and a half-empty bottle of Glenmorangie she knew I kept hidden there.

'You'll need it,' she said, pouring out a peg. I didn't protest.

'Has Mini called?' Sylvia asked, taking a tentative sip.

'No. We haven't told her yet. Ma's with her.'

'And Ruchi?'

'The boys are trying to locate her.'

'I heard Shobeeta's harangue. Cheers!'

I turned my face away.

'You'll have to face the whole shebang sooner or later, my girl.

Bellboys of yesteryears, Burra sahibs of today! When do you want to come down and meet the whole caboodle?'

'In a bit,' I sighed and took a long sip. The whisky warmed my gullet.

'I'll nip out and see what's happening,' said Sylvia. 'Just give me a shout when you're ready.'

Back and forth, back and forth I rocked gently, trying to concentrate on the ache slowly coiling around my head. Here I was, widowed and wasted, and they kept coming through the main door, enveloped in perfume and perfidy, to pay their condolences.

How was I to know, wading through all the tensions, that life and death are too resolute, too implacable to be mere accidents? That nothing could be added or taken away from the eternal scheme of things? Neither the beauty nor the degradation; neither the innocence nor the obscenity. Who could you blame for the allegiances or the betrayals? For the privileges or the poverty? The loosely threaded sentences like strings of pearls whispered in love or hate that could mend or snap relationships? All the worthless, devious games would come to a sudden end one day – the lies, the ruses, the regrets and retributions when we would return, ashes to ashes, shattered and empty-handed. It was all so magically, brutally pre-ordained; every story a soft eclipse written in the stars.

'Ma,' said Vicky, tiptoeing in with the cordless phone. 'We've just managed to get through to Ruchi didi. Will you speak to her?'

'Ma?' over the crackle of the phone I heard my daughter's voice reaching out to me all the way from Frankfurt. 'Ma, are you there?'

'Yes, Ruchi,' I said.

'Oh, Ma,' Ruchi's voice was unbearably heavy.

'He died the way he'd lived, darling. Impetuously, and without a care.'

'What happened?'

'Collapsed on the golf course this morning. A massive heart attack.'

There was a long pause. A stifled sob. Time stood still.

'Hello?' I said.

'Hello, Ma? Hello? Are you there?' asked Ruchi.

'Yes, darling. They did everything to save him. But it was so futile…' I was aware of the tears crowding my eyes.

'Did they take him to the hospital?'

'Yes, darling. But he didn't give us a chance.'

'Ma,' sobbed Ruchi without a care. 'Ma. Are you alright?'

I bit my lips.

'I'll get by, darling,' I whispered. 'Don't worry.'

'Ma, I know what you're going through. I understand. I love you,' said Ruchi, thousands of miles away from home.

'I know. You're my first born. I know that you know, my baby. How's Guy?'

'He's fine, Ma. He's very upset. He sends you his love.'

Another pause. Then Ruchi said, 'I'm glad the twins are home.'

'So am I,' I said.

'I'll come on the first available flight, Ma,' Ruchi's voice was very faint now, almost broken.

'Are you sure?'

'Of course I'll come,' said Ruchi over her useless tears. 'I'll let you know tonight by which airlines.'

'Alright, darling.'

'Bye, Ma, just hang in there!'

'I will. Bye…'

In the drawing room, those who had gathered to witness the drama were sorely disappointed. The emotions were too hushed, too civilised. They were dying to see some high-voltage histrionics they could bitch about later. None of them had imagined I would sweep in like a tragic heroine, red-eyed but in complete control.

The servants had pushed the heavy sofas against the walls and spread spotless white sheets over the carpets. The curtains had been drawn, the stage had been set, the farce was about to begin. Some of the crystal vases spilled over with fresh tuberoses, white and smelling of death. Their fragrance mingled with a bunch of incense sticks burning on a side table, discreetly out of sight, crowed in a delicate brass holder. The Ganesh Pynes and the Anjoli Ela Menons remained undisturbed.

Someone coughed. In a patch of shadow a solitaire sparkled. A sniff was hurriedly drowned into a perfumed handkerchief. The women were dressed in pale French chiffons. They refused to take off their shades, wary of letting their gloating become public too soon. Most of the men had changed into white kurta-pyjamas. But, inevitably, the kurtas had started to crush around their ample buttocks.

Pretty Burman, sans eye makeup and in her best tragedy queen mode, leaned over to have a quick word with the RajRani. 'Terrible! Terrible!' she whispered. 'Bobby shouldn't have done this to her!'

Sunanda Devi grinned and whispered back, 'Are you still fucking your Anglo-Indian gigolo?'

Stung, Pretty sighed and turned away. Sunanda Devi gave her a sidelong glance, unscrewed her lipstick and carefully applied a fresh coat.

The mourners waited in anticipation to see me perform my swansong. Of course they'd forget me the minute my use was over! With Bobby gone, there'd be no more parties, no more business deals, no more drinking till the wee hours. Why, I would have to leave the company house within the next six months and move to Southern Avenue. At least Bobby had had the wisdom to invest in an apartment. I would be comfortable but completely anonymous, my circle of so-called friends drastically whittled down to a handful. There'd be no distractions; no large galas and junkets, with people looking the same, talking the same, drinking the same gin-slings and planters' punches and gossiping about things that would not affect me, now that I was stripped and widowed and exposed for the world to snigger at and tut-tut about. I'd continue to sit on a few philanthropic committees dabbling with raped women and spastic children, trying to keep my back straight and nodding my head or raising my index finger every time a resolution was passed. But beyond infrequent appearances during lunchtime at the Saturday Club veranda and a few more at charity fetes, I'd be swept under the social carpet. The middle-class mob would, inevitably, consume me with alacrity.

Startled like a bunch of sparrows, the mourners stared at me framed against the door. They had been so absorbed in their whispering and gossiping that they hadn't seen me enter. Now they didn't know what to say to me. I must have looked so defenceless and young. Condolences were harder to handle than congratulations, particularly as I felt they were more insincere. But I was ready for the onslaught.

PomPom lowered her eyes and let out a sob, the bitch! Pretty Burman followed. Queenie smiled weakly. Den Dhingra appeared thoroughly out of his depth standing at the far end of the room with a bunch of Bobby's office colleagues, ill-at-ease and with their hands carelessly folded over their crotches. Shobeeta Mitra, about to launch into a fresh monologue, was savagely reduced to a yelp by Purnendu as he clasped her wrist in an iron grip.

'Thank you for coming,' I said, folding my hands together. Sylvia sprang to her feet and guided me to a chair.

'They are bringing the body in the next hour,' announced Den. 'Paddy just called. Goli Singh and Sammy are on their way.'

The body?

How suddenly could a living, laughing, quarrelling, ambitious, deceiving, egotistical person – so alive and kicking – become an object without dignity and gender?

The body! That is what Bobby had been reduced to in minutes, freed of all ties.

No more the flesh-and-blood father of my children, no more the hot-tempered husband whom I never knew, no more the devious, conniving, single-minded Bobby who had made such a song and dance about becoming chairman. It all seemed so vulgar, now that Bobby was dead! Bobby, without his artillery of arrogance and sarcasm, withering contempt, sharp irascibility and full-throated roarings. They were bringing home the body – an empty shell – with a heart that had stopped beating and a temper and libido forever cooled. A carcass that would be strung with wilting flowers; with scraps of inconsequential remembrances. And drenched temporarily in inconsequential tears shed by his crowd who'd go on and on about his passion for golf and single malt whiskies and dirty jokes. Who'd dole out free advice to the twins over cups of tea and then, leaving the sandwiches untouched, peck my cheek and disappear into Calcutta's corporate mist.

Bobby was now a silhouette soon to be thrown to the fire. He was half-a-dozen sentences and just a crooked smile. But I was already losing out on the details, unable to drag back all those silly, funny, foolish little things he did or said – the way he'd stub out his cigarettes, the way he'd glare at me after an argument, the way he'd suck in his tummy before walking into a party. I couldn't for the life of me recall whether he slept on his belly or sipped water throughout his meals; whether he ever said a silent prayer after his bath. Whether his formal suits were brown or grey.

A jumble of faces rose before my eyes. But who were they? Who were these strangers who called themselves Bobby's friends? Men who had doubled-crossed their bosom buddies by helping themselves to their wives or getting a foot one rung higher on the commercial ladder. Ladies of leisure who had blasphemed their philandering husbands when they were alive, only to change their tune within weeks of their passing away. Mothers who had turned their children into confused, vulnerable drug addicts, only because they didn't find time to tell them that they were always unconditionally loved. Nouveau riche wives dripping with diamonds who pointed fingers at other nouveau riche wives, dripping, perhaps, with bigger diamonds, for snaffling their fiancés hours before the wedding, blind to the fact that their husbands now spent sultry afternoons with their favourite toy-boys or bimbettes. So-called entrepreneurs who exploited poor village women. Quasi fashionistas who shamelessly stole designs. Society ladies who ran some of the city's best little whore-houses in the suburbs for the exclusive pleasure of influential, pot-bellied ministers. Shrewd political sidekicks who changed colour with the times, pimping for those who came into power. Model consorts who had mastered the ancient art of mithridatism made popular by the Maurya kings – our local bunch of Visha Kanyas, toxic and lurking in the dark, out to poison unsuspecting victims.

What a menagerie! What a delectable display of fiercely plucked eyebrows, Paloma Picasso shades, painted lips and polished nails that would pounce on me like rapacious vultures given half a chance! They were all there, sitting in front of me like ruins – a pathetic, cunning, inconsiderate lot, without a thought for the morrow.

All I could see were hidden welts and festering gashes. I could see women trying to catch my eye. Women who had been dumped by their husbands after twenty-six years of so-called 'happy' marriages. I could see men who had lived their lives in constant subterfuge, trying to keep things smooth between spouse and mistress. Yes, they were all there – the gamblers and the dipsomaniacs; the literati and the self-styled illustrious; the drama queens and the devout, wearing their permanent blinkers; the nymphos and the nihilists; the good, the bad and the ugly. The tawdry jet-set of Calcutta.

I had been trapped in their snare. Trapped in their petty affairs and jealousies and all the sordid tales they liked to spread about so-called friends the minute backs were turned. Now I waited for them to come up and spout empty words of commiseration, telling me how they'd stand by my side through my troubles. I waited to smart under their unspoken taunts. I also waited for the wreaths to be laid on the hearse before Vicky and Sunny took the body away.

The body!

One part of me felt like shouting and saying, 'Don't let's do this to him! He'll really have none of this! Please, at least let Bobby go with dignity!' But only silence collided with my unuttered cries.

Bobby. Husband. Father. Lover. Cheat. And now Body!

I was suddenly exhausted. And I didn't give a damn. Somehow I'd swim through the coming years, empty and filled with regret. I'd stop going to PomPom's to colour my hair and allow the grey to take over. I'd succumb to the stillness in my life once the whispers faded. I'd let my world fall softly apart, like the notes of those songs Ruchi liked to sing.

The cortege finally left the house over murmurs of 'Who's got the death certificate?', 'Have the newspapers been informed?', 'Will you get Vicky and Sunny to change into dhutis?', 'Do they mourn for eleven days or thirteen?' I stood with my nervous sons on either side, watching Bobby go away forever. There was such a gaunt expression on my face, such a mask, that the mourners must have been forced to envy my self-possession. Paddy waited for the twins who were silently weeping by my side. I patted their shoulders and told them to do what needed to be done. Faithful Paddy Uncle would accompany them to the crematorium. And they'd return in a few hours with just an urnful of wasted ashes.

As my parting gift, I had hung a garland of memories around Bobby's neck. Now I stood before the mirror, staring at myself, unimpeachable at last. Gently, as if I were putting a baby to sleep, I took off the thin noa-bangle wrapped in gold foil from my wrist, the symbol of my marriage, and placed it in a drawer in the dressing table. I found a handkerchief and deliberately wiped the vermilion spot off my forehead.

All my life I had been somebody's daughter or somebody's wife. Now I was simply Mohini. Now I was free. But what was I to do with my freedom? Where could I go without being followed by Bobby's shadow? I didn't want to think about my future right then. I didn't want to think about Vicky and Sunny going back to their respective universities in America. I didn't want to think about the bother of shifting house and setting up a new life in the frugal little flat on Southern Avenue or getting swallowed by the multitudinous crowds at Gariahat. Would I be able to afford a car? An air-conditioner during the gruelling months of summer? A shampoo and blow dry? Would I be able to afford all that I had, so far, taken for granted? How would it be now to live a life of truth after all these years of lies, I wondered – the truth of knowing that I had been reduced to an object of pity, trying to be a good daughter and a good wife.

Would I be able to face the reality of living alone? Of trying to make friends with new neighbours who'd whisper surreptitiously among themselves, nodding their heads and clicking their tongues at the Bara Mem who had suddenly been demoted? Would some of them find out about PomPom? Would they laugh, seeing me going up and down the lift in a crushed sari, wiping sweat from my face and carrying a loaf of bread or a plastic basket with wilting vegetables? Would I shed bitter tears night after night for all that was gone? Would I be able to challenge the looks of empty sympathy, the empty promises of visits that would never materialise? Perhaps the girls at Sarojini Memorial Women's Union would help me forget my predicament. And perhaps, when evenings descended without any distractions, I'd write another book. New stories crafted from my imagination.

Please, God, save me from the tedium of widowhood!

Perchance I'd dream of my childhood at Amherst Street. I'd recall the kite-flying sessions with Dibaakor-da flooded by soft autumn sunlight; the laughter ringing down the corridors during Durga Pujo, chased by the heady fragrance of incense. I'd remember our card sessions on sweltering summer Sundays with Dolly-kaakima ruling the roost. On wet monsoon afternoons I'd recollect the aroma of hot khichuri drizzled with ghee served for lunch, accompanied by pumpkin fritters and fried eelish fish. There'd be Ma in the kitchen again as if by some miracle, ordering Beejeepishi to put more coconut into the stuffing for patishapta pancakes. And there'd be Baba in his study, lording it over and holding court, surrounded by his faithful clients. Oh, I'd bring to mind so many insignificant details that had made me laugh and cry! But most of all, I'd remember my school days at Loreto Convent dominated by the nuns. There'd be magic now in the mundane past, stirred by a flutter of wings in the marble birdbath. And I'd wait for Ruchi.

Ruchi would come in the next couple of days from France,

bringing with her the gift of her wonderful songs. She'd sing them for me in the hush of twilight and soothe my hurts.

'Amaar shokol dukher prodeep jeley dibosh geley korbo nibeydon/ Amaar byathaar pujo hoy ni shomaapon...'

I'll light the lamp of all my sorrows and at the close of day make you humbly know/ That it has not yet ended, this worship of my woes...

Ruchi, my first-born – my poor, neglected Rooch-Pooch – she'd finally make friends with me. She was a woman. She'd understand. And, together, we'd walk away from the past, hand in hand, leaving behind the menacing shadows.

We'd watch raindrops dribble down the windowpane on dark monsoon afternoons. And against the rustle of indiscernible pinions we'd fly to undiscovered seashores where rainbows would bridge the silent distances. We'd visit places we had not visited in years – vineyards and churches in Bellagio overlooking Lake Como; the Riviera at Nice where Isadora Duncan had snapped her neck, letting her silk scarf get entangled in the open-spoked wheels of her boyfriend's Buggatti; the university town of Heidelberg in the Rhine Rift Valley where General Patton had died in the US Army Hospital; the theatres in London where, way back in 1895, *The Importance of Being Earnest* had played to a packed audience even as Oscar Wilde was accused of sodomy by the Marquess of Queensbury; the Musee Rodin in Paris where that famous kiss still stands forever frozen in marble; Las Ventas during the festivities of San Isidro, where Hemingway's heroines would watch bull-fights; and the Spanish Steps – gosh! How could I forget the Spanish Steps in Rome, where a debutant Audrey Hepburn had licked at a gelato in the company of the gorgeous Gregory Peck? With luck, we'd go everywhere, sitting on our rocking chairs, here in the bedroom, nursing a drink and allowing the shadows to lengthen.

I caught myself nodding in the mirror and stopped, shaken. I had a horror for gestures that old women made in confirmation of their private decisions. Had I grown old already? Had the wrinkles begun their onslaught? My heart started beating furiously. I wondered whether I had already suffered my exile in hell. Was I done with the burning? Would God spare me now? Spare me the anguish at long last?

A voice from nowhere abruptly asked, 'As a conventional spouse, what did you do with your life?'

And I wiped my tears and whispered, 'I learnt to endure.'

'Was that enough?' the voice demanded.

'Perhaps not,' I said, 'but I have my life before me now. And I have the gift of light and dreams and music.'

'But what about the compromises?'

'I'll learn to ignore them and live anew. I'll put the past behind me. For the past is over and done with. Only some beautiful memories linger through the darkness. And I'll make them my talisman, my beacon of hope and joy!'

If I were to succumb to the flute again, to the notes of the flute from long ago, the pain would lessen. But pain was always a prelude to love, I reasoned. Pain was so real that it was the only thing you could ever trust. And with every invisible bruise on my wrist left all those years ago by a bunch of broken glass bangles, with every gentle laceration from the past, memories of an enchanted, long-forgotten autumn returned to haunt me – haunt me and hurt me awake with its marvellous echoes snatched out of oblivion. The snow-covered peaks, the gentle landscape, a road lazily winding through the hills, the bustling marketplace – why did they seem so real once more? And yet so hallucinatory? Would I have to go through life endlessly searching? Endlessly looking for a face I could barely remember?

While Sunny and Vicky slept fitfully in their bedroom after the funeral and the last visitors had departed, slowly, very slowly, as if drawn to a magnet, I returned to my desk and started writing again.

EPILOGUE

'What though the radiance
Which was once so bright
Be now for ever taken from my sight,
Though nothing can bring back the hour
Of splendour in the grass,
Of glory in the flower,
We will grieve not, rather find
Strength in what remains behind...'

—WILLIAM WORDSWORTH

Three years after Bobby died and I settled into the apartment on Southern Avenue, I finished with the book and put away my manuscript, uncertain whether I wanted to share it with the world after all. Then Sylvia came to Calcutta for the summer and decided to stay with me. One evening, my impetuosity took over and shyly I placed the sheaves of paper before her.

'My, my!' Sylvia exclaimed, looking at me, amused. 'You've actually written a book!'

But when she started reading the typed sheets, she couldn't help her tears from spilling over.

'Darling, this is too good to lie neglected. I'm taking this back with me to England. I've very dear friends in a literary agency and I want to show it to them.'

Within six months events escalated into a veritable storm.

It started one sultry afternoon when I got a phone call from the London agency where Sylvia had placed my book. A young woman, with the very unusual name, Petronella Kavanaugh, introduced herself and then proceeded to enthusiastically talk about my story that had unexpectedly become a literary novelty. How was I to tell her that it was only about my mundane life; my humdrum joys and sorrows? I had neither taken any creative writing classes nor intended to share my innermost emotions with the public. All stories, after all, were about love and pain and redemption, and people liked to tell them in their own, eccentric ways.

Ms Kavanaugh gushed on and on. Not only had they loved what I had written but the agency had also negotiated its sale at a considerable sum with one of the biggest publishing houses that boasted a huge distribution network in America, Europe and Australia. I needed to sign the necessary contracts and the managing director of Morris & Gordon was flying out to India straight from New York the following weekend to meet me.

I was completely thrown. Would the world really understand my feelings? Would the children be happy? What difference would this make to them, my life being shared on such a public platform?

That Saturday I found myself hurrying in a car sent for me to keep the appointment made by Petronella Kavanaugh. Soon I was ushered into one of the plush offices at the Business Centre of the Taj Bengal by a smart young woman from the reception desk. And before I could catch my breath, I was staring at the tall frame of a man who stood with his back to me, gazing out at a small patch of sunlight flooding the garden that lay beyond the window.

My legs suddenly melted. I had this terrible impulse to run away and lick my wounds in peace. How I wished I hadn't allowed Sylvia to bully me into this! Of what worth would my tale be to this outsider or to anyone for that matter – anonymous readers who'd flip through the pages, temporarily curious, and then carelessly tuck me away on a dusty bookshelf once they had gloated over my life so ruthlessly disemboweled? How many in that faceless crowd would truly understand the isolation and agony of being part of a travesty the world lauds as the corporate El Dorado? Was this stripping of my middle-class honour, this uninhibited exposé, going to be my ultimate karma? My passport to fame?

Yet, beyond the millions of doubts assailing my mind, I saw the mountains again – the breathtaking, snow-capped mountains. I quickly tried to think of something else – anything else – fighting the enormous fug of emotion building up inside me. I tried to concentrate on the plants in the room, the paintings, the patterns on the carpet.

But I could only see a road veer sharply around the hills, climbing higher and higher, past fields yellow with mustard flowers dancing in the breeze, fleeing from the present like a lover on the run.

'You've written a wonderful book, Mrs Sen,' said the stranger. 'It has moved me deeply. But we need to edit it further. Where would you like to work with our editor?'

'I'd like to go to the mountains,' I whispered, as if in a dream. 'I'd like to go to Kathmandu.'

He turned. And in that insufficient light I saw him smile.

'Would you, Moh?' he asked softly, and in a flash I could see those blue eyes again – those cobalt blue eyes, reflecting his boundless energy even though there was a hint of grey on his sideburns now, and tiny wrinkles around the mouth.

When Bobby had filled the parting in my hair with sindur at the end of the wedding ceremony, I had tried to kill a love that refused to die. That love was replaced by loneliness. Loneliness in the garb of a name, a secret voice, a constant presence. Today, after a lifetime, or so it seemed to me, I dared to give it utterance.

'Paul!'

Pushing aside the soft mist, I was able to see him clearly now, standing before me in a rhombus of light, as the long-forgotten scent of wet wood shavings on a crowded lane in Thamel overtook my senses.

He came over and held my hand. There was so much I wanted to say but I became hopelessly tongue-tied. Was this the miracle I had been waiting for all my life? Miracles could happen, couldn't they? I wanted to trust in miracles. In the miraculous dreams Ma used to speak about – the unfathomable visions peopled with caparisoned elephants and magnificent palaces and temples and gods and goddesses with impassive, painted faces. Ma lived on hope, in the belief that it would all turn out fine for us girls some day. Yet she had been betrayed. Today, I wanted to change all that. I wanted to embrace my fate and humbly accept that what was happening to my life was, indeed, a prophecy; an intricate culmination of events that was most magically predestined.

Once upon a time, in a kingdom by the mountains, there was Moh, young and madly in love. There was enchantment. There was thrill. And there was wonder and innocence and beauty. Today, after a lifetime, there was just Mohini. She was middle-aged and tired, with sallow skin, crow's feet and streaks of white in her hair. And she was unable to think clearly.

Maybe, at long last, the fog would clear and I would see the mountain peaks again turning pink in the first light of day.

I held Paul's fingers, felt the warmth of his touch and looked into his moist eyes, unaware that my eyes too were full of tears. Suddenly inadequate and shy, I turned away to scan the garden visible beyond the half-drawn curtains. I suppose I was looking for a tangible confirmation of what was happening to me. A little reprieve. Some scrap of affirmation to reassure me that love could do no wrong.

But all I could spot was a tipsy bee tumble into the heart of a rose.

ACKNOWLEDGEMENTS

Encouraged by my women friends, I have dared to take on the female voice to write *A Soft Eclipse*. The feminine side embedded in my heart has tried to see the world through their eyes and the characters, as long as they live within the pages of this book, are as real as my dreams. However, when they escape – unbidden – into the real world, I am not responsible for their existence!

I have been privy to numerous stories told to me sotto voce by my baandhobis that are now part of this book. These belong, by and large, to the corporate world of the seventies. Many of them were revelations, seen against upper crust Calcutta's hypocritical standards. I have, of course, fictionalised the anecdotes most shamelessly to suit my characters. But thank you, kind ladies, for letting me enter your vulnerable worlds and live there for a while, not as a clinical outsider but as part of what you have seen, felt and suffered, every hair in your bouffants in place. I am grateful that you let me glimpse the pain hidden behind your shadowed eyes and heartrending smiles. And observe your claws; yes, your catty, wonderful, deliciously painted and manicured claws! I don't know if I have emerged a better, more compassionate man after the experience. But I have, most certainly, beheld with wonder your fragile yet perfect facades and stood utterly humbled.

I have to also thank my daughter, Shahana, for meticulously tooth-combing the manuscript and licking it into shape. Jane Conway-

Gordon, my literary agent in London, read an early draft and gave pertinent suggestions. Manoj Kulkarni at Amaryllis needs a big 'high-five' for believing in *A Soft Eclipse* and guiding it through many stormy seas so that it could finally see the light of day. And how can I forget Rashmi Menon, my editor, for crossing the 't's and dotting the 'i's and giving the manuscript a final edit? Onek dhonnobaad! Thank you, Shobhaa and Kishwar, two writers I admire, for reading the manuscript and for your generous comments. Now I can laugh without any qualms, remembering how this, my third novel, came about, emerging from a rush of thrashing waves like Botticelli's proud Venus floating on a shell!

As the wise Osho said, 'A buddha laughs too, but his laughter has the quality of a smile. His laughter has the feminine quality of grace. When an ignorant person laughs, his laughter is very aggressive, egotistic. The ignorant person always laughs at others. On the other hand, the contented person, the person who knows life a little, laughs at himself, at the whole play of life itself. It is not addressed to anybody in particular. He just laughs at the absurdity of it all... the impossibility of it all.'